War on Humanity

Robbie Dorman

For apple fritters.

1

"What are your plans?"

The commander sat bound in the chair, bleeding from multiple places in his face. His mottled gray skin was bruised and broken around his mouth, and small, alien nose. He bled black blood, like everyone here. Still, even sitting, his size dominated the room.

He stared at the rebel who interrogated him with impertinent eyes. His black crescent moon irises were hard to read, but he didn't answer. It was easy to guess what the stare meant. It meant that he wouldn't answer any questions, not questions from these *Kajahar* scum, these poor nothings that he wouldn't let clean his boots.

He finally spit, a wad of dark blood sailing through the air. Anjar, the interrogator, dodged, their reflexes good enough to move in time. They sighed. The room was quiet, and no sounds bled in from outside. The fighting was long over and this commander knew that. Knew that his troops had abandoned him here, either thinking him dead or a lost cause. They wouldn't welcome him back.

But still, the Oukan leadership were hard, raised through brutality and pain, and they wouldn't give up information, and this was an officer. He had endured unimaginable torment to get to his position.

"I don't want to hurt you," said Anjar. Anjar told the truth. They were peaceful and kind.

"Hurt me?" asked the commander. "You cannot hurt me. The Oukan are strong, in all the ways that you are not. You are subjugated because you are weak. You are poor because you are weak. You are dominated because you are weak. Kill me now. It will save you time."

He spit again, another thick wad of black blood.

Mike watched it soar, and hit the back wall of the small hut they sat in. It was only the three of them.

The battle had been long and hard, and the Kajahar cleaned up outside, nursing their wounded as best they could. A few short months ago, Mike wasn't allowed out of his own hut. But in that time, he'd proved his worth to the leadership of the Kajahar. Many times over.

He held The Book. He never let it go, not anymore. Not here. It kept him safe. It would get him home. He knew it would.

Anjar looked at him, a long look. Mike hadn't been able to read the Kajahar, not at first. But with time, he could piece together body language. Anjar's better than most.

Anjar *was* peaceful and kind.

But now, they wanted Mike to hurt the commander. To punish him.

To make him talk.

Mike walked forward and laid The Book on the small table in the center of the room. The commander didn't look at Mike. He stared at The Book, his hard, black eyes only looking at the cursed and powerful object.

It told Mike a lot. But he needed the commander to say it.

"This is your chance," said Mike. "Answer Anjar's questions."

The commander's gaze cut away from The Book, and looked at Mike, and the brief moment of vulnerability, of fear, it vanished. The commander shoved it away, back in control. The Oukan didn't know fear. *He* didn't know fear.

But Mike knew that wasn't true. And soon he would prove it.

The commander stared at Mike, and then back to Anjar. "You think this foreigner scares me? Do you think I haven't crossed worlds?"

Mike stared back at him. "Have it your way."

Mike looked down at The Book. It was the right page. He had never practiced on the Oukan before, but it should work. Mike drew the dagger he kept on his side. It had only tasted his blood, and he whetted it once more, sliding the blade across his palm, squeezing the blood onto the page. The scar tissue in his hand had grown thicker, and each slice took more force, but the dagger was sharp, and soon the page was covered in red.

Mike sheathed his dagger, and looked down, and watched The Book drink. The same book Laurel had used, in what seemed so long ago.

How long had it been?

He pushed the thought away and looked at the page, and read. The words ripped through the air like snarls, because Mike spoke the language of The Book. Tenuous ribbons formed, rising from the paper, indestructible. Mike didn't stop. This was only the beginning.

The commander stared now, not at Mike, or at Anjar, but at the ribbons of energy that rose from the book, and floated toward him. Mike saw his crescent irises waver, but he had made his choice.

Mike read more, thinking of the atrocities this officer had ordered. The enslavement. The brutality and torture.

What had he ordered, what had he condoned in his career with the Oukan? To rise to this station?

A lot. Too much.

And it made it easier, as Mike's throat ripped apart, exhaling smoke and fire, the smell of sulfur filling the hut. The ribbons filled the air, and floated over to the commander, and unfurled around him, energy dancing delicately, cutting toward the Oukan. They were invisible angles, air above the desert sand, an illusion of substance, of something.

They floated around him, dancing, and the commander thought to speak, but then they floated inside his ear, an ear unrecognizable as human, a blank lump of bone, to protect the ear canal, but the ribbon floated right inside, and then the commander whimpered.

It wasn't a human whimper, but Mike had learned much in his time there, and the noise the commander made wasn't one any human would recognize, but it was a whimper all the same, and the ribbon floated deeper in.

Soon the whimper turned to moans of pain, but more than pain.

Pain was too simple a word.

Mike had felt pain when he sliced his palm, the dagger cutting through his flesh.

What the commander felt was sorrow, deep and cutting.

The Book contained all horror of otherworldly power, and some of it was physical torment. But it would do nothing to the commander, who had known physical torture his whole life, the Oukan knowing only pain from an early age.

And that brutality would have forced him to lock away his fear, and the things that truly terrified him. The things that would unlock mourning.

The ribbon slid inside the officer, and then he wailed.

He wailed, and even after Mike had learned their language, this sound crossed all barriers of linguistics.

It was the sound of a mother mourning a child.

The sound of an abandoned life.

The sound of hope dying.

But Mike did not stop.

The officer hadn't answered, and so he would experience it all. He wailed, a deeper sorrowful cry, and black tears covered his face, dripping from him.

No one interrupted them. Anjar stared. Mike finished reading, the ribbon disapparating, finally sliding away back into The Book, into nothingness.

The commander stopped moaning, breathing hard, dark breaths.

They all waited, in silence, letting the commander linger in the vanishing sorrow that had ripped through him.

Mike didn't know what he felt, what he saw, to pull those

feelings out of him. But he would do it again, and again, until the commander spoke.

"What are your plans?" asked Anjar, again. "How did you find us? Why did you attack us?"

"You have a mole," said the commander, finally, not looking up at them.

"Who?"

"Biliq," said the commander. Anjar cursed. Mike said nothing. Biliq had been welcoming of him. But the commander wasn't lying. "He gave us your location. Told us when to attack."

Anjar looked away from the commander. Mike gave them the time. They were close to Biliq.

Anjar looked back. "Why? We are small. We aren't worth the effort."

The commander looked up, finally, his eyes different now. All the hardness was gone from them.

"You know the answer to that already," he said.

"I would not ask if I knew," said Anjar. "Tell me."

"The Book, kaja," said the commander. "We know it had returned. We wanted it." Anjar's eyes went to The Book, on the table, Mike still leaning over it. "We don't care about your encampment. You are nothing. Well, you *were* nothing. Now, you have that. You are a threat."

Anjar didn't ask why they wanted The Book.

"You made yourself a target," said the commander. "And we won't stop. You'd be smarter to hand him and The Book over. We will only double our attack next time."

"And you will lose double the soldiers," said Anjar. "With The Book, we can defend any amount."

The commander smiled, or what passed for a smile.

"That may be true," he said. He looked at Mike. "But it has a cost, doesn't it? And you're the only among them that knows how to use it. You are not infinite."

Mike stared at him, but said nothing.

"Go ahead, kill me," said the commander. "Do it before I do it myself. But it won't stop us." He still stared at Mike. "We are coming for your home, foreigner."

"Are we done, Anjar?" asked Mike, ignoring him.

"Earth," said the commander, in English. Mike looked back at him. The commander smiled wider still. "Surprised I know the word? We know a lot. And soon, it will be ours as well. It is rich and will be easy conquest. A vast people, split and divided. Simple."

"You're lying," said Mike.

"No," said the commander. "We have someone preparing the way. They will open a portal, and we will spill through, and take it all. And you cannot stop us." He smiled. "Don't worry, foreigner. You won't see it. You'll only see the insides of these kaja tents."

"Ignore him," said Anjar. They poked their head out of the hut and yelled for help.

The commander started laughing, laughing loudly, what passed for Oukan laughter, and Mike wanted to read The Book again, he wanted to punish this son of a bitch, and he drew the dagger—

Loud thumps woke him up.

Mike opened bleary eyes and reached for the bedside lamp. The clock read 7 AM. More thumps.

Someone knocked on their door.

Mike pushed himself out of bed and threw on a t-shirt, leaving his small bedroom. Marion stood at her door, still in her pajamas. Daniel opened his door as Mike walked past it.

"Stay here," said Mike. Their residence was comfortable for what it was.

Mike opened the door. Two guards stood there in their plain uniforms, without insignia of any kind.

"Strickland wants to talk to you," said one.

"It's 7 AM," said Mike. "It can't wait?"

"He wants to talk to you," said the same guard, repeating himself.

Mike stared at them. "Let me get dressed."

"We'll be waiting," the guard said, and Mike closed the door.

"Go back to bed," said Mike, to Daniel and Marion. Marion nodded and closed her door. Daniel held his gaze for a second, and then nodded. Daniel wanted to go with him, but it was better for Mike to talk to Strickland alone. At least for now.

Mike got dressed, taking clothes from his bag in his small bedroom. It was comfortable, for what it was.

What it was, was a cage.

<h1 style="text-align:center">2</h1>

Mike walked with the men. They were taking him somewhere new. He had spoken with Strickland before, but only briefly. Most of his interviews had been with rank-and-file officers.

Officers of what, Mike didn't know. They had never identified what agency they work for, only that they handle such things.

Things like The Book.

He could feel it, still. They had taken it from him, but it wasn't far.

He had returned to Earth right where he had left it, in the ruins of the Laurel City Baptist Church. Well, what was left of it.

It had been hell to get back, and it had seemed like an

eternity gone, but it had only been seven months. There was no way to be sure, but Mike didn't think time passed the same over there. He felt like it had been years. The extra gray hairs, the additional wrinkles. It had aged him.

He *had* gotten back, though. Gotten back to Earth, and back to Daniel and Marion.

But they'd been watching.

Daniel and Marion had told him about the government's intervention in the aftermath of Halloween night. About the agents who swept the town. Who'd paid off everyone to keep their mouths shut.

But Mike had only been back a day before they came back, in force.

It had been six months since then. Six months they'd been here, in their comfortable cage.

Where were they?

Mike didn't know. They'd kept the three of them in the dark. They'd taken The Book away from him, no matter how he protested, and he wouldn't use it, not here. Not with Marion or Daniel at risk, with sub-machine guns held at ease, but ready to be raised and fired at any moment.

He still felt it, though.

The feeling made him queasy. Made him feel shame.

It was the want that did it. Because he craved The Book again, now without it. And as the days passed, in their new residence, he thought the want would fade. The urge to hold it again, to bleed again, would disappear with time.

But it hadn't. It stayed there, a gnawing hunger inside his chest, an itch that couldn't be scratched, no other way to soothe that need. And over time, he got used it, but it didn't go away.

And he realized this was what Laurel felt like all the time, and without realizing, he felt a kinship with the man, the man who had tried to kill him and his children and to invite hell into their world.

It made him queasy, and ashamed, but he had needed The Book to survive, and to get back. And would need it more still, if he was right.

The agents wouldn't tell him what agency they represented, and they took The Book from him, and they ferreted them away to a compound, where they had comfortable beds, and food, and exercise, but couldn't leave.

And they asked them questions.

They asked *him* questions.

Marion and Daniel had told them what they knew, back when they were first interviewed. They had seen nothing more, and knew only about The Book and its magicks from the little exposure they had seen. Daniel had touched it, had handled it briefly. He got a glimpse.

But he had no idea. Only Mike and the Laurels knew it, and so they mostly asked Mike questions.

Where did you go?

How did you get back?

How does The Book work?

Can you translate it?

And Mike would answer, over and over again, that he didn't remember.

He took The Book across because he wanted its power away from Earth, and to close the portal. He remembered that.

No, he couldn't recall what was on the other side.

He couldn't remember studying The Book, and learning

how to get back.

He couldn't read it, still, so no, a translation wasn't possible.

Once a week, they averaged. Marion and Daniel were left alone, after a while.

The agents still questioned Mike, once a week.

And he repeated his answers.

Today, they were bringing him somewhere new. Typically the interviews took place in a small room.

By taking him, they escorted him. There were never handcuffs. Never restraints.

But Mike knew that was only because they didn't have to use them. If they needed to, they would.

But they hadn't. They'd kept them comfortable, comfortable as they could be, imprisoned in their velvet cage. They could have made them uncomfortable, or threatened him, or either of the kids. Not yet, though. And Mike thought he knew why.

Because they didn't want to resort to that unless absolutely necessary. Because Mike was their way into The Book.

How long would that last, though? How much longer would their cage be covered in velvet?

Down multiple hallways, and then a big set of wooden double doors, and into an office, a small room, with a secretary, and she exchanged a glance and a nod with the two men that escorted Mike, and through another heavy door, and then they were in Strickland's office, big, with a bar on one side, and a massive red, wooden desk. Two simple chairs sat across from Strickland himself, perched above them in a large office chair. He smiled and rose as they entered.

"Mr. Dawson," said Strickland. "It's been a while. I wanted to speak to you." Strickland had introduced himself when they first came. He'd been polite. Had acted like they were guests. Not prisoners.

Strickland was tall, and lanky, and his suit fit him weirdly because of it. His head was shaved bald, and his skin was pale and pallid. His massive hand enveloped Mike's as he shook. Strickland's eyes bore into him. They were gray, almost silver.

Mike didn't trust them.

"Leave us," Strickland said to the two men, and then gestured to one of the chairs. Mike took a seat, like he had a choice. The men left them. Probably waiting on the other side of the door.

Mike stared at Strickland. Strickland stared back. He smiled without smiling, a look that Strickland had learned to make himself look less threatening, Mike guessed. It didn't work.

"I wanted to check in on you," said Strickland.

"Check in?" asked Mike. "What do you mean?"

"Just to see how you and your family are doing," said Strickland, the smile plastered on his face. "If you need anything."

Mike stared back. This was the game they would play. Mike could answer honestly, of course. He could say they wanted to fucking leave, and to give him back The Book, so he could find someone he trusted to talk about what he knew.

But Strickland wanted that. He wanted leverage against Mike.

"We're doing fine," said Mike. "Everything's comfortable." He wouldn't lie. He'd played this damn game before.

Strickland's face didn't change. Mike would give him credit for that.

"Oh, well, that's good to hear," said Strickland. "We just want to make sure you're safe and sound, you know. After you returned with The Book, we were worried. Worried that more of those creatures would come through after you."

"Creatures?" asked Mike.

"Yes," said Strickland. "The things that attacked Laurel City on Halloween night. Fear eaters."

Mike pressed his tongue to the roof of his mouth, pushing himself into a poker face.

"Has there been anything?"

"Oh, no," said Strickland. "Not yet, at least. But that's why we brought you and your children here. And why we took The Book. We wanted to ensure your safety. And the safety of the good people of America."

"Of course."

"You know, Mike, we could really use your help," said Strickland. "We think The Book is the key to all of this. To making sure those things don't come back across." He paused. "Are you sure you remember nothing about your journey?"

Mike stared back. "Not a thing."

"Because it seems very strange, Mr. Dawson. You traveled across, with The Book. Very selflessly, I might add. Seven months pass, and you re-emerge, back with The Book, the very one you left with. Why did you bring it back? What did you encounter on the other side?"

"I don't know," said Mike. "It's all a haze."

The smile finally dropped off of Strickland's face. "I think you're lying, Mr. Dawson. You know more than you say. And every moment you don't share that information with us, the more danger we are all in. And my patience is wearing thin."

"What danger would that be?"

"Those things, those creatures," said Strickland. "They could come back across. The Book is all that can stop them, clearly."

"Bullets stopped them, actually."

"Joke all you want, Mr. Dawson," said Strickland. "But we've been waiting for you to tell us the truth—"

"You've been waiting?" asked Mike. "*You've* been waiting? I was back a single day before we were taken away, kidnapped by people who wouldn't identify themselves, and stuck here, away from the world. My daughter away from her high school. My son away from his job. And every time I've asked, I get the same damn answer. Who are you with, Mr. Strickland? What agency do you represent?"

Strickland stared at him. "We cannot tell you, it's classified information—"

"And yet you expect me to cooperate with you? You expect me to tell you how that thing works? To tell you what happened to me over there?"

Strickland still stared. "You're a civilian, Mr. Dawson. We can't involve you in matters like this—"

"Who the hell is we?" asked Mike. "Are you in charge? If you're not, who is?"

Strickland looked away for a second, and Mike saw a hint of anger on his face, of frustration bubbling. Good. At least it was something.

"You want me to talk?" asked Mike. "Let me go. Let my kids go."

Strickland looked back. "That's impossible. It's a security

risk—"

"Then I don't remember what happened after I passed through that portal. And I sure as hell don't remember what The Book says."

Strickland's face was plain again, all his emotion swallowed up. "Why are your palms covered in scars, Mr. Dawson?"

Mike stared back. "I don't remember."

Strickland's nose flared. He exhaled. He hit the intercom button, and the two men came in and escorted Mike to his cage.

"The next time we meet, Mr. Dawson, it won't be in my office," said Strickland. "Unless you get your memory back."

3

Marion's heart thumped in her chest. She pulled herself up, her chin above the metal bar.

"Seven," she said, breathlessly, so quiet she herself could barely hear it. Her arms trembled, and she hung for a second, taking a deep breath. She pulled herself up again, slow, her arms quaking, but she didn't stop, her muscles screaming, and then her chin was above the bar, and she lowered herself back down, and she hung.

"Eight," she said. She tried to pull again, but there was nothing left, and she dropped, her feet touching the ground. Her arms twitched, and she paced, catching her breath. She wanted to bend over, and put her hands on her knees, but Daniel had told her it was counterproductive, that it was better to stay upright.

Daniel did push-ups, his large frame horizontal. Sweat dripped off him, but he pushed hard, up and down, up and down.

They worked out in a small gym, the floor covered in mats, with a modest array of workout equipment. A few sets of dumbbells, the pull-up bar, a standard bench. Not much, though. This wasn't a luxury gym.

It was a prison gym.

Marion hadn't wanted to do anything at first. She was angry, furious, afraid, confused. They had left so quickly, pulled away from their house, with only ten minutes to pack, her phone stolen from her. No time to tell Cara. What would she think? The entire family, gone in an instant?

They had asked her questions, and she had told them the same answers she had told the agent who had visited before. She had told them what she knew.

They asked her where Dad went, and how he got back, and why he had brought The Book back.

She told them the truth, and the truth was she didn't know. In the short day since he had returned, he had been raving, out of it. They had spent that time keeping him calm, and making sure he had food. He had mentioned *them* coming back, but had said nothing else.

They hadn't been arrested, hadn't been charged with anything, but they were prisoners. She wanted to spit on the guards, but knew it would accomplish nothing.

She had expected the same rage from Daniel, but he'd withheld his anger. He had asked her if she would work out with him, and she had said no.

Marion didn't want to work out. She wanted to go back to her life. She wanted to see Cara, to go to school, the life they had fought for in Laurel City, now taken from her again.

But Daniel had kept asking, and eventually she gave in, and through the months, it became a daily ritual. She had no idea how to do all the exercises, but Daniel taught her the basics, and with the equipment they had, the basics were all they could do.

She couldn't do one pull-up at first. Her arms shook and trembled, but her chin couldn't get close to the bar. But she started slow and small, and eventually, she did one.

They celebrated her first pull-up, but now she could do ten on her first set, and every week, every month, she got stronger. Pull-ups, push-ups, Hindu squats. She had been soft, but now, her body showed the progress of her work. Marion felt the strength of her back and shoulders, of her hips and core.

In the time Dad was gone, they had grown closer. They'd had to, they were all they had. Sure, she had Cara, and their circle of friends and allies were still there, and still support-ive—but they weren't family.

They'd kept each other going while Dad was gone. Mar-ion and Daniel were the only two who truly understood what it felt like, and they made do. They got through it.

And now Dad was back. And if you had asked her to trade their lives in Laurel City for what this was, with their father returned, she would take that trade, every time. Pro-vided they got out of here, at some point.

But the bond between her and Daniel was still there. Stronger now, than ever. It had been forged alone, but it persisted, even with Dad back.

A part of it was them realizing their strength together, and truly cherishing what they had as brother and sister.

They'd always loved each other growing up, but never were close. After Halloween in Laurel City, after what they went through—they were as close as they could be.

The other part was that Dad *had* come back, and they loved him, and they had missed him, missed him so, so much. They loved him, and *were* glad he was back.

But the Dad that had come back was not the same Dad that had left.

Daniel finished his final push-up, the last few labored, and then pushed himself up to his knees. Daniel was big, and strong, and fit, from playing football and lifting weights, but his months working out here had strengthened him further. He'd gotten lean, in a way Marion wasn't used to. Daniel's face always had the smallest amount of baby fat, no matter how much he worked out.

Not anymore. The time here had hardened them.

"We doing more?" asked Marion.

Daniel looked at her and then plunked down on the bench. "I don't think so. I'm done."

Marion sat down next to him. Her breath had caught up to her raging heart.

"Dad was talking to Strickland," said Marion.

"Yeah," said Daniel. "They're tired of him stonewalling them."

Marion cast an eye at him. "How do you know that?"

"Why else would they send him to the boss?" asked Daniel. He looked up, and around the small gym. Marion followed his eyes. They'd never seen or found any bugs, listening devices, or cameras. But that didn't mean they weren't here. Didn't matter. There was nothing they could say that they hadn't said already.

"You think he'll tell them anything?"

Daniel paused, and then answered. "No. Why would he start now?"

"You know why," said Marion. Daniel raised an eyebrow. "Us. If they threatened us, or promised to let us go."

"They won't let us go."

"What do you mean?"

"Why would they?" asked Daniel. "I've touched The Book, Marion. Sure, nothing like the Laurels, or Dad, but I still touched it. Held it, even. It spoke to me, for a time. With what they know about Halloween night, why would they let me back out there, now that The Book is back?"

"I haven't touched it," said Marion. "And they *have* The Book. Why does it matter if you're free? Or Dad?"

"It's potential knowledge that someone else might want," said Daniel. "It doesn't cost them anything to keep us here. At least nothing substantial."

"So what, we'll just stay here forever?" asked Marion. "Or until Dad loses his patience and tells them whatever happened when he went through that portal? Provided he actually remembers any of it."

Daniel turned and looked at her. He didn't look angry, or frustrated, which is how she felt. She was tired of staying here, tired of losing her life, and she missed Cara. She hadn't even gotten to say goodbye.

Daniel looked unbothered.

"He's not going to tell them."

"What if they threaten us?"

"Hurting us will ensure that Dad never helps them," said Daniel. "So they won't do that either. They'll think of another way to sway him. Or try. As to if he we'll just end up staying here forever—"

He looked at her, and winked.

Winked.

Daniel didn't wink. He wasn't playful like that. What was going on?

"I don't think we'll be here forever," said Daniel. "Eventually, something will change, and we'll be out." Daniel said with finality. With confidence. He looked at her again, but didn't wink. Once was enough, and she understood.

He knows something.

But Marion couldn't ask. At least not directly.

"You think Dad will be okay?"

"I don't know," said Daniel. His face changed immediately. The confidence was gone.

"He's—"

"He's struggling," said Daniel. "I think that much is clear. With what? I don't know."

"He won't tell us," said Marion. "They would hear."

"I don't think he would tell us anyway," said Daniel. "When he stopped me, at the portal, on Halloween—he had already made that choice a thousand times. He'd never let me, or you, pay a price when he could do it instead."

"But he didn't know what was on the other side," said Marion. "He only knew that he was taking The Book across, and saving us from whatever was coming through."

"But that's part of it," said Daniel. "If it was easy to say, if it didn't matter, he'd have already told us. Told them." Daniel motioned with his head toward the compound, toward *them,* as a whole. "But he hasn't said a word. Hasn't even mentioned what it was like."

"He went to Hell," said Marion.

"That's what we imagined," said Daniel. "But we don't know. And whatever happened over there, Dad considers that a part of the burden. And there's more to it than just that. If he tells us, they'd be getting us up at 7 AM to talk to Strickland, just like him. He's protecting us. He protected us then, and he's protecting us now."

"We don't need protecting," said Marion. "We can handle it."

"You say that," said Daniel. "You haven't touched that thing. You've seen his hands."

Marion didn't answer. They both had noticed it right away, the day Dad appeared on their doorstep, haggard, and wild-eyed. They had brought him inside, and got him some water, and calmed him down. He wouldn't drop The Book, wouldn't let it away from him, not at first. And then they saw his palms. Thick, crossing scars, on both of them.

Enough that his hands weren't recognizable as his anymore.

"Maybe eventually we'll know," said Daniel. "But for now, it's probably best that we don't."

Marion desperately wanted to ask Daniel what he knew. How he knew that they'd get out of there. But she said nothing.

"Ready to head back?" asked Marion.

"Yeah," said Daniel. The guard waiting on the other side of the door escorted them back to their quarters.

Dad was already there. He had made them sandwiches.

"I made some chicken salad," he said. "Hope you don't mind."

"No, that sounds great," said Marion. They sat down at the little dining table, and ate, all three of them. The ritual felt good. Marion caught Daniel's eye. She thought to ask Dad how his "interview" went. If Strickland had said anything about them leaving.

But Daniel told her no with his eyes. If Dad had news, he would tell them. And she trusted Daniel, trusted him fully. If he knew something, and wanted her to stay quiet, she would.

And she did trust Daniel, with every fiber of her being.

And she had trusted her dad, before, in the same way. He had always supported her, protected her, defended her.

She glanced over, and the criss-crossing scars on his palms stood out, the scar tissue bright white.

Dad wasn't the same as when he had left, and neither was her trust in him.

As she ate her sandwich, she looked at him. His eyes stared straight ahead.

4

Daniel's feet were killing him as he ran hard through the forest. They ached with every step. His heart beat hard in his chest, the beat echoing through his body, his breath hot, but he felt his feet more than anything.

His tennis shoes were okay, they weren't running shoes, but he didn't believe it was the shoes that were the problem.

The problem was him.

He was big, and no matter how much weight he lost, no matter how good of shape he was in, he was still big, tall, broad-shouldered, and that was a lot of weight to put on his feet, especially over and over, as he ran.

At first, he had run only to get away from the compound. No matter how many exercises he did in their tiny gym, it wasn't the same as working out in the open air. He had never enjoyed running. He had run a lot because of football practice, but it had only been a thing to do to get ready for the games.

But in the months here, as he had run more and more, he grew to like it. The heat of his breath, as it burned through his lungs, the rhythmic pounding of his feet on the dirt path, even the aching pain in his feet, as they carried his large frame across the ground. While he was running, they kept his mind off of—well, off of everything.

He could focus on the pain in his feet, instead of the fact they'd been imprisoned for six months. Six months away from their lives, away from their friends, away from the world. Imprisoned by the government.

The government was all they knew, because they still had seen no logo, no agency, no official word on who held them. He'd had the thought of it not being the government at all. It could be some other shadowy organization, pretending to be the government, only to use The Book for their own means.

But he didn't think that was true. They had too many resources, too much manpower. The only other explanation was a large corporation, but they wouldn't know about The Book.

Would they?

He ran. The intrusive thoughts about why they were being held, and when they would get out, if ever, pushed and pulled at the edges of his mind, but the pain in his feet and the burning in his chest kept him grounded and centered, and kept those thoughts at bay.

The questions of what had happened to his dad on the other side of that portal. Of his relationship with The Book.

Of the words he'd said when he'd come back.

They're coming. I have to stop them.

Of the thick sets of scars on the palms of his hands.

Daniel ran, pushing those thoughts away. It was the only part of the day when he could get away from them, away from the compound, away from everything. His sweat and toil kept his mind free as he ran through the path in the forest.

The forest was dense, and the trail never led to anywhere with any height, so Daniel couldn't really get a lay of the land. But it was still chilly in the late morning, and with this type of forest, Daniel would bet they were East somewhere. Based on this being a government facility, he would guess Virginia, or somewhere nearby.

But that's all the information he could glean from his surroundings. The path was well tread, and he suspected the workers here used it to run on like he did. No signs, though, and no trash cans, and no other evidence of habitation.

A branch cracked behind him.

"You're giving yourself away today," said Daniel, loudly, with what little air he had to give. There was no response from behind him. There never was.

When he'd asked if he could go running, they had said yes, but only supervised. So during his hour of outside time a day, an agent would accompany Daniel on his runs.

The agent would run behind him, never close, never far, but almost always out of sight, and almost always silent. And at first, Daniel had hated the agent running behind him, lurking just out of sight.

It had made him feel like a rabbit, running through the woods, with a wolf behind him.

Despite his size, he felt like a prey animal, being hunted. No matter how fast he ran, the agent would always be there, just out of sight.

And maybe there were more out there, keeping an eye on him. Making sure he didn't stray too far from the path, or try to escape on foot, if he even could, and the agent that accompanied him was just a distraction, just someone there for Daniel to think about. Mind games.

Daniel had never been a good runner. His form was sloppy, and running with his teammates had frustrated him, all smaller and faster than him.

But he couldn't deny that in these six months, he'd become a better runner. In fact, he was a *good* runner now, and his cardio was top-notch. Finishing the five-mile trail had been a task at first, and he would slow down a lot on the last leg of the path, but now, his only test was how fast he could run it. He was running eight minute miles, and for his size, he was proud of his achievement.

He ran, trying to outrun his thoughts, when he realized he was nearing the spot. He slowed down incrementally and started breathing harder. As he neared the tree, the tree that bent in a Y, catty-corner from the huge boulder, Daniel slowed, and stopped. He heard the footsteps approach him from behind.

"We don't have much time today," said the agent. Daniel turned and looked at him. He was above average height, with close cut black hair, and eyes hidden behind sunglasses. He wore standard issue athletic shorts, shirt, and shoes.

"What are they planning for my father?"

"I don't know," said the agent. "But it's not good. Your dad still hasn't given them any answers, not even after talking to Strickland himself. He's doing the right thing, but it also means we expect action, and soon."

Daniel stared at the agent. He'd never gotten his name. Daniel had asked, but the agent had never given it. It wasn't safe, he had said, and it was to protect Daniel. If Daniel didn't know his name, he couldn't give it up if he was pressured.

The first time they'd spoken, the agent had caught up to him, at exactly this spot, and told him to stop, quickly. This spot was safe, safe for them to talk, without being seen or heard. An overlooked gap in surveillance coverage, helped along with a dampener the agent had hidden near the boulder, in a nook no one would see.

"Soon? How soon?" asked Daniel.

"We don't know," said the agent. "There's been pressure from up above to get answers about The Book, and so we expect it soon."

"What will they do?"

"It'll be bad," said the agent. "We suspect they'll at least separate the three of you. If the honey doesn't work, they'll try vinegar."

"Dad won't help them if he thinks we're being hurt."

"I realize that," said the agent. "But they have a different line of thinking. And they need what's in The Book." He stared at Daniel. "And your father, right now, is the only way inside."

"So?" asked Daniel. "What do we do?"

The agent looked at Daniel. For the first time, he took off his sunglasses, and Daniel saw his eyes. They were green, a low green the color of a tropical fern.

At first, Daniel didn't trust the man. It felt like a trap,

laid to get Daniel to give him information. Information that Daniel didn't have, but maybe they thought he did. But as time went by, Daniel looked forward to their little meetings, where the agent would leak him information about the outside world, about why they were there. Daniel couldn't tell anyone this information, but it helped, knowing that there was someone out there looking out for them.

"I got word, just now," said the agent. He took a breath. "We're going to try something."

"What does that mean?" The clock was ticking in Daniel's mind. They could stand here for another minute or so without raising suspicion.

"We're getting you out," said the agent. "Your family, and The Book."

"How the hell are you going to do that?" asked Daniel.

"Good question," said the agent. He took another deep breath. "We're still working on it. We had hoped that everything would work out without the need. That you'd be out of here already. But it's gone the other direction. And if we don't do something now—well, we might not get a chance at all."

A thousand questions danced through Daniel's mind.

"We need to get moving," said the agent. "Be ready tonight. Don't tell your family, not until we knock on your door. It'll be late, maybe 2 or 3 AM, when everyone with high enough knowledge is asleep. Don't fight us, do what we say, and hopefully, we'll get you all out of here."

"Who are you with?" asked Daniel. "What is—"

"I can't tell you, Daniel," said the agent. "But don't worry, we're the good guys. Or at least, the less bad guys. Hopefully, everything goes smoothly tonight, and there's no bloodshed."

"Bloodshed?"

"No more questions," said the agent. "We stay here any longer, and it'll jeopardize everything. But you needed a heads up. Get running."

"Will I see you again?"

The agent stared at him again, and put his sunglasses back on. "If everything goes right, maybe." Daniel looked at him for a second longer, and then ran, holding his side, feigning a pulled muscle or a cramp. As he ran, he slowly resumed his normal behavior, and the agent stayed the same, safe distance behind him.

As he ran, both the pounding of his feet on the path and his hard breathing couldn't push away the thoughts, not anymore. He ran hard, as hard as he could, forcing himself to his limits, to escape those thoughts, but he couldn't. The questions whirled in his mind.

Who or what did this agent represent?

How were they going to break them out?

And finally, the question of bloodshed.

After Halloween, Daniel wanted no more of it. He had seen too much death, too much violence. Remembering the Laurels, and what they used to justify using The Book, and the blood they shed for it. Violence begets violence.

Daniel still remembered his father's words.

They're coming. I have to stop them.

No matter how hard Daniel ran, he couldn't outrun the thought that there would be more blood before the end of this.

5

Mike holds his hand over The Book, and runs the dagger over his palm, working to get through the layer of scar tissue that has built up over time.

The blade is sharp, honed, and with the smallest amount of pressure, it slices cleanly through Mike's skin, blood welling up from the cut, no pain, not yet, but it would come, it always trailed behind the wound.

The blood poured from Mike's hand, and he held it over The Book. He had to use The Book, it was the only way, the only way they had a chance.

The blood spilled onto The Book, and it lapped it up greedily, absorbing it, using it to fuel its dark magicks. With it, Mike could punish the unjust. Could summon an infinite amount of soldiers to fight for them. Could use it for good, not just evil. It was a tool, that's all it was.

It just needed blood, the requisite amount, and so Mike poured his life into it, but The Book needed more, and so Mike squeezed his hand, forcing the blood out, and then he looked and both hands were bleeding, palms down, bleeding straight down into The Book, because it needed more. For what he wanted, it would need more blood.

No, this wasn't right, he had never needed this much, no, he would bleed out, he would die, The Book would suckle him dry, and he went to retreat, to leave The Book, but he couldn't escape, no.

He was shackled to the table, his hands suspended, trapped there, held there. Mike tried to pull them back, but no, The Book hadn't had its fill yet, and it needed more.

More and more. Fountains of blood poured from Mike, and it was impossible, this was more blood than he had, but that's what The Book required. It needed all his blood and more, and if he wanted to use The Book, he would have to get more blood, find it, from the willing and unwilling alike. The Book did not require consent to sate its appetite.

Give me Daniel. Give me Marion. Give me a thousand more. The sons and daughters of the Earth.

No, no, Mike tried to yell, tried to scream, but there was no voice, because The Book did not suffer dissent, and Mike would obey, Mike would bleed the Earth for The Book, he would bleed—

Thumps on the door woke him up in a haze.

He blinked away the nightmare, the blood, and he looked at his palms in the dim light of his bedroom, and they were clean, no slices. Only scars.

He looked at the clock. 2:03. Had he imagined the

sounds, that woke him up?

Then more thumps from the door. They were here for him, it had to be. His time had run out. But they would have barged in, wouldn't they?

Mike got up, and threw on clothes hastily, exiting into the common area, where Daniel was there, dressed, waiting for him.

"Daniel? What's going on?"

Daniel looked him in the eyes. Mike had a hard time reading his face, but Daniel wasn't surprised. He had expected this.

"Dad, they're here to take us away. I couldn't tell you before. You can trust them. We have to hurry."

Mike looked at him and blinked away the sleep as best he could. Daniel had known this was coming.

"Get your sister ready," said Mike, and went to the front door, not knowing what was on the other side. He opened it, and two agents stood there, wearing black suits. Both were of average height, one with black hair, one brown, but both looked similarly nondescript.

"Mr. Dawson," the black-haired man said. "We're getting you and your family out. Bring only what you can carry."

"That's all we have anyway," said Mike. "How much time do we have?"

"Not much," said the man. "Take only what can't be replaced."

Mike nodded and retreated into their residence, and went into his bedroom. He grabbed the same backpack he had brought here, and shoved what clothes he could grab inside, along with his notebook, that he'd been using in their time here. There was nothing else of import, and by the time he was out, Daniel and Marion were ready. They went to the front door. The agents were still alone, keeping their eyes up and away, looking for any interruptions. There'd been none so far.

"Why—"

"No time for questions," said the agent. "There will be time later, if we get you out. Stay between us, and let us handle all the talking. Understand?"

Mike looked in his eyes. Both agents knew what they were doing, but there was no hiding the small glimmer of fear there. Mike nodded.

"Understood," said Mike.

"Good, let's go," said the agent. He took point, while the brown-haired agent fell in behind them. They moved with purpose, not hesitating at any intersection. Mike had seen these hallways only in passing, and the place was a labyrinth, but the agents knew the layout, and led the three of them out toward the exit, long forgotten, only seen once before, when they had first arrived six months ago.

They came upon a checkpoint with a guard who looked tired. Annoyed that something had happened on his shift. He stared at them as he approached, and Mike suddenly had the question if these two agents were armed, or if they'd had their guns taken from them, and then he realized he knew nothing about them, about who was taking him and his kids away from here, or why, or if they were the good guys or not, but he realized that this place was prison, and in this case, he'd take the devil he didn't know.

All these thoughts came in a flash, but it was too late to do much about them, and just as quickly, the checkpoint guards eyed them but said nothing, did nothing to stop them.

Maybe it would be that easy.

But then Mike realized there was another checkpoint before the exit, and he wouldn't feel at ease until they were off this compound, driving away, driving to anywhere else.

Marion and Daniel were there, moving silently with him, and he studied Daniel's face, but saw no more answers. Like the agent said, they would have to wait until they were out of here.

But then, The Book.

They couldn't leave without it, and a panic seized him. They couldn't leave it behind, not with these men, who desperately wanted to unlock its secrets, who wanted him to unlock it for them. They couldn't be trusted with it. Who knows what they would use it for, what blood they would find to feed it—they couldn't leave it behind, *they couldn't leave it behind*, and he looked to the agents, but they were only focused on getting them out of there, and Mike couldn't do anything, not if he wanted freedom, and Marion and Daniel were here, and getting them out was the most important thing.

That need superseded the desperate urge for The Book, and he would find it, but only after the kids were safe, despite the aching itch in his palms—

They kept moving, through hallways, through places Mike had forgotten, past other offices and prisons, and then they were at the front door, a big double door, but you couldn't miss the blast doors hidden in the walls, and the bulletproof glass that covered the windows. This place could withstand a war.

Two guards stood at this checkpoint. They looked tired

as well, something that didn't surprise Mike, here at 2 AM, but they didn't look overwhelmed like the last guard. They looked pissed.

The black-haired agent that led them moved straight to the front door, not even sharing a glance with them. They can be pissed all they want behind them. Mike looked out and saw their freedom through the bulletproof glass.

The doors weren't open though, and needed the two guards to buzz them through.

"Could you please release the door?" asked the black-haired agent.

The guard stared at him. "I'm not letting them out of here," he said, his voice cold.

"Excuse me?" asked the agent.

"I'm not letting them leave," said the guard. "I've received no notification or approval for movement of prisoners. Why should I let them go?"

"We told you when we came in, we have approval—"

"Yes," said the guard. "Yes, and you bull rushed us, and pushed inside, but I have received no approval, and until I get it from my superiors, they are not going anywhere."

"We don't have time—"

"We have all the time in the world," said the guard. "I'll sit right here until I get approval."

The brown-haired agent turned, and Mike saw the black-haired agent do the same, both of them subtly positioning themselves in front of Mike and the kids. The two guards both carried pistols holstered at their waists, and both of them had a hand near their hip, and Mike realized they were about to be in the middle of a gunfight, and he looked to Daniel and Marion, and Daniel had slid in front of Marion, and he did the same for Daniel. His heart rate jumped up, and his guts sank, there would be blood—

"Are we having a problem?"

Everyone turned to the source of the voice, another black suited agent, who walked in from the depths of the compound. But Mike's eyes went to what he carried.

The Book.

"I'm not letting these people go, or that book, without prior approval—"

The new agent walked up, thin, carrying The Book, wearing leather gloves. He walked straight to Mike, his eyes never leaving the guard, and he casually handed The Book to Mike, and Mike took it, and a void he didn't know existed inside him was suddenly filled, and he held The Book with two hands, the itching in his palms stronger.

"Prior approval from who?" asked the agent.

"From Director Strickland—"

"Do you think Strickland is as high as it goes, Sergeant?" asked the agent.

"Well, no, but—"

The agent reached into his coat pocket and pulled out a folded piece of paper, which he unfolded.

"This is approval by the President of the United States. He authorizes us to take possession of these prisoners, and of this book." The agent held the paper up, and Mike saw the seal on the bottom.

"Well, I still—"

"You still what?" asked the agent. "This goes above Strickland. He is not the biggest shark in the sea. I have a very limited time table, Sergeant. Do you want to be transferred to Hazardous Artifacts Testing? I hear they have constant turnover, and I'm sure you're quite capable—"

The guard's stern demeanor finally dropped, replaced by fear.

"No, sir, I don't—"

"That's what I thought," said the agent. "Now, please, buzz the door, so we can be on our way. We have the proper paperwork. Don't delay us further."

The guard looked at him for a moment longer and then reached below the counter and the door buzzed. The agent smiled then.

"Thank you for your cooperation," and opened the door, and gestured everyone through. They hurried through, and the agent fell in beside Mike and the kids.

"Keep walking," said the agent. "Don't look back."

The agents led them to a black SUV, and the lead agent got into the front passenger seat. A driver was already there, waiting. The two other agents got into a separate vehicle. Mike and the kids got into the back, Mike still cradling The Book.

The driver pulled out as soon as the doors closed, and they left the small circular driveway, the car heading for the exit to the compound.

They drove quickly, and soon got to the gate at the exit to the compound, a huge thick iron reinforced gate, their final boundary. There was no guard here, only the gate, along with a camera, and they waited.

They were all silent inside the car, all watching the gate, all waiting for it to open.

Mike felt The Book in his hands.

A little blood, and nothing will stand in your way. No construction of man can stop you—

And then the gates rattled and shook and moved out of their way, and rolled all the way open, and the two SUVs roared away, out of the compound.

The lead agent let out a deep breath.

"Well, it worked," he said. He looked back at the three of them in the back seat. "Hello, Mr. Dawson. I'm Agent Bowman. Marion, Daniel. Nice to see you again."

6

Daniel took a deep breath in the back seat of the car. They were driving through the dark, headlights piercing the shadows.

"Where are we?" he asked.

"Virginia," said Bowman.

"I knew it," said Daniel.

"I'm sorry for all that," said Bowman. "But it couldn't be helped."

"You're sorry for getting us out of there?" asked Dad.

"No, I'm sorry they had you in the first place," said Bowman. "But there have been constraints on us lately."

"We met you," said Daniel. "Back in Laurel City. After Halloween."

"Yes," said Bowman. "We didn't think you'd come back."

He looked at Dad.

"I wasn't sure myself," said Dad.

"Is that letter actually from the President?" asked Marion.

He glanced at her and smiled for the first time. "Oh, no. In fact, he'd probably be upset if he knew this was happening. But it worked. And that was the most important thing."

"What is going on?" asked Dad.

"Yeah, where are we headed?" asked Daniel.

Bowman looked at the three of them. "We have a few hours drive. We're heading to our base. It's a safe place."

"So into another cage?" asked Dad.

Bowman stared at him. "Well, I'll let you go, if you want. But Strickland will find you, and take you again. And you cannot leave with The Book." His eyes went to it, still in Dad's hands. "It took a lot of doing to get you out of there, Mr. Dawson. We have a facility in the mountains. Near Thunder Ridge. Did you expect to come back with that—" Bowman gestured toward The Book. "—and not attract attention? Did you expect for no one to notice?"

Daniel looked to Dad, who said nothing.

"It's late," said Bowman. "Or early. We have a few hours of driving. I know it's not ideal, but try and get some shut-eye. I'll debrief you on everything when we're safe. Alright?"

Daniel's eyes stayed on his dad, who paused, and then softly nodded. But his hands stayed wrapped around The Book.

The car went silent as it glided through the night, and they did their best to lean back and fall asleep.

Daniel closed his eyes. He hadn't slept that night at all, anticipating the rescue. He should be exhausted, as the adrenaline wore off, and they were driven away from their cage.

But he couldn't sleep. His thoughts were only about The Book. He had touched it back in Laurel City. It had spoken to him. It had been gone, and out of sight while they were imprisoned, and existed only in the abstract.

But here it was, back in Dad's hands, and Daniel felt its pull.

He didn't sleep.

*

They arrived at the Thunder Ridge facility as the sun rose. The mountains came into view as they approached, the rising sun coming from behind them, banishing the dark behind the peaks. The roads were long and winding through forest and woods, as they crossed through small towns.

Marion slept next to Daniel, and he nudged her awake as they approached the first chain-link fence. It was a double chain-link fence, with a gap in between, with razor wire running over both sets of fencing. Gates opened as they drew near, with cameras watching them as they entered.

The road winded more, and the mountains loomed over them, and the road ended, leading to a large gate set into the side of the mountain, right in a cliff wall.

"When you said it was in the mountains, I didn't think you meant literally," said Marion.

"Extra land mass is an important buffer," said Bowman.

"A buffer for what?" asked Dad.

"Threats," said Bowman, but didn't elaborate, and no one

pressed him. The gate opened slowly, the big metal doors sliding to the side, enough for the SUVs to pass through. They drove into a big open area with dozens of vehicles parked. Most were similar SUVs to the one they rode in, but there were also smaller sedans, motorcycles, and even a larger armored vehicle with a turret on top.

The driver pulled into a spot. Daniel got out and looked around, trying to take in the size of the space. It felt like a hangar, and he looked to see the huge metal gates closing behind them. On foot, the sheer size and thickness of them was intimidating. It'd take a tank to get through them.

Bowman was out.

"Welcome to Thunder Ridge," he said. "Do you want to get settled in, or do you want to talk first?"

Dad looked at them. Daniel was exhausted. He hadn't slept all night, and all the adrenaline had worn off. His body ached, and his eyes were heavy.

But he didn't want a bed.

"Talk," he said.

"Talk," said Marion.

Dad looked at Bowman. "I think we'll talk."

*

"This is your office?" asked Daniel, as they sat in front of Bowman's desk. The room was big enough for them, but big enough wasn't what he expected.

"They've offered to move me to a bigger space, but I like this spot," said Bowman. "It's close to everything. Location, location, location."

They had walked down many hallways, and taken multiple elevator rides to get here, and honestly, Daniel didn't know how far they were into the mountain, or even if they were close to the surface at all.

Dad still held The Book. He carried it the entire way, and hadn't let go since he had regained possession.

Bowman sat behind his desk and seemed at ease. His shoulders weren't so tight, and he seemed relaxed. Or as relaxed as he could be. His office was neat, well organized, with everything in its place. Two screens sat to the side of his desk, both off.

"So," said Bowman. "We're safe. We can talk."

"Talk about what?" asked Dad.

"Everything," said Bowman. "But let's start with the Laurels."

"We told you everything we knew, last year," said Marion. "You investigated. What else is there?"

"Yes, you told me everything *you* knew," said Bowman. "I wasn't authorized to fill you in then. I am now."

"Fill us in about what?" asked Daniel.

Bowman looked at them, his eyes jumping between all three. "We first detected an extra-dimensional presence in Laurel City in the 80s. Presumably the work of David Laurel as a young man, or perhaps his father, before he passed." Bowman waved it away. "Impossible to know, but that was our first clue to the presence of The Book."

"Detected?" asked Dad. "Detected how?"

"We came into possession of another artifact in the late 70s," said Bowman. "We didn't quite know what it was at first, but it's proved itself valuable. It can detect a wide array of energies that are—I wouldn't say foreign to our world, because that's not accurate, but energies that exist outside of perspective. It doesn't matter. That was the first time we were aware of The Book."

"Who's we?" asked Daniel. "Where are we? Who do you work for?"

"Thunder Ridge, Virginia. We're about a mile or so inside the mountainside. I work for the Internal Protection Agency."

"Never heard of it," said Marion.

"Most haven't," said Bowman. "We're off the books."

"Like the Men in Black?" asked Marion.

"Not quite," said Bowman. "Only humans work for the IPA. And we don't have memory erasing tools. It'd make the job a hell of a lot easier."

"What does internal protection even mean?" asked Dad.

"It's vague on purpose," said Bowman. "And the name, well, it doesn't really matter. We protect America from the things that go bump in the night."

"Monsters?" asked Daniel.

"Sometimes," said Bowman, looking at him. "Things you can't categorize. Things too powerful for humans. Creatures that come from—other places. We step in when necessary, and do what must be done."

Dad stared at him. "You keep things under wraps."

Bowman stared back. "Do you think the entire world should know about werewolves, Mr. Dawson? Or the threat of vampires? Or shape-shifting fish men?"

"Fish men?" asked Marion.

"Our world barely holds together as it is without all that," said Bowman. "We do our best to keep things tidy. It gets more and more difficult by the day."

Daniel stared at him. He had suspected a lot about Agent

Bowman, and his visit with them after Halloween night. But hearing it from him, in the middle of a mountain base—it was a lot to take in.

"You said you first detected The Book in the 80s," said Dad. "Why didn't you step in then?"

"There are a lot of factors," said Bowman. "Some of it is about priority. We're firemen. We go to the biggest fire, put it out, and repeat. If there's not a fire, we won't necessarily show up."

"He was summoning demons," said Marion.

Bowman said nothing, and then looked at Dad. "Was he, Mr. Dawson?"

Dad stared back, but didn't answer.

"It's not as simple as right or wrong," said Bowman. "Believe me, I understand. But if every time some bumpkin slipped and fell into some monstrous threat, we'd lose focus. Marching into Laurel City and trying to take it from the Laurels probably would have resulted in a lot of death, probably more than on Halloween night. And might have blown up in our faces, and maybe even made the news, and we couldn't have that. We have to be tactical and precise."

He paused. "But, that book is in our purview," said Bowman. "I meant it when I apologized. We were caught with our pants down when you came back, Mr. Dawson. It's never happened before. We thought you and The Book were gone."

"I wasn't entirely sure I'd ever come back, either," said Dad.

"But you're here now," said Bowman. "That's all that matters."

"Who does Strickland work for?" asked Dad.

Bowman looked at him and sighed. "For the majority of the history of this America, the IPA has been the only agency who handles artifacts like that book, or active paranormal threats. But then 9/11 happened, and the Department of Homeland Security was created. And alongside that, another agency was created. The Bureau of Extra Normal Threats."

"BENT?" asked Daniel. "Really?"

"I didn't come up with the name," said Bowman. "I was a junior agent then, and had no pull. But the IPA disapproved as a whole, because why do you need two agencies handling the same thing? Of course, all of this was out of the public's eye. And if we knew then what we know now, we would have pushed back harder. But we were busy, and we wanted to be optimistic, and there were even a few of us who were supportive of BENT. Maybe they would lighten our load."

"Let me guess," said Dad. "They didn't."

"No," said Bowman. "They've made our jobs a hundred times harder. They challenge us for jurisdiction, they're reckless, and they're power hungry."

"Power hungry?" asked Dad.

"Yes," said Bowman. "It wasn't an accident that they wanted that." Bowman pointed at The Book. "Or were asking you how to use it."

"I told them nothing," said Dad. "I didn't trust them."

"You were right," said Bowman. "These things we've captured, or discovered—" Bowman shook his head. "—they're too big for us. Some are innocuous. A handful are safe for use under very careful circumstances. But most are impossible to replicate, and too big a weapon for any human to use."

Daniel's eyes went to The Book, clutched tightly in his dad's hands.

"Strickland would weaponize The Book, Mr. Dawson," said Bowman. "And all our work would be undone. The next time some penny dictator rose up and became annoying to the US, there'd be someone there with The Book, and they'd use to it to get rid of them. And maybe, just maybe, it'd be quiet, and no one would notice the difference."

"Or, someone would get caught, and The Book would belong to another country."

"Yes," said Bowman. "Or it'd blow up on the news. Or all of the above. Most of the major world powers have their own respective agencies, and we've managed to maintain a relative peace accord with them since the end of World War II. But BENT changed everything."

"Well, we're here now," said Daniel. "We made it."

"You did," said Bowman. "It was close, but we got you out."

"Why did it take so long?" asked Marion. "We were in there for six months."

"We knew almost immediately they had you," said Bowman. "It wasn't a mystery. It was navigating bureaucracy. There's a lot of politics at play, and if we stepped on too many toes, it might create even bigger problems. We couldn't have that."

"But you said you faked that letter," said Marion. "Did no one approve the transfer?"

"The President didn't," said Bowman. "I don't even know if he knows you exist. But we, the IPA, are looked at as stodgy, and old-fashioned. BENT has been favored by every president since Bush Jr, and probably will continue to be so. But it was becoming urgent we got you out of there, so I invented the letter. If pushed about it, I'll lie and say I said no such thing. Technically, neither BENT nor the IPA exist, nor have any power over each other. So us having you, and The Book, breaks no laws."

"You just said you didn't want to step on toes," said Daniel. "Isn't that what you did?"

"Yes," said Bowman. "Undoubtedly. But our patience was at an end. *My* patience was at an end. So I pushed for permission to get you out."

"Strickland threatened us," said Dad, finally. "Unless I gave him information."

"Were we in danger?" asked Marion.

"You haven't stopped being in danger," said Bowman. "Ever since The Book entered your lives. But yes, Strickland would hurt you, if necessary. We try and intervene, when appropriate, but we haven't been able to stop him all the time."

"We're safer here, though, right?" asked Marion.

"Safer, yes," said Bowman. "Thunder Ridge is heavily guarded and easily defended. Getting you and The Book here was paramount. Your lives were absolutely a part of the decision. But I'd be lying if I said it was our only motivation."

"The Book," said Dad.

"Yes," said Bowman. "It's too powerful. We couldn't let them have it, even in normal circumstances. But after our discovery, we have to move quickly. Hopefully, it'll pay off."

"Discovery? What discovery?" asked Daniel.

Bowman looked at them.

"The artifact I mentioned, that detects other energies. Well, it pinged again."

Bowman took a deep breath.

"There's another Book. And we couldn't let them have both."

7

Marion and Daniel scoured the room. Daniel poked and prodded along the ceiling, in high light fixtures, being tall where Marion couldn't.

Marion searched underneath tables and chairs, in the outlets, wherever she could think.

She found nothing, and neither did Daniel. After an hour of searching, they hadn't found anything.

"Either it isn't bugged, or we don't know what to look for," said Daniel.

"Both could be true," said Marion. They sat at the small dining table. Dad had been gone for an hour, off to talk with Bowman, and she had no idea when he'd be back. She had wanted to talk to Daniel—without Dad around.

"They might be listening," said Daniel.

"They might," said Marion. She sighed. "I mean, it is the question. Can we trust Bowman?" Marion stared at Daniel, whose face betrayed nothing.

"He saved us," said Daniel.

"He transferred us," said Marion. "This isn't home. This is another prison."

"You heard what he said," said Daniel. "And he's right. If we went home, we'd be pursued again. Because of The Book. Because of what Dad knows about it."

Marion took a deep breath, struggling with her thoughts.

"I hate it," she said, finally. "I hate that damn book. I want to go home. I miss Cara—God knows what she's thinking—"

"Ask Bowman, he might let us call."

"It'd be something," said Marion. "But it doesn't change that we can't go home—"

"Not yet."

"When, then?" asked Marion. "Hell, give it to Bowman, then, and we can leave—"

"Dad knows things," said Daniel. "Strickland doesn't just want The Book. He wants that knowledge. And Dad can't give it to him."

Marion sighed again. They were stuck.

"I know you're frustrated," said Daniel. "I think we can trust Bowman. He's been open with us. Strickland kept us in the dark."

"That's true," said Marion. "But still—"

"What's wrong?"

Marion hesitated. She looked down at her hands, unblemished, her father's hands flashing through her mind. A stark contrast. Layers and layers of scar tissue in his palms. How many times had he cut them?

She looked back at Daniel. "I think you're right—I *think* we can trust Bowman. But—but he gave The Book back to Dad. And you could see it on Dad's face. The relief. And the way he held it. It's not just a book to him. He holds it—holds it like an infant."

Daniel looked at her, worry showing on his face. Something, at least.

"You trust Bowman," he said. "You just don't trust Dad."

Marion swallowed. The pain of hearing it out loud rose in her stomach, and into her heart, and she felt a tear well in the corner of her eye. She blinked hard and forced it away.

"Not when he has that book," she said. "You've seen it, I know you have. I'm glad he's back, I am, but he's not the same. He hasn't joked with me once. It's been months, and there's just no happiness in him. Wherever he went, whatever happened, he used The Book, God knows how many times, and it changed him. It pulled something from him. And you ask if I trust him? How could I trust him? After everything we went through in Laurel City, after whatever hell Laurel summoned, and now Dad is no better."

"We don't know where he went," said Daniel. "We don't know—"

"Because he won't tell us!" said Marion, finding herself yelling. She stopped.

"We don't know what he went through," said Daniel. "He's not Laurel. You know that. Laurel was an authoritarian, trying to use The Book to control his own fiefdom, to enforce his own way of life. Dad isn't that. He knows something is coming, something from the other side, and he wants to protect us. He wants to protect everyone. Whatever he went through—"

"Daniel—"

"Whatever he went through, I know it was bad," said Daniel. "I touched The Book, Marion. I held it. I paid into it. I know what it takes. I know how it feels. It's awful, and addictive, and I know Dad wouldn't do it, knowing what he knew, unless it was the only way. Do I want him to have The Book? No. I want it destroyed, or banished. But if there is anyone I trust to hold it, it is Dad."

Marion said nothing.

"It's not safe," said Marion, quietly. "Not for anyone. Not ever."

"It's not a gun, Marion—"

"It's *worse* than a gun, *Daniel*," said Marion. "A gun uses bullets, made from metal, and gunpowder, and lead. Mundane things, made by man. The Book uses blood, absorbed, and driven into darkness, summoning things that torture and kill and devour. There is no use case—"

"Someone else having it is worse—"

"Is it?" asked Marion. "Because that's the same argument Dad is having with himself, I guarantee it. He's told himself someone else having it is worse, that they'll use the power inside it for worse things. They'll get corrupted by it. And if we asked him, that's exactly what he would say. But the problem is that he's the one being changed. Dad is not invulnerable to its influence, and yes, I'm glad he's back, but I'm only glad if the person we're getting back is *still our dad!*"

Marion breathed hard, her heart thumping in her chest. She was yelling again, and she realized she'd been holding this back for months, months and months of sitting in their velvet cage.

"Then what do we do with it?" asked Daniel, finally, staring at her. "Give it to Bowman? You just said you're not sure if you trust him."

"Sure," said Marion. "Give it to him."

"What if someone—"

"I'm tired of being selfless. I'm tired of sacrificing. I'm tired of having to fight just to have a normal life. We did it in Laurel City, having to battle just to exist. Give it to someone else. Let someone else fight that darkness."

Daniel took a deep breath. "We can't decide that for him. Only he can."

Marion shook her head. "Maybe Bowman should have The Book. He knows these things. Dad's a small town cop. A father. Why is he trying to save the world?" She paused. "And how do we know if the world even needs saving?"

"What do you mean?" asked Daniel.

"Dad is the one who said something is coming," said Marion. "There's no proof of it, anywhere else. We don't know what happened to him. We're taking him on his word." She locked eyes with Daniel. "That portal, that Book—it has done things to him, and we don't know what. He seems roughly the same—but we don't know if he's right."

Daniel met her eyes. "I trust him."

"Why?" asked Marion. "And don't tell me you trust your instincts."

"Because he is still our Dad, no matter what else. And yes, The Book has changed him, but it hasn't changed how he feels about us. He fought for Laurel City, for us, and he's still doing that. If you're asking for evidence, it's the way he talks, the way he looks at us. The silence when he doesn't know what to say. He's still our dad. He's human. That is the evidence."

Marion took a breath. Daniel's face tried to reset, back to the stoic expression Marion had grown used to. But it didn't. Instead it wavered, and Daniel's hand went to his face, and then he broke. He cried, softly, tears rolling down his cheeks.

Marion said nothing, going to him, holding him, his face to her shoulder, as he cried. She held him, Daniel twice her size, until he was done.

"I'm sorry—"

"No," she said, and grabbed a box of tissues from the bathroom, and he wiped his face and blew his nose. His eyes were red. "Don't apologize. It's hard."

"I've tried to stay strong," said Daniel. "But being watched, for months, and not knowing anything. I want to go home, too—"

He stopped and took another deep breath, before he lost control again.

"I'm sorry," said Marion. "For yelling. But like you said, holding everything for so long—"

"I do trust Dad," said Daniel. "I do. And I can't force you to do the same. But you trust me, right?"

"Yes," said Marion. She did.

"Then that's all I ask," said Daniel. "We'll get through this. We will live a normal life again. We'll get back to Cara, and to our friends."

"But what about Dad?" asked Marion.

Daniel took a breath and let it out. He looked her in the eyes. "We'll get him back. Our Dad. We will." Marion met his gaze. He didn't believe what he said.

"What's wrong?" asked Marion. "You're not telling me something."

Daniel started. "I—" He paused. "I shouldn't."

"Say it," she said. "Don't hold it in."

"You're worried about not trusting Dad. That he's being corrupted by The Book, or by the government, or chasing phantoms—"

He paused.

"—I won't say that's dumb to worry about. But it's never what *I've* been worried about. And it started right away, right when Dad came back. And it's only gotten worse over time. How did we lose him in the first place?"

Marion looked at him. "He took The Book back across. Away. To close the portal, and keep that thing out."

"Yeah," said Daniel. "And he succeeded. But The Book was the only way. And it had to be carried. And that's been my worry—no, my nightmare. That it'll happen again. And with there now being a second Book, it's worse. Let's say he's right. That there are people here, trying to bring those demons back across. That they want to open another portal."

A single tear rolled down his cheek, and Daniel wiped it away.

"What if we have to close it? What if we face that choice again? Because if we do, I know what Dad will pick. Because as much as you're tired of sacrifice—Dad isn't. If he has the ability, he will do it again. To keep those things out. We'll lose him. And—I can't face that again, not after everything."

Marion looked at him, and felt her own tears fall. "What did you say? We'll get through this. We will. Together. And we'll get Dad back, and keep him. We'll find a way."

8

"Hello?" answered Cara.

Marion had been afraid that Cara wouldn't answer. Marion's phone was new, given to her by Agent Bowman. He'd given them all their own phones, to do with what they wished. He knew Dad had called Jenny.

She had been excited to get the phone, to talk to Cara again, but she was also anxious, a nervous energy in her gut. She had paced for an hour before she called.

"Hey, it's Marion," she said quietly, trying to stay calm. Butterflies did swan dives in her stomach.

There was silence on the other end.

"Cara?" asked Marion. She looked at the phone. Did they have reception here? Marion had come to the surface to make the call, but still—

"I'm here, I'm here! Oh my god, Marion, are you safe? Where are you? Where's Daniel and your dad? I got your text, about your dad coming back, and I went to your house, and you weren't there, and no one in town knows where you went—"

"I'm safe. We're safe," said Marion. "Safe now. We were taken by the government."

"Jesus," said Cara. "Why? Your dad?"

"Well, yes," said Marion. "I don't know what I should tell you. We're still with the government, I guess, but we got transferred to somewhere more friendly."

"What you can tell me?" she asked. "What happened to your dad? Where did he go? What was on the other side of the portal?"

Marion took a deep breath. "I don't really know. He still hasn't told us. He came back over, and said that they were coming, and he had to stop them."

"Who?"

"I don't know," said Marion. "The enemy on the other side. But he brought back The Book with him."

There was a silence from Cara. "Oh no."

"Yeah," said Marion. "His hands—they're all scarred up. And it's why they took us. They wanted what he knew. About The Book—about using it."

They talked for hours, until the phone burned hot against Marion's face. She told Cara everything she could. And a hollow spot inside her, one she hadn't recognized, slowly filled.

"When are you coming back?" asked Cara.

"I don't know," said Marion. "I think we're working on it. But until the stuff with The Book is settled, I don't think we can leave."

"I miss you," said Cara.

"I miss you too," said Marion. "I promise, we'll come back as soon as it's safe. Love you."

"Love you too," said Cara, and the call ended.

*

"Do you have a minute, Agent Bowman?" asked Marion. He looked at her from his computer monitors, his face measured as always.

"Marion," he said. "Surprised to see you. Please, have a seat. Close the door."

Marion had found her way back to his office. After her conversation with Daniel, after talking to Cara—she needed to know if she could trust Bowman.

In more ways than one.

Marion closed the door and sat down opposite him.

"I need to talk to you about The Book," she said, looking at him.

"Well, I do appreciate your directness," said Bowman. "What about it?"

"You gave it to my dad."

"I did, yes," said Bowman. He raised an eyebrow. "And?"

Marion took a breath. In a certain way, it was easy to talk to Agent Bowman. She didn't have to be careful about anyone's feelings.

"You trust him with it?" she asked, finally.

"Yeah, I think I do," he said. "Why? You don't?"

"You've seen his hands," said Marion. "It's impossible not to notice."

"Yes," said Bowman. He said nothing else.

"Well?"

"I need to earn your father's trust," he said. "Only he knows what went on through that portal. It won't do if he won't tell me."

"You're bribing him."

"I'm earning his trust."

Marion stared at him. "I trust the man that went through the portal."

"But not the man who came back?"

"I don't know yet," said Marion. "But he seemed more himself the further he was from that Book. Even if we were stuck."

"He won't be keeping it long term," said Bowman. "But he has to give it to me. I can't take it."

"What about after he talks to you?"

"You want me to take it from him, after getting the information from him?"

"You weren't there," said Marion. "In Laurel City. You didn't see what damage it caused. It almost ripped us apart."

"Believe me, I want to lock it away," said Bowman. "And I will, as soon as feasibly possible. But I believe your father, and we might just need that Book before this is over."

"Did he tell you what he saw on the other side?"

"Not yet," said Bowman. "Our full debriefing is scheduled for tomorrow."

"I don't want him using it."

"I don't either," said Bowman. "And I'll do my best to make sure it doesn't happen."

Marion read his face. Still inscrutable.

"Promise me."

"Promise you?" asked Bowman. "I can't promise anything."

"If you want our cooperation, both me and Daniel, you'll promise." Marion stared at him. Bowman stared back, considering her. He took a small breath, and she sensed the smallest amount of frustration.

"Alright," he said, finally breaking eye contact, and then looking at her again. "I promise I won't let your father use The Book."

"Okay," she said. "Thank you."

"Anything else?"

"No."

"I thought you were going to ask about your brother."

"What about him?"

Bowman raised an eyebrow. "I thought you were going to ask permission, like he did."

"Permission for what?"

"For firing range access," said Bowman. "To practice shooting. He came in here a few hours ago and asked for it. I gave it to him."

"You have a firing range?"

"Of course," said Bowman. "He's probably still there." He paused. "You have permission, too, if you want."

"I don't like guns," said Marion.

"Neither do I," said Bowman. "But I still use them."

*

They gave her ear protection on the way in, but it was still loud inside the firing range. There were only a handful of agents inside, practicing their shot. A handful of agents, scattered throughout the dozen stalls. Plus Daniel.

He was taller than any of them, and he held a pistol at arm's length, in two hands, and fired at a mid-range target, squeezing the trigger with each shot. Marion stood behind him, watching him as he fired. He had good enough aim, but he didn't fire quickly, taking a moment between each shot. Within a minute, his cartridge was empty, and he casually examined the empty gun, and then placed it down on the small table in front of him. He turned casually, and then saw Marion, his eyes widening. He gestured for her to come over. Shots rang out around them.

He yelled over the gunfire. If she looked at him while he talked, she could understand.

"Marion—"

"Why are you shooting?" she yelled.

He looked at her quizzically. "What do you mean?"

"Dad didn't want us shooting guns," she said.

"After everything that's happened to us, you don't think we should know how to handle a gun?"

There was a moment of silence, as coincidentally everyone stopped firing. It only lasted a moment, and more bullets flew.

"They just let you start shooting?" asked Marion.

"No," said Daniel. "There are a couple agents here who are qualified as instructors. They showed me the ropes, gave me some safety lessons. It's all common sense."

Marion stared at the empty pistol on the table. She'd never fired a gun before. Dad had never let them.

"It's not a snake," said Daniel. "It won't bite you."

"They're dangerous," said Marion.

Daniel nodded. "They are," he said. "You should learn,

while you have the chance."

Marion took a deep breath. The gunfire kept up around her. He was right.

"Okay," she said, over the din. "Where do I start?"

9

"What happened on the other side, Mr. Dawson?"

They had settled into their new digs at Thunder Ridge. It was a nice apartment, fully furnished. They had the run of the dormitories, and the cafeteria. Anything the employees of Thunder Ridge could use, so could they.

Agent Bowman had filled them in with all the need-to-knows, but he said they were still gathering more information. They had rested. But Bowman had requested he speak to Mike separately from the kids.

Mike stared at him now, in Bowman's small but tidy office. The Book was back in their apartment, in Mike's bedroom. Bowman hadn't forced the issue. Not yet, at least.

"Something is coming," said Bowman. "I know, I know. The forces on the other side. But what are they? *Who* are they? How did you get back?"

Mike looked away from Bowman's eyes.

"Please, Mr. Dawson," said Bowman. "I'm not going to torture you, and I'm not going to hurt your children, but we need to know what you know."

Mike looked back and Bowman's eyes seemed sincere.

"I can't trust you," said Mike, finally.

"Mr. Dawson—"

"Please, please, just call me Mike," he said. "And yes, this cage is better than the last one, and you're much nicer than Strickland, so far at least, and you've told us what you know, but—that might all be a ruse."

"Mr. Daws—I mean, Mike," said Bowman. "I took an enormous risk getting you away from Strickland. And I wasn't lying when I said that you were free to go, you and both your children, if you wanted to leave. But I also wasn't lying when I said that Strickland would come for you. You're the only living person who can hold that book. That has come back from the other side. And as long as you are, you're too valuable for them to let you live a normal life."

Mike looked at him. He remembered the alien laughter of the Oukan commander, echoing in his mind. Earth, he had said, in his broken English.

Bowman stared back, but then his face changed. He was thinking. Bowman picked up his phone and pressed a few numbers.

"Clive, yeah, it's me," said Bowman. "I'm coming down with a guest. Open it up. Yeah, yeah, it'll be fine." He hung up.

"What was that?"

"We're going for a walk," said Bowman.

"A walk? Where?"

"Trust me."

Bowman led him out of the office and down sets of hallways. As they passed other employees, Bowman nodded at them.

"The IPA has been around for a long, long time," said Bowman. "Initially founded during the Civil War, we've been protecting the belly of the United States ever since."

"Why the Civil War?" asked Mike. He continued to follow Bowman, as they came to an elevator, and Bowman pushed the down button, holding a key card next to the sensor. It beeped, and the door opened, and they went inside. Bowman used his key card again, and pushed a button with a large "A" on it. The elevator silently moved down.

"Whenever there has been wide scale conflict, the losing side will often resort to desperate measures," said Bowman. "In the dying days of the Civil War, the South was losing. They knew it was at an end, and they would do anything to win. Including using a supernatural artifact to even the odds."

"The Book?"

"No," said Bowman. "The Book had been in the Laurels care for as long as we knew. If someone else had it, we weren't aware. But the Southern leadership had gotten a hold of a weapon. A powerful one."

"What was it?"

"It was a construct," said Bowman. "Give it a task, and it would execute it, to the best of its ability."

"A terminator," said Mike. The elevator went down.

"A golem."

"Like, from Jewish folklore?"

"No, but similar," said Bowman. "But effectively invulnerable, and could be tasked to do any number of terrible things."

"It didn't kill Lincoln, did it?"

"No, Mike, that was John Wilkes Booth."

"I thought, you know, maybe it was a cover-up."

"No, that stupid truth is fact, as far as I know," said Bowman. "Stopping mediocre actors from killing the President was not in our purview at the time." Bowman paused. "The construct didn't *do* anything. We found its location, killed the men who were learning to operate it, and took it from them."

The elevator stopped then, and the doors slid open. It opened into a small lobby. One man sat at a desk.

"This your guest, Stu?" he asked. Mike guessed this was Clive.

"Yeah," said Bowman. "Mike Dawson."

"Ah," said Clive. Clive was black, bald, and looked to be in his mid-40s. He dressed the same as Bowman, but Mike saw the muscles straining at his shirt, and also the pistol strapped to his hip. "The Bookmaster. We going to get that in here any time soon?"

"Hopefully," said Bowman.

"You'll be alright in there?" asked Clive.

"He's not a threat," said Bowman. "At least not to us."

"Fair enough," said Clive, as his eyes finally went to Mike, gave him a wink, and pushed a hidden button, that buzzed open the only other door in the room, a full metal door that Bowman pulled open and stepped through, and looked back to Mike to follow him.

The door slammed shut behind them, and Mike heard it

click locked.

"Can't let anything out," said Bowman. "Even on accident."

"Does that happen often?"

"Often?" asked Bowman. "No. But once in a great while, something will worm its way out. We have to be vigilant."

Hallways stretched in three directions from them, left, right, and dead ahead, with intersecting hallways, cutting across as far as Mike could see. Dozens, if not hundreds, if not thousands of rooms were here.

"How far does this go?"

"I don't know," said Bowman. "We expand constantly. We always want a buffer of empty space, just in case we need it. But there's over a thousand rooms, I can tell you that."

"Why are we down here?"

"I wanted to show you," said Bowman, and walked next to the first room. Bowman pushed a button, and a thin wall panel slid down, revealing an observation window. A humanoid shape stood in the room, immobile, made of stone. It stared ahead, blankly, its mouth slightly agape.

"That's the golem," said Mike.

"It's traveled a lot," said Bowman. "This facility was built relatively recently. But this was the first, and so it stays here, under lock and key."

"Do all the rooms have windows?"

"No," said Bowman. "Case by case basis. But the construct doesn't do anything unless instructed, and very few people have access to this room. And no one can open it by themselves."

"Is it alive?" asked Mike, staring at its blank expression, its open eyes. Was it thinking? Waiting?

"No," said Bowman. "At least not by any measurable standard. And that's all we can go by." Bowman pushed the button, and the panel slid up again. "All these rooms are shielded in a dozen different ways, some of them specially to guard against whatever is inside." Bowman walked away, and Mike followed him. He went down the central hallway, and turned corner after corner, past a dozen different rooms. Mike quickly lost his sense of direction.

"Every single one of these rooms has something in it," said Bowman. "Something powerful, or dangerous, or both." Bowman turned down another hallway, and walked past a dozen rooms until he stopped at another. He pushed a button, and the same panel slid away, revealing a window into the room. Bowman gestured inside.

Mike looked. The room was empty, except for a table in the center of the room. On it sat a cup. A drinking glass, filled with a golden liquid. The glass was tinged green. It looked to be from the 70s.

"What's that?" asked Mike.

"It's a cup, filled with ambrosia," said Bowman.

"Ambrosia?"

"Nectar of the gods," said Bowman. "The sweetest, purest substance to ever exist."

"What does it do?"

"What do you mean?" asked Bowman. "It's doing it right now. It contains ambrosia. It will always contain ambrosia. No matter how much anyone drinks, there will always be ambrosia in it."

"But what does it do? If you drink it?"

"It's restorative," said Bowman. "Like super powered steroids. You heal faster. You need less sleep. Seemingly cures all illness and disease. And we haven't been able to study it well, but we also think it will extend your lifetime. Maybe infinitely."

"Then why is it in there?" asked Mike. "Couldn't we use it?"

"Well, for starters, it stops working if you dump it out," said Bowman. "No transferring the substance. So although it may seem infinite, it's really not. Unless it passes from that cup onto someone's lips, it's worthless."

"There's some other catch, isn't there?"

Bowman stared at the cup. "Where do you think we found this?"

"The Middle East, somewhere?"

"No," said Bowman. "California."

"California?" asked Mike. "How?"

"We don't know," said Bowman. "We keep our ears to the ground. We heard reports of a long-lived man. Not only long-lived, but someone who never aged. We came to his home, and he opened fire on us before we could even speak to him."

"He knew you were there for the cup."

"Oh, definitely," said Bowman. "This was well before my time. We tried to capture him non-violently, but he wouldn't allow it. Killed himself with a shotgun. He was convinced we were going to take the cup from him, and he decided he'd rather die."

Bowman closed the window.

"It's addictive," said Bowman. "Naturally, it would be. But our limited research showed that it's the most addictive substance to ever exist. So let's say we want to use it to cure cancer. We line up every cancer patient in the world, and give them a sip. They'll want more, but unfortunately, there's only one cup. And they would kill to get more of it. Kill, or die in the process."

Bowman looked at Mike. "Like I said, there's thousands of rooms in here, and every item has that potential. But every single one of them would upend the status quo, in deadly ways. And this isn't the worst of it. The truly bad stuff, the memetic viruses, the dimensional pathogens, the impossible geometry—that's somewhere else. A prison no one visits. Not even me."

Mike understood. He asked the question Bowman wanted him to ask. "Why haven't you put The Book in here?"

Bowman looked at him and raised an eyebrow. "What would you do if I took The Book from you, all of a sudden?"

Mike didn't have to think about the answer. "I'd be upset. Especially knowing what I know. I would think you're the same as Strickland."

"Strickland, and BENT, has wanted access to these items for as long as they've existed. They wanted to use them when we invaded Afghanistan, and Iraq, and a dozen other conflicts that the public doesn't know about. But we've never let them, and we never will. All of them are beyond humanity. We are not equipped to use them properly, and we do our best to ensure that. It's why we got you and The Book away from him." Bowman looked at him in the eyes. "Mike, please tell me what happened on the other side. Please tell me what's coming for us."

Mike looked down the hallway, at the innumerable rooms he couldn't see the end of. Each containing danger. The Book surely belonged here.

He sighed. "Alright."

10

"It's not Hell," said Mike. "I don't know what Hell is or isn't. I used to believe that Hell was real. After crossing over, and then coming back—I don't know anymore." Mike paused. "Sorry, I haven't told anyone this, not even the kids. It's hard to talk about."

"Take your time," said Bowman. Mike took a deep breath. Silence hung in the room.

"It's not Hell," said Mike. "But it's hellish. Not much food or water. Very little oxygen, which is only a problem for humans. The people there, I don't know what they breathe, but it's not oxygen."

"How did you survive?" asked Bowman.

"It's a world at war," said Mike. "For how long, I don't really know. They don't measure time the same way we do.

They can't because they're not in our solar system. And I think traveling between worlds distorts time as well. I may have only been gone seven months, but I'd guess that I was there for way more than seven months."

"We've noticed a time dilation effect in the few experiments we've done with interplanar travel. Inconsistent, though."

Mike glanced at him. "Interplanar?"

"It's as good a term as any," said Bowman. "It's only a handful of times, over decades. We've never come away with any useful information, and usually it's cost us. So we stopped tinkering. But we don't think it's a different planet. We think it's a different plane."

"A different dimension?" asked Mike.

"Maybe," said Bowman. "But physics doesn't apply. At least not our physics. There might be laws that govern it, but we don't know. Any sufficiently advanced technology is indistinguishable from magic. We've encountered technology that skirts around magic, like The Book, but any kind of experimentation would prove too costly. Best to just shut the door. We had hoped you'd be able to tell us."

"I don't know where I went," said Mike. "Well, that's not true. The place I went is called Ulum. For as long as they can remember, they've been at war."

"Who's they?"

"The Kajahar," said Mike. "They took me in. They're the reason I'm still alive. I would have died without them. They fed me, and used their magic to keep me breathing."

"Who are they?"

"I spent a lot of time there," said Mike. "Like I said, I don't really know how long. But the entire time, I was talking to them, and living with them. I don't think I ever got a handle on everything. A part of it is that they themselves don't know."

"They don't know who they are?" asked Bowman.

"No," said Mike. "Their history has been taken from them. By the Oukan."

"Who—"

Mike stared at Bowman. "They rule. The Kaja are rebels, trying to stop them. And failing. They were failing. Until I arrived, and I helped them, with The Book."

Bowman's eyes went to Mike's hands. The thick scars, laced through his palms. Mike squeezed them. He felt the scar tissue.

"I had to," said Mike. "They would have lost without my help. They might have fallen now, now that I'm not there. After I took The Book from them."

You can't leave us, not now. We need you.

"You said they were coming," said Bowman. "Who is coming?"

"The Oukan," said Mike. "They're not the same race as the Kaja. I pieced together that they conquered Ulum. They've built up an army of monsters. Those creatures, that we saw in Laurel City—those are some of them. But there are others. And—and there's no end to them. And that's before you get to the Oukan themselves, who are incredibly dangerous. They're conquerors."

Bowman stared at him. "No end to them?"

"I mean, I don't know that," said Mike. "But it felt like they were infinite. I was able to stop them with The Book, but it was always temporary. They always came back with more. The Kaja suffered many losses. And it was more than the fear eaters. There were these massive things, that towered on two legs, with battering rams for arms. They functioned only to smash, to destroy—"

"Mr. Dawson, I mean, Mike—" interrupted Bowman. "I do want the details of that, but who told you they were invading? How? When?"

Mike looked at him. "We captured a commander," he said. "We interrogated him. He said they were coming for Earth."

"He said that specifically?"

"Yes," said Mike. "And—and he said that they had someone here, preparing for their arrival."

Bowman said nothing at first, only staring at Mike. His eyes wavered for a moment, his facade breaking. Mike saw the fear. And then his facade returned.

"Who?" asked Bowman.

"He wouldn't say," said Mike. "No matter what we did. He laughed in my face. He said they would transform our world. And—and that it would be soon."

"Jesus," said Bowman. "Jesus Christ." He put his head down into his hands, rubbing over his eyes, and squeezing the bridge of his nose. He looked up again. "Do you think he was talking about the Laurels?"

"I don't think so," said Mike. "I doubt they knew about the Laurels at all."

"Then who?" asked Bowman.

"I don't know," said Mike. "I didn't have a day before I was taken by Strickland, and locked away. You tell me."

Bowman looked at him, his eyes wide. He didn't know. "I could make guesses—but that's all they'd be. And we don't work with guesses. Not unless we absolutely have to."

Mike stared back at him. "An officer said they had people here, preparing for their arrival. I come back, and I'm immediately taken. Six months go by, and you get me out of there. And sure, you're nicer than Strickland, I'll give you that. And certainly smarter. And you seem to be telling the truth. You seem to be laying all your cards on the table. But you tell me, Agent Bowman. Who can I trust?"

Bowman stared at him.

"Because Strickland and his people were pretty demanding. For prisoners, we were treated fairly well, but still, it was always clear they wanted what The Book contained. You tell me they want to turn it into a weapon. Fair enough. I believe you. But it doesn't mean that *you* don't want what's inside The Book. That you don't want to turn it against us, and open a portal to their world, and this time, instead of summoning a handful of creatures, you won't bring over the entire Oukan army, to take over the Earth. And sure Strickland was willing to do god knows what to get me to cooperate—but I just spent months, or years, or I don't know, using The Book to fight a war, because it was the only way."

Silence hung in the room.

"They are coming, Agent Bowman. I don't know when, or how, but he wasn't lying. I bent reality to get back here, and put my body through fresh hell to do it. I left the Kaja behind, without a hope in the world, because I wasn't going to let Earth be overrun. You tell me, who can I trust?"

Bowman stared at him. His face was calm again, after the burst of fear that Mike had caught. But that single burst of fear proved a lot. Maybe more than Bowman knew.

"There's nothing I can say that can prove I'm not an inside man, so to speak," said Bowman. "But I don't care about the circumstances, I don't want you to use that Book. Ever. I want to lock it away, for good. The only reason it's not down in some depths that no one will find is because I want your trust. If you hand me The Book, no one will see it again."

Mike read Bowman's eyes again. He saw only the truth in them. Bowman had spoken plainly about what he wanted, and how they were involved.

But Mike couldn't give him The Book. Not yet. Doubt still lingered somewhere inside him, a slight feeling of fear and concern, a small piece that he worried would unravel. He wasn't sure, and he couldn't give up The Book, not until he was confident it was safe.

You don't want to give it up. It's got its hooks *in you.*

"Where's the second Book?" asked Mike.

Bowman held his gaze for a second, and then grabbed a folder off his desk, and opened it, flipping through it.

"A small town in the suburbs of Colorado Springs called Night Hill," said Bowman. "We detected the same energy we did from Laurel City."

"A new Book?" asked Mike.

"We don't know," said Bowman. "But we've never detected it before. Our suspicion is that its source is the same as The Book we have, just that this new one hasn't been used since we've been looking."

"How does it stay hidden for so long?"

"Maybe it wanted to," said Bowman, eyeing Mike. "Maybe it waited, out of sight, in someone's attic, or in the backroom of a library, or bookshop, and when it sensed someone desperate, or weak, or compatible, it sent out feelers."

"Have you found it?" asked Mike.

"No," said Bowman. "We sent two scouts, for reconnaissance. At first glance, the town seemed completely normal. Small place, standard western small town."

"But—"

"But with some snooping they quickly realized it was all a facade. The whole town is on edge. Having normal conversations with anyone is impossible. The scouts are smart. They know what questions to ask, and how to get information from people. It took a while, but they finally got some info. And talked to the person with The Book."

"And?"

"It's a little girl, named Lyssa."

"How old?"

"Eight or so," said Bowman. "At least, that's what the scouts reported."

"A little girl has a Book?" asked Mike. "That seems dangerous."

"I would agree."

"What else have they learned?"

"I don't know," said Bowman. "We lost touch with them, two days ago." Bowman paused. "We think they're dead."

"Jesus."

"We don't know what happened," said Bowman. "But it's hard not to suspect the worse."

"The Book—or Books—they're—they're overwhelming," said Mike. "Even for me, or the Laurels, adults, who know what they're facing. I can't imagine what it's doing to a little kid."

"That's why we want to get it," said Bowman. "And fast. We're not waiting on this one. And I know Strickland wants it too. The faster we move, and get out with it, the better off we'll be." He put down the folder, and looked again at Mike.

"We're sending a full team in, and I want you with them."

"When?"

"As soon as they're all here," said Bowman. "I'll be going with you. The last few people should arrive tomorrow. We'll debrief here, and then take a private plane to Colorado. Are you on board?"

"There's someone on the inside, Agent, someone who is going to betray humanity."

"Controlling the Books is the surest way to control any potential invasion," said Bowman. "If there is a Judas in our midst, they will want The Books for their own means. We control The Books, and we will ferret out whoever is working with the other side."

"Then I'm aboard."

"I'm not taking this lightly," said Bowman. "It's why I got you out from under Strickland's thumb, and why you're coming with me to Colorado. This is my job, Mike. It's life or death, every day."

11

The trip through the portal was hell.

Mike didn't know what lay on the other side, or if he would even survive the journey, but he jumped through, taking The Book with him.

The portal was not intended for humanity.

It pulled at him, pulled at every piece of him, time moving instantly and infinitely, both at once, and Mike wouldn't remember the experience on the other side, only the agony, the pain, the torture of his body as it traveled.

He vomited when he arrived, throwing up bile from an empty stomach. It splashed onto the red earth below him. He coughed it up, until his gut was empty, still sore and roiling, but the urge was gone, and he looked up.

Black mountains stood on the horizon, sharp, cutting

into a violet sky. The light was dim, but there was no apparent sun, no star in the sky that provided it. The ground was red, a dark crimson close to the color of blood, hard and rocky, with little sand. He bent to touch it, to make sure this was real, but then he thought better. He didn't wear gloves, still wearing the disheveled clothes of his Halloween costume. He shouldn't touch anything. It might be poison—

He staggered, suddenly, the world tilting, and he caught himself. Mike took a deep breath, and it hurt, his lungs aching. He realized the question—was there oxygen here?—but he could breathe, even if it hurt. It might not be a lot, but it was something.

Visions from the portal flashed in front of his eyes, a quick succession of pain and torment and existential torture that had torn his mind apart in an instant but had lasted for years but he couldn't remember it, but it lurked there behind his eyes, but he blinked them away, and tried to take in his surroundings, he—

He needed to get back.

The black mountains stood against the violet sky, and the ground was red, and he stood in the middle of a primitive henge, with standing stones, carved from the same black stone of the distant mountains, and he was alone.

Mike tried to focus, but his mind shook and trembled, and his feet were unsteady. He moved outside of the standing stones, away from the site of his travel. He didn't know what to look for, or where he was, but if this was the home of the harvesters of sorrow, of whatever else was coming through that portal, he needed to find shelter. They would tear him apart, out in the open.

Outside of the henge, his view was still limited. The terrain was rocky. He stood among foothills that led to the mountains in the distance. But how far were they? How tall were they?

Mike pushed those questions away, even as his lungs ached. There wasn't enough oxygen in this air, and his lungs strained to get even the barest taste of it as he panted.

He could barely stand, but he pushed away from the henge, away from his arrival. If they knew he'd come through, it wouldn't be safe to stay there. They'd be here soon enough.

He had to get his bearings. The foothills rose ahead of him. If he could get to the top, he could get a sense of his surroundings—

This place is alien, Mike. There is no air. There is no food. You will die here, alone, suffering, starving.

Mike pushed past his thoughts. He would get to the top of this hill, and take it from there. One step at a time.

Then he heard it. The ominous sound of the harvesters of sorrow. Or more accurately, the sound of his terrible memory, the phone ringing, but he pushed it away. If he let the memory overwhelm him, he'd be dead on his feet, devoured while his mind was trapped in his trauma.

He kept moving, away from the sound of the terrible ringing phone, onto rockier terrain, and he moved as fast as he could, as fast as his aching lungs would allow, away from the scrabbling maws of fear and trauma.

He pushed himself hard, away from them, but his vision was fading, going in and out, and he had to find somewhere to hide, somewhere to catch his breath—

There is no catching your breath. Your lungs will forever ache until they give out, this place is not meant for you—

He scrambled over the rocks, over the red earth, away from the ringing sound of the fear eaters, the black mountains still piercing the sky in the distance, still as far as ever—

Mike's foot caught a rock, and he fell, tumbling, and the sharp rocks cut him as he fell. His chest rose fast and hard, as he finally came to a stop, laying on the ground.

Get up. Get up, or you're going to die here.

But he couldn't. He wasn't getting enough oxygen, and his blood wouldn't go, his heart wouldn't take it, could barely take just laying there, and the sound of ringing phones got louder, and his vision faded—

Footsteps approached.

"Scarv na grash," said an alien voice, words that Mike couldn't understand, words that strained his ears just to hear.

"Mar kov, mar kov," said another voice, and Mike felt hands grab him, and pick him up. Their grip was strong, and Mike tried to open his eyes, tried to speak, to see who or what had grabbed him, but his lungs ached.

"Please, no," he said, and his eyes got a brief glimpse, of skin the same color of the earth here, of inhuman features, of black eyes with white pupils, shaped like an oval, and they looked at him, and said a handful of alien words, and his eyes were closed for him.

*

Mike woke up in the dark.

He reached for his phone, looking for the time. Why had he woken up?

And then he realized he was not in his bedroom, not in

his comfortable bed, and his phone was out of reach. He was in a small cot, not uncomfortable, but not his bed.

His lungs didn't hurt, not now. He breathed clear and easy. Then he remembered his arrival in this world, and his harried journey away from the henge, and—

Someone had picked him up.

"Hello?" he shouted. "Hello?"

There was no answer, but the room was dark. As much as Mike strained his eyes, he saw nothing.

"Hello?" he shouted again, louder. He heard a shuffling noise and then suddenly a dim light filled the room as the door opened, and Mike saw he laid in a small hut, with dark red walls of an unknown material.

A shape came into the hut, humanoid, but with red skin, with black eyes and white oval pupils. Their figure was lithe and lean, but moved with quiet precision.

"Mai naash," they said. "Mai naash." They spoke quietly, and with a subtle gesture to the corner, a soft yellow light lit the room, a cold yellow crystal emitting a pleasant glow.

"Hello?" he asked, his eyes straining. His whole body ached, and he strained to push himself up. The alien—Mike didn't know what else to call them—walked over, with their webbed hands out, cautioning him to stay put.

"Mai naash," they said again.

"I can't understand you," he said, as he laid back, doing his best to prop himself up on the cot. Everything hurt. The alien handed him a cup and motioned for him to drink. His throat burned, dry and rough, and he would kill for water. He smelled the liquid in the cup, and it smelled faintly like milk. He took a small sip.

It wasn't water, but it tasted pleasant, like a peppermint

tea, and he drank a few more swallows. While he drank, the alien watched him, quietly. He handed the cup back to them.

"Thank you," he said. "But I doubt you can understand me."

The alien stared at him, and then moved next to him, a slow, graceful movement. They slowly reached for him with a webbed hand.

"What are you doing?" he asked.

The alien put out their hand, palm out, and with their other, pointed at their own throat.

"Toowe noi, toowe noi," they said, and nodded at him.

"Um—I don't know what that means," he said. The alien reached for him again, and Mike only watched as their hand slowly rested against his throat, and then put their other hand against their own.

The alien sang then, a soft low rhythmic sound that Mike wasn't sure humans were capable of, and the creature's hand warmed against his throat, and he felt something shift inside him, something he couldn't calculate or even feel until it moved.

The alien sang, soft and sweet, and then their hand cooled down again, their skin dry and soft. They pulled it away.

"What did you do?" asked Mike.

The creature looked at him, with their wide, entrancing eyes. "Can you understand me?"

"I—I can," said Mike. "How did you do that?"

"Language was the first thing the Oukan used to separate us," they said. "We had to find a way to bridge the division."

"Where am I?" he asked. "Who are you?"

"You are in a hut," they said. "We are the Kajahar. I am Anjar."

"No, but where am I?"

"Ulum is our name for our world," said Anjar. "I eased your lungs. It'll make breathing possible. This world was not meant for you."

"I realize that," he said. "I'm Mike. Wait a minute—wait, where's The Book? Where is it? It's dangerous, don't—"

"We have it," said Anjar. "It's safe."

"I need it," said Mike.

Anjar stared at him. "It's a weapon of the oppressors, of the Oukan. No one should handle it."

"I need it if I want to go home," said Mike. "Please."

"You cannot go home," said Anjar. "There is no way back."

An alarm rang, loud, blaring in his ear, and Mike woke up.

He bolted upright, his eyes opening, looking for the source of the noise.

He was in a bed. A human bed. In Thunder Ridge.

12

Alarms and gunshots woke them up that night.

Marion woke with a start. Did she hear the sudden noise?

And then there was another, and another, and the alarms rang, loud.

Marion pushed herself out of bed, and out of her bedroom. Daniel and Dad were already there.

"What's happening?" she asked.

"I don't know," said Dad. He had grabbed a knife from the kitchen, and Daniel carried the fire extinguisher.

"What should we do?" asked Marion.

"Get dressed," said Dad. They waited at the door. It was locked, but still, if someone with a gun wanted in, they could get in.

Marion quickly changed. The gunshots had stopped, for

now, but the alarms still rang, piercing her ears.

"Should we barricade the door?" asked Daniel.

"I don't know," said Dad. "We still don't know what's happening."

They had only been there for five days and already, disaster.

"Maybe they'll take care of it," said Marion. "There hasn't been a gunshot in a while—"

Several gunshots rang through the air, louder now.

"That was close," said Dad. "Help me with the couch."

They moved to the couch. It wasn't that heavy, but it was something, and they had to try. They had to try.

They shouldered the couch over to the door, trying to push it into place when three loud thumps shook the door. Someone was knocking.

They all froze, looking at each other. The alarms rang over them.

"It's Bowman," said a voice from the other side. "Please open. Hurry."

Dad looked at the both of them, and cracked the door, his knife ready to strike. He opened it wider, the couch still not in the way. Bowman stood there, a pistol in his hand. He was dressed in plainclothes, in jeans and a white polo, a splatter of red across the chest.

"You're bleeding," said Daniel.

"It's not mine," said Bowman. He looked at Dad. "Get The Book. We're leaving. Now."

"What's happening?" asked Marion. "We just got here—"

"We don't have time," said Bowman. "I was stupid. We were infiltrated. BENT is here. We have to go." Bowman looked at Dad, and his body language immediately changed.

He charged off into his bedroom, and came back clutching The Book to his chest. Marion eyed it, the dark leather cover touching Dad's hands. She hated it. Hated that they were connected to it like they were.

"Follow me," said Bowman. "There's a back door. I think the path is clear, but let me handle any problems."

The alarms still rang, louder now that the door was open. Marion hadn't any time to get settled in, with her meager belongings, and now she was leaving even those behind. With one quick glance behind, she followed Bowman, with Dad in front of her and Daniel behind.

The hallways were dark, the emergency lighting on, everything cast in various shades of crimson. More gunshots rang out behind them. Bowman moved fast, not quite jogging, but walking as fast as he could, his gun out, covering every corner as they passed down hallways, and through doors that she didn't recognize. The dormitories were expansive, sheltering most of the employees.

"Oh my God," she said, as they passed their first body. A female agent, shot in the chest with something big.

"She was one of ours," said Bowman, still moving.

"Did they get to the artifacts?" asked Dad.

Artifacts?

"No," said Bowman. "The emergency lockdown will keep it isolated. It was the first thing they went for. It cost us two agents. This way."

Bowman turned, and they found themselves in another long hallway, filled with doors, none of them labeled. The alarms were quieter now, as they moved deeper into the facility. Bowman pulled a single key from his pocket and slid it into the lock of one of the many doors. Marion saw no difference in it. He opened the door to reveal the sliding metal door of an elevator. He inserted the same key into another lock and the door slid open, revealing the elevator. Bowman moved inside, and they all followed.

He pushed a manual close button, and doors closed. There was only one destination button, and he pushed that next. He took a deep breath as the doors shut. The elevator moved upward, slowly.

"It's an old elevator, but it'll get us there," he said.

"Get us where?" asked Daniel.

"An exit. There will be a vehicle and some supplies. Enough to get us out of here."

"What's the plan after that?" asked Dad.

"I—I don't know that yet," said Bowman. "I need some time to think."

"I thought we were safe here," said Marion.

Bowman looked at her. His eyes were harried, and for the first time, Marion saw worry in his face.

"I thought we were too," said Bowman. "We'll find a way through. Once we get out of here, we can reorganize."

The elevator slowed, and then stopped, the metal doors sliding open.

"Put the fucking gun down now!" yelled the man waiting on the other side, an assault rifle held to his shoulder. It pointed at Bowman, who stepped in front of the three of them. "Now!"

Bowman put his hands up, slowly stepping out of the elevator. "Hey, we don't want any trouble."

"I told you to put the fucking gun down!" yelled the man. He wore all black, dressed in tactical gear, a helmet. His face was barely visible.

"I'm putting it down, okay?" said Bowman. "I'm going to slowly lower it to the floor, alright? The people behind me are civilians. They aren't armed."

Dad slowly moved to the side of the elevator, trying to move out of the line of sight of the armed man. He was alone, covering this exit by himself. Dad put his arm around her, pulling her to the side.

"You're Agent Bowman," said the armed man, as Bowman slowly lowered his pistol to the floor. "And he's got the fucking Book. You stupid son-of-a-bitch, did you really think—"

Bowman moved fast, faster than Marion thought possible, and within a moment was inside of the gunman's reach, grabbing the rifle out of his hands and tossing it aside. The gunman tried to grab Bowman but the agent was too quick and too strong, then he ripped off the gunman's helmet and Bowman slammed it into his head CLUNK CLUNK CLUNK, the hard shell of the helmet smashing into the gunman's skull.

He fell, dazed, blood leaking from his head, and Bowman didn't hesitate, dropping his knee onto the gunman's throat, crushing his windpipe. He reached out, his arms trying to grasp Bowman, but within a minute, he was dead. Bowman retrieved his pistol from the ground.

"Jesus," said Daniel.

"He would have killed us," said Bowman. "A lot of good people died today. Let's go."

Bowman continued down the hallway, and they followed, past the dead gunman. This hallway was different than the ones they'd seen before, less finished, with concrete floors, and unfinished drywall.

It was only a short walk until another door, needing another key. This opened into the open night time air, in a small alcove in the mountainside. A jeep was parked in the space, protected by a chain link fence, and a double rolling gate.

"Get in the jeep," said Bowman. "I'll unlock the gate."

They got inside, with Marion and Daniel in the backseat, and Dad in the front. Bowman joined them after rolling open the gate. A dirt road led out past it, through the thick cover of trees.

"They didn't know about the exit," said Bowman. "Thank Christ." He glanced at them all and started up the jeep, and roared away, piloting in the dark, down the winding dirt road, the jeep bumping on the gravel. It led to a small, two lane paved road, and Bowman turned to the left.

"Where are we going?" asked Marion.

"I don't know," said Bowman. He stared out into the darkness.

"I don't know."

13

Let me think.

That's all that Bowman said, when they asked what the plan was. Or where they were headed. He said they were headed to a safe house, far from here. That they would be on the road for a while. Try to get some shuteye.

But mostly, he said let me think. He stared ahead, still wearing other people's blood, as they drove through the night.

Daniel tried to sleep, he tried, but his adrenaline ran hard through his body, and no matter how exhausted he was, he couldn't. Marion fell asleep against him, and he let her.

He looked to Dad in the front seat. The Book still sat in his lap. They were connected to that cursed thing, and now they were being hunted for it.

They had come for them. Daniel didn't need Bowman to confirm it. Bowman's eyes, once calm and confident, now were harried and concerned, and there was no doubt in Daniel's mind that Strickland had come for them, and had gone through Bowman and the IPA to get The Book.

And there was a second one out there, somewhere in Colorado.

His dad hadn't given them the specifics, only telling them he was going to help them retrieve it.

Daniel's eyes were glued to The Book. It remembered his touch.

Your blood is still inside it.

Daniel remembered the feeling of the Laurel's dagger slicing through his skin, of his blood fueling The Book, of seeing the shadows ripple and churn as those terrible creatures emerged from them.

It had been a year, and both he and Marion had seen a therapist, processing the trauma they had gone through in Laurel City, and their father's disappearance. But still, those memories would not go away. They were a part of him. The only bright side to his dad going through the portal, carrying that cursed item, was that it was gone, too.

But he had brought it back. The albatross around their neck. They couldn't get rid of it.

Daniel stared out the window, to the dim forest rushing by. They drove on a two-lane road, rarely passing another vehicle. He thought he heard the whooping sound of a helicopter above at one point, but when he looked, he saw no lights, and the sound passed.

There was no way he could sleep, not after that night, no matter how tired he was, but he closed his eyes.

The sound of a car door closing opened them. Marion was rubbing her own. Bowman was pumping gas, his on the horizon. Dad was already on his way inside.

Daniel climbed out of the car, stretching. The sun had risen. The car's clock pegged it at just after 8. They looked to be in the middle of nowhere, with clusters of trees on the other sides of plains.

"Where are we?" asked Daniel, looking at Bowman.

"Kentucky," said Bowman. Bowman answered without looking at him.

"How much farther are we going?"

"We'll be driving all day," said Bowman. "And into the night. The longer we stay moving, the harder it'll be to find us."

"Do you want me to drive?" asked Daniel. "I don't mind."

"Maybe later in the day," said Bowman, still not looking at him. His eyes scanned the road passing by the gas station, the parking lot, the sky.

"Have you seen anyone tracking us?"

"No," said Bowman. "But it doesn't mean they're not." He looked at Daniel, then. "There's a briefcase in the back. There's cash inside, if you want to buy something. Can't be traced. Use the bathroom, get food and drinks. We'll be driving until we need gas again." His eyes went back to the horizon.

Nice talk.

Daniel went to the trunk, and opened it. There was a slew of bins back there, all carefully stacked and organized. A metal briefcase laid among them, and he opened it.

Jesus.

He'd never seen so much cash in his life. Stacks of bundled bills, in all denominations. Someone had already ripped open a stack of twenties, and Daniel grabbed a hundred dollars worth. There had to be ten thousand dollars in the briefcase, at least.

He pocketed the money and closed the briefcase, after one more glance at the stacks of money.

Marion had exited the jeep by then, and he slipped her a couple twenties. "Cash, for food." Marion blearily nodded, and they went inside. The gas station was almost empty, with a single bored woman in her early 20s behind the counter, staring at her phone. Dad left the bathroom as they came in. He winked at Daniel and Marion, and then started picking through the assorted warm food options, which were limited.

By the time they left the interior of the gas station, Bowman had finished pumping gas, and went inside, to pay and use the bathroom. They were back on the road within ten minutes, Bowman still behind the wheel.

They all ate while he drove. Daniel looked to Bowman. He stared, his eyes focused on the road ahead. He'd been driving for over six hours now, but Daniel saw no sign of fatigue. He had to be tired.

He hadn't seen him eat, either.

"Where are we headed?" asked Dad, as they finished up their breakfast of gas station burritos and hot dogs.

"Kansas," said Bowman. "A safe house."

"Do we have a plan?"

"A semblance of one," said Bowman. "We can talk about it once we're safe."

His dad looked at Bowman, and he wanted to ask more questions, just like Daniel did, but Bowman had done what he could to keep them safe so far. They would trust him, at least for now.

The jeep went silent, and Dad turned on the radio, finding a station playing 80s one-hit wonders, and left it. No one complained.

Daniel stared out the window.

*

They entered Kansas with the sun already set, the temperature dropping.

Daniel had no idea where they were. They had stopped for gas multiple times. Bowman drove the entire time, always demurring when anyone would offer to drive. Daniel realized Bowman wouldn't take them up on it, and stopped asking.

They pulled into the driveway of the small bungalow in a suburb of Wichita, in a quiet neighborhood.

It was dark, almost midnight, and they were all exhausted.

"Let's unload everything," said Bowman. "And then we can sleep."

They each helped carry the bins into the small house. The bins contained food, water, extra sets of clothes, and survival supplies for all situations.

The house only had two bedrooms. Bowman took the couch, and Dad gave Marion the master bedroom, leaving the room with two twins to him and Daniel. They all retreated to their beds. It was late, and they were all weary. Even Bowman, who seemed tireless and inhuman, was sluggish. He had driven for nearly 24 hours straight, and

Daniel couldn't imagine the concentration needed.

Daniel watched as Dad slid The Book underneath the bed, near the headboard. He would sleep right above it.

The twin bed barely contained him, and Daniel's feet were right at the edge. There was a part of him that wondered if they'd be woken by gunshots in the night again.

"Ready for lights out?" asked Dad.

"Yeah," said Daniel, trying to get comfortable. He turned the light off. The dark was welcoming, after such a long day.

He closed his eyes and tried to sleep.

—

—

—

The Book called to him in the dark.

It was quiet, a subtle whisper, a gentle pull.

It had been a long time since he'd touched The Book. He'd avoided it since, never letting it close to him, ever since Dad took it from him on Halloween night.

But it hadn't forgotten him. Or maybe his body hadn't forgotten it. He didn't see the difference, but as he laid there, The Book pulled at him, impossible to ignore. It was soft, and gentle, the undertow of the ocean, standing in ankle deep water. Not a riptide, not overpowering, but always there. Always reminding him of his part.

He turned to his other side. He had slept in the car with it, surely he could do it now as well, farther away.

But the jeep was different, it wasn't dark, they weren't alone—

You're not alone. Dad is three feet from you.

—But his palms. His palms.

Daniel rolled again, the bed was too damn small, he'd

never sleep in this damn thing—

"You alright?" asked Dad, in the dark.

"I—I can't get comfortable."

"Is the bed too small?" asked Dad. "I'm sure Marion would swap with you if you asked—"

"I guess, yeah, it's too small, but—" Daniel started, and then stopped himself. The room was silent.

"You can feel it, can't you?"

"Yeah," said Daniel. "Just a little. Just enough."

Another long pause in the dark.

"I don't want to keep it," he said. "I hate the damned thing."

"You don't have to," said Daniel. "Give it to Bowman. I trust him."

"I do too," said Dad. "Except—" He stopped.

"Except what?"

"Except that this damned thing beneath my bed, it—it breeds distrust. It inspires betrayal. Its power—its unlike anything else. It corrupts. And no matter what I do, I know that me handing it off to anyone else is just spreading that distrust. Spreading that corruption."

"You can't save everyone, Dad," said Daniel.

Another long moment of silence. Long enough to think that the conversation had ended.

"That's the thing," he said, finally. "With that Book, I can. I can do anything."

"That's what it tells you," said Daniel. "But it's not true."

"On the other side, Daniel," said his dad. "I saved people. A lot of them. I helped. I fought for what I thought was right. Just like I did in Laurel City. And I left them—I left them to come back, to save you, and your sister, and—"

"Dad—"

"And look where we are," said Dad. "Running for our lives, with a target on our backs. And now—now there's another Book? If it has all the same power as this one—" He trailed off. "One is too many. What if there are more? What do we do? And—and I've only put you two in the line of fire."

"We're where we want to be, Dad. At your side. Helping you. Just like in Laurel City. You always said we fight together. This is no different. If there's one more, or a dozen, or a hundred, it's the same thing. We try and stop whatever it is from coming through."

His dad sighed next to him. "When I have trouble sleeping, because of The Book—I think about love. I think about you, and Marion, and your mom. About Jenny. It helps. It keeps that pull a little further away."

"We'll get through this," said Daniel. "Together. I love you."

"I love you too, son," he said. "Get some rest. We're going to need it."

Daniel rolled back over, and the pull of The Book was still there, amplified in the silence, but he thought about Dad, and Marion, and Mom, and then he was asleep.

14

Mike woke early, the next morning, and crept from his bedroom, leaving Daniel to sleep.

Bowman was already awake. He had brewed coffee, and Mike grabbed a mug. Bowman sat outside in the cold, his breath steaming into the air. His coffee sat next to him on a small table, same steaming. The small patio had one other chair. Bowman didn't look back as Mike stepped outside. Mike shivered once to the sudden chill, and pulled the blanket he carried around him close. The neighborhood was quiet.

"Do you ever sleep?" asked Mike, his voice low. He sat in the other chair, the small table between them.

"I don't need much," said Bowman. Bowman was dressed in casual clothes.

They sat there, as the world woke up. The light slowly grew to dim. Mike drank his coffee, and his mind awoke, the coffee warming him.

"I was stupid, Mike," said Bowman, finally. He looked out to the street, but his eyes were somewhere else.

"You shouldn't—"

"I was stupid, and it cost people their lives," said Bowman. His voice was measured, and calm, the same even tone that hid sorrow and rage.

"You saved us," said Mike. "And we have The Book."

"Small miracle," said Bowman. He took a deep breath and breathed out a plume of steam into the cold morning. "I should have seen the signs. The fact they moved on you so quickly. The rhetoric coming to us from leadership. Trying to take our budget. But I was stupid. We are old and used to the old ways. Despite everything, despite disagreements between leadership over the years, everyone has always understood the necessity of what we do. And maybe they disagreed with our intent, or our methods, but we always found a compromise, and never sacrificed anything important. We stayed true to our intent as an organization. We protected people from impossible things, and we thought—*I* thought—that no matter the opposition, no matter the politics, they would understand the necessity. They would understand the danger."

"Do you know it was Strickland?"

"Yes," said Bowman. "It all matches up. It's my fault. I got you out from under him, and he wanted you back. He wanted The Book back. But I didn't expect this to be the straw that broke the camel. I thought we had more time. I thought we would forestall him long enough."

"He attacked you. He killed agents," said Mike. "There has to be consequences, right? He can't get away with it. BENT can't get away with it. It'd be like the CIA attacking the FBI."

"He had approval," said Bowman, quietly.

"From who?" asked Mike.

Bowman looked at him, finally, with a soft and earnest eye. It delivered the message.

"The President?"

"He's in his ear," said Bowman. "Strickland is convinced we're sitting on a cache of incredible weaponry, and that we're fools for not using it." Bowman paused. "And he's not wrong. If we used some of the things we have—we'd be unbeatable. Any pissant dictator, any skirmish, we'd brutalize them. We'd break their backs."

"But there'd be a cost," said Mike. "There's always a cost."

"Yes," said Bowman. "In every way. Beyond ethical questions, beyond the cost to anyone using those things, to their soul—we are not the only ones with these items. Russia. China. North Korea, Iran. And of course, all our beloved allies, who are our friends now, but may not be in ten years. It'd be an arms race. And even one of these artifacts is too powerful. Imagine dozens of them. If one of them breaks containment, gains authority—it's the end of the world as we know it."

"Is he—"

"The turncoat?" asked Bowman. "I don't know."

"He wants The Book," said Mike. "He's already killed for it."

"If that's the deciding factor, so have I," said Bowman. "And you as well."

"That's different."

"Is it?" asked Bowman. Bowman looked back across the street, at nothing in particular. The sun was rising. "I don't know if Strickland is the turncoat. He might just be a power hungry hawk with bad intentions. There are many of them, at all levels of government. Either way, we can't let him have it."

"Can we not go to your superiors in the IPA?" asked Mike. "Can't they protect us? Can't they fight back?"

"They would try," said Bowman. "They might be doing it now. I stay out of politics. I stay on the ground. And *I* might be okay, if I surface. Probably could bargain my way out of it, as long as I leave my job, take a pension, and quietly retire. And hand over all the artifacts to Strickland and BENT." Bowman looked at him again. "But they would want you and the kids. And eventually, they would break you, or kill you. And that's non-negotiable. If we raise our heads above the surface, they'll be cut off."

"Then what do we do?" asked Mike. "Wait here? Stay hidden?"

"They'll find us," said Bowman. "Enough time, and they'll ferret us out. They're already working on it."

"So run?" asked Mike. "And how long will that last? I didn't come back to run for my whole life—"

"We're not going to run," said Bowman, a small smirk on his face. "We're going to get the second Book."

"What?"

"We're going to Colorado," said Bowman. "Today. After Daniel and Marion get up, and we get a good meal in us, we're heading for Colorado Springs."

"You said you had gotten a whole team together," said

Mike. "Are we meeting up with them?"

"No," said Bowman. "They're spread to the wind. We got a message out to them, luckily, but they can't help us. I told them to keep their heads down. Strickland will want their help."

"We're doing this alone?" asked Mike. "Isn't that dangerous?"

"Yes," said Bowman. "But we have to. Strickland is already preparing his own team. He's surely pieced together our intel, and is planning to do the same. We can't let him have The Book, turncoat or not."

"You're serious."

"Of course," said Bowman. "I was stupid. This is my fault. I'm going to set things straight. And I'm for damn sure not letting that son of a bitch kill my people *and* get a hold of that damn Book. Not happening."

"So, we're going to Colorado? All of us?"

"Well, I can't *make* you go," said Bowman. "But I'll need your help. There are only two people on Earth who have intimate knowledge of The Book, and you're one of them. The other is in Colorado. And we can't leave the kids behind." Bowman took a breath. "If you want to stop Strickland, or whoever the Judas is, your best bet is with me."

"I'm on board," said Mike. "I never said I wasn't."

Bowman looked at Mike in the eye. "I won't lie to you. BENT attacking us was a rude awakening, and it won't be roses and sunshine from here on out. It will be dangerous. Strickland won't play nice. And that's before whatever the hell is waiting for us in Night Hill. But I'll do my best to keep us safe."

"What else can we do?" asked Mike.

"When I told you I needed to think, I wasn't lying. I weighed our options. This is our best bet."

The sun rose, and the neighborhood woke up. People started going by with their dogs, and leaving for work. The temperature warmed, slightly, and they both finished their coffee.

"So—let's say we succeed," said Mike. "We avoid BENT agents. We survive whatever hell is brewing in Night Hill, and we get out with the second Book. What then?"

"That's taking a lot for granted."

"I want to know what we're getting into," said Mike. "If you've thought that far ahead."

"The Archive is locked. They can't open it, and they can't blast it open or drill into it unless they want to crack the mountain in half. They won't do that, not yet at least. If Strickland is the turncoat, who wants to open that portal and let Hell into this world, he needs a Book. If we have them both, we have the power. Once we have them both, we leverage them into drawing out whoever is the traitor, and then we stop them."

"How do we do that?"

"That's a question I don't have an answer to," said Bowman. "Not yet, at least. I have options open, but which one we use depends entirely on how successful we are in Night Hill. And how much interference we face from BENT. Maybe we get there fast enough, and they don't see us at all. Or we have to go through them. Either way, I have resources at my disposal. But I don't want to commit to them, without knowing the rest of the equation."

"Fair enough," said Mike. "What are our chances?"

"Chances of what?"

"Succeeding," said Mike.

"It depends what you consider success."

Mike watched as a happy dog walked past. It stopped to look at them, its tail wagging at the mere sight of another person. The owner smiled at them, and urged the dog along.

"Keeping the second Book from Strickland. Finding the traitor, and stopping them for good. All of us surviving."

"All of those?" asked Bowman. "Very low."

"That's encouraging."

"I'm just being honest with you," said Bowman. "But it's not impossible. The threat of failure or of death hasn't stopped me before. Or you, for that matter. You did something great in Laurel City. We can do it again."

"Do you have kids, Agent?"

"You can call me Stu," he said. "And no."

"Well, Stu, you'd make a good dad," said Mike.

"I'll keep that in mind," said Stu. "Do you want me to tell the kids, or do you?"

"I'll tell them," said Mike. "Back on the road, to save the world."

15

"Can we change the radio station?" asked Marion.

It was the middle of the day, and they'd already been driving for hours. They had just left a gas station.

"I just changed it," said Dad.

"I know, but I don't want the best hits of the 80s, 90s, and today," said Marion.

"We're in the middle of nowhere," said Dad. "There's not much else to listen to, unless you want farm reports or to be preached at."

"Alright, alright," said Marion.

Daniel stared out the window at the passing farmland. He felt better now, after a good night of sleep, but his eyes still looked to his father in the front seat, and to The Book still in his grasp.

Back in Kansas, and soon they'd be gone again. They were headed to Colorado, to get the second Book, even without the support of the IPA agents. Neither Marion nor he had questioned Dad when he told them. They trusted him.

Daniel did trust his father, with every fiber of his being.

He trusted Stu as well, at least enough. Stu wanted to lock away The Book, and keep it there, and that was enough.

But Daniel didn't trust The Book. This one, or the one in Colorado, or any others that might surface. They wanted blood, and they didn't care how they got it.

The plains passed by, endless fields, with an occasional herd of cattle dotting the landscape. A few more hours, and they'd be in Colorado.

Marion read a paperback book next to him, her nose deep in it. She'd taken it from the safe house, which functioned as an AirBnB for cover, whenever it wasn't being used. He'd thought to take something to distract him, but he didn't feel like reading.

His gaze settled on Agent Bowman—no, on Stu. He was dressed in a slacks and button-up shirt again, his eyes on the road. He had insisted on driving, and none of them had argued. But Stu's eyes weren't on the road, or not only on the road. They kept bouncing back and forth between his mirrors.

They cruised in the right lane, and then Stu put on his blinker, shifted to the fast lane and accelerated, passing the big truck in front of them, and then back over. He gassed it a little more and then stayed steady. His eyes stayed glued to the rear-view mirror. Finally, they shifted back to the road ahead.

"We're being followed," said Stu, finally.

"What?" asked Dad. "How?"

"The grey sedan," said Stu. "It was at the gas station with us. It's staying with us, but never passing."

"BENT?" asked Dad.

"Most likely," said Stu. "Or another agency assisting. But probably BENT. It was a risk, using the highway. But I wanted to get there quickly."

"What do we do?" asked Dad. "Can we lose them?"

"No," said Stu. "It's risky, and would only alert them we know they're following us. Best to play dumb."

"We can't do that forever," said Daniel.

"No, we can't," said Stu. "We have to stop them before we get to Colorado. Hopefully get some info, too."

"How do we that?" asked Marion.

"Trust me," said Stu.

*

They drove for another few hours until the gas tank was under a quarter full.

"It'll have to be believable," said Stu. "We'll take our time."

The gas station they stopped at was isolated, a single building off a lonely exit on the interstate. It was a few miles away from the highway.

"The more isolated, the better," said Stu. "It works to our advantage."

The gas station was quiet, a single other car in the parking lot, presumably the vehicle of the person manning the till inside. Stu pulled the jeep up to the pump.

Less than a minute later, the sedan drove by and pulled in. The agent parked on the other end of the small parking lot near the store. He got out and walked inside, without even a glance in their direction.

"Daniel, go inside, and go into the bathroom," said Stu. "Leave it unlocked."

"Unlocked?" asked Daniel. "Are we setting a trap?"

"Yes," said Stu. "He's going to get the drop on you. He'll have a gun. Do what he says. I'll be right behind him, and take him out. We will kindly escort him out of the gas station, and back to his car. I will take it, and him. Mike, you follow the sedan in the jeep. It will happen quickly once it happens. Everyone understand?"

"What do I do?" asked Marion.

"The same thing as your dad," said Stu. "Think positive thoughts."

"But what if something goes wrong?" asked Dad.

"It won't," said Stu. "Now go inside, Daniel."

Daniel looked at him for a long moment, and then went inside, stepping around the potholes and puddles of oil in the parking lot. On a normal trip, he would have driven right past this place. It's the type of gas station you went to when you were desperate or you lived nearby, and had no other options. Shards of glass piled in one of the parking spots, and the dumpster reeked even from a dozen feet away.

A bell dinged as Daniel stepped inside and surveyed the store. An older woman sat behind the counter and gave him a quick glance as he entered.

"Welcome in," she said in a vague midwestern accent, and then looked back at her phone. She sat on a stool, and Daniel wondered if she saw more than a dozen people in any given day. She sat in front of a wall of tobacco options, with vape pens, cigarettes, and chewing tobacco well stocked. The rest of the store looked normal, and relatively clean, which surprised him.

Daniel's height let him see the agent, who browsed the back wall, which was full of beer. The agent had already seen Daniel, or was waiting for Daniel to make a move before looking.

"Does your bathroom need a key?" asked Daniel.

"No," said the cashier, without looking up from her phone. "Feel free."

Daniel tried to stay calm and casual, and not to look at the agent, who was wearing a polo shirt and jeans, and sunglasses, and had light brown hair, cut short, and Daniel averted his eyes, and his stomach tightened.

Don't think about it, behave normally.

Daniel kept his head straight, his eyes on the bathroom, which was down a short hallway, across the hall from the ladies room. He pushed the door open, and the light was already on, the fan struggling to work. The bathroom was clean, thank God, but Daniel didn't lock the door, but he didn't want to pee. He opted to wash his hands at the sink, keeping his head down.

His heart beat hard in his chest. He'd never been in this situation before, even in Laurel City, and sure, he trusted Stu, after he had bailed them out, twice now, but still—

The door creaked open behind him, and he jumped.

"Occupied," he said.

"Don't move, kid," said the voice, and Daniel didn't need to look to know it was the agent. He felt something cold and metal in his back. "It's a gun. If you behave, everything will go smoothly."

"I don't—"

"Tut tut tut," said the agent. "We know who you are, and we know what you're doing. Where's The Book?"

"I don't know what you're talking about—"

The agent pushed the gun harder in his back, by a handful of degrees.

"Wrong answer, kid," said the agent. "Don't lie to me. I won't give you another chance—"

And then the door creaked open again, and the gun left his back, and Daniel turned to see Stu come into the bathroom, and the BENT agent swung his gun at him, trying to pistol whip him, Stu coming in too close to shoot. Would the agent shoot his gun here, with a witness out front?

Daniel didn't know, but Stu grabbed the agent's wrist, and racked it against the doorframe, and the gun went flying, clacking onto the tile floor.

"You bastard—" started the BENT agent, and then headbutted Stu, once, twice, with an awful noise, and blood was welling out of a contusion on Stu's forehead, but he was still conscious, and he dodged the third headbutt, and then the BENT agent shifted position, and Stu threw elbows into his torso, but the agent didn't budge, and up close Daniel saw he was strong, with thick shoulders, and Stu had lost position.

"You picked the wrong team," said the BENT agent, and then Daniel smashed him in the temple with the butt of the pistol, and he went down like a sack of potatoes, completely unconscious.

Stu bent over, catching his breath, his face red.

"Thank you, Daniel," said Stu. He breathed deeply, his hand at his throat. After another moment of recovery, he rifled through the agent's pockets, and took his keys, and

ID. "Can I have his gun, please?"

Daniel handed it over sheepishly. Stu tucked it into his waistband along his back, and then grabbed the BENT agent's wrists. "You take his ankles. We'll put him in the trunk of his sedan. You ride with me."

"What about the lady out front?"

"Ignore her, and move quickly, and she'll never say a word. She doesn't get paid enough to make this a problem."

16

The BENT agent was conscious when they opened the trunk. He stared at them with angry eyes, blood leaking from the contusion on his temple where Daniel had pistol whipped him.

Stu gripped the gun, pointed at the agent.

"You fucker—"

"Quiet," said Stu, his voice calm. "Get out of the trunk. Move slowly, and I won't shoot you."

Mike stood behind Stu, in the abandoned barn they had pulled the cars into. Sun peaked through holes in the ceiling, and spider webs hung in every corner of the building. Mike had followed Stu as he drove the BENT agent's sedan a few miles farther down this farm road, until he pulled off, down a dirt road that ended at this half collapsed barn. If anyone owned this place, they hadn't visited in quite some time. Daniel and Marion were outside. They didn't need to see this.

The BENT agent climbed out of the trunk, considering every movement. Stu took a single step back, and Mike did the same.

"On your knees," said Stu. "Hands on your head."

The agent fell to his knees and obeyed. His eyes went to Mike, and stayed there, staring at him.

"You look at me," said Stu. The BENT agent shifted his gaze, lingering for a second longer on Mike. He flared his nostrils. "What's your name?"

The BENT agent stared at him. Said nothing.

"This will be easier if you talk," said Stu.

The agent still said nothing, only staring at him.

Stu took a deep breath. He still held the pistol out, not wavering.

"I don't want to hurt you, but I will," said Stu. "You killed my men. I will make this painful. And I know how."

The agent stared for a second longer. "Harrison."

"See, that wasn't hard, was it?" asked Stu. "Why are you after us, Harrison?"

"You know why—"

"Why are you after us, Harrison?"

"You have The Book," said Harrison. "You have him." He nodded his head at Mike. "Did you think you could take them without consequences?"

"Consequences?" asked Stu. "You attacked a government installation, and killed government agents, good people, who have risked their lives countless times against the shadows—"

"Oh, please," said Harrison. His eyes were still filled with anger. "You people. So high and mighty. Not willing to get dirt under your fingernails. You sit on an incredible resource, a vault filled with tools that could solve the world's problems, but you refuse to open it. What did you think would happen? Did you think there wouldn't be someone who wanted them, eventually?"

"They're too dangerous. They are beyond us—"

"You would have stopped the Wrights from developing flight, because it was too dangerous—"

"I'm not arguing with you," said Stu, holding the gun firm. "Are there any more BENT agents in the area?"

Harrison stared at him. "No," he said, finally.

"Why does Strickland want The Book?" asked Stu.

"What kind of question is that?"

"Tell me," said Stu, inching the gun closer.

"I don't know," said Harrison, and Stu blinked his eyes hard, holding them closed, and then opening them.

"Tell me," said Stu. "I know that you know. You wouldn't be sent to retrieve The Book unless you were trusted."

"I don't know," said Harrison, still staring, and Stu reeled back and hit him with the pistol, a sharp thud, and Harrison grunted in pain. Blood leaked from the welt on his temple.

"Tell me," said Stu.

"Go fuck yourself," said Harrison.

Mike stared at the agent. "You think he knows more?"

"Yes," said Stu. "He does."

He knows who's behind it. Get him to talk, and we can stop them. For good.

"I can help," said Mike.

"What do you mean?" asked Stu, looking at him, finally.

"If he has the info we need, I can get it," said Mike. "With some help."

Stu took a deep breath. His face barely shifted.

"Go get it."

Mike nodded and went back to the jeep, The Book sitting in the passenger seat where he had left it. He grabbed it with two hands, and it felt good, the scars in his palms rubbing against the red leather cover.

Marion and Daniel watched him.

"What are you doing?" asked Marion.

"Dad—" started Daniel.

"Stay out here," he said. He didn't want them seeing this.

"What are you doing?" asked Marion again, and she followed him into the barn.

"Marion, go outside," said Stu, looking at her. Daniel trailed her, coming in after.

"Marion—" he said, his hand on her shoulder.

Mike's stomach ached, ice cutting inside him. But this agent had what they needed. He could help. She couldn't understand.

"Dad, please—"

"Marion," he said, meeting her eyes, his voice hard. "Go outside. You don't want to see this."

She went to speak, and a tear fell down her face, but she said nothing, and turned quickly, and left.

Mike's stomach fell. It was hurting her, he knew. She would understand, eventually. Daniel looked at him, and then followed her, closing the door behind him.

Harrison's eyes stared at The Book, not breaking away.

"I'll ask again," said Stu. "What are Strickland's plans with The Book?"

"I don't know," said Harrison, but now he didn't look at Stu. He looked at The Book. His eyes wavered. The mere presence of it was doing something to him.

"I don't believe you," said Stu. "Mike, can you make him tell the truth?" Stu's eyes were only on Harrison now, and Mike saw something new in Harrison's face, something he hadn't seen before, and that was fear. The presence of the pistol hadn't fazed him, not at all, but the threat of The Book—he was afraid.

"What are Strickland's plans with The Book?" asked Stu, again. Harrison stared at him and then looked back at The Book.

"I don't know."

Stu looked at Mike. "What can you do?"

"I need a knife," said Mike. "Something sharp."

Stu pulled a knife from his belt, near his holster, and flicked it open with one swift motion, and handed it to Mike, handle first.

Mike took the knife from Stu. He placed The Book on the hood of the sedan, and flipped to the correct page, a page he'd used before

—the sound of mourning, the sound of gnashed teeth—

Mike took the blade in hand and ran it across his palm, a motion once routine, just like riding a bike, and blood flowed from his hand, dropping onto the page, and Mike read, read the words in whips and snarls, and the language tore through the air, and from The Book ribbons of pink and red spiraled up and out.

"What the hell is that?" asked Harrison, staring. "No, no—"

"What is Strickland's plan for The Book?" asked Stu.

"I can't tell you, I can't—"

"Tell me, Harrison," said Stu. The ribbons spun through the air, as Mike continued to read. His heart pounded in his ears, his fist squeezed, blood still dripping onto the page.

"I can't—"

The blistering sounds stopped from Mike's mouth, and the ribbon left the page, and flew through the air, and snaked into Harrison's ear, and he screamed at first, but that was only the fear.

The true sorrow came next, the ribbon pulling out the worst trauma, the deepest terror, and inflicting it on him, over and over again, an infinite well of sorrow and trauma—

"Please, please," Harrison begged, tears pouring down his face, his hands grasping at his ears, trying to stop the assault. He pulled at his hair, and Stu kept the gun pointed at him. The ribbon was gone, inside his mind, and Harrison sobbed, his face wet. He wept, he moaned, he wailed, and then he stopped, as the magic faded.

Harrison sat there, in the abandoned barn, on his knees. He stared down at the ground, his chin dripping.

"I can't tell you," said Harrison. "I can't, he won't let me—"

"Do it again, Mike," said Stu.

"No," said Harrison. "Please—"

"What are Strickland's plans?"

Harrison took a deep breath.

"He said we can use it to do whatever we want," said Harrison. "That it's an infinite resource. We can take over with it. No more petty squabbles. Sheer brute force, to take what we want. To make things better."

"Is that what he said?"

"Yes," said Harrison, still not looking up.

"Did he mention anything about where The Book came from? About the other side?" asked Mike, suddenly. Stu glanced at him, before looking back at Harrison.

"He said—"

Harrison took a breath.

"—I can't," he said, finally. He looked up. "I can't."

Mike raised the knife, and brought it to his other hand.

"No, no, no no," said Harrison. "Okay. Okay."

Mike stopped, the blade an inch from his skin.

"The President—the President," said Harrison. "He said they had made a deal. He said—he said—" and then he paused, his hands going to his chest. He moaned in pain.

"Harrison," said Stu. "What did he say?"

"He said—" Harrison grabbed his chest. "The White House, use The Book to take over, the President—" He stopped. "Can't bre—"

He grabbed his chest, both his hands squeezing the skin there. He tried to pull in breath, in big whoops. Harrison wheezed, and wheezed, and inhaled, a deep, harrowing breath.

"Harrison," said Stu. "What's happening?"

"I can't—" he started. "I told you—"

And then he coughed, a gout of blood spitting out onto the wooden floor, and he coughed again, and he vomited, blood pouring out of him, with chunks of flesh and viscera, and he choked as he tried to breathe, and then he fell over.

Stu holstered his gun, and kneeled next to him.

"He's dead."

Mike sighed. "Did I—?"

"No," said Stu. "Whatever it was, it wasn't you that killed

him."

"He said the White House," said Mike. "The President."

"They're going to use The Book to take over," said Stu. "That's what he said. Take over the White House. Take the President. Or kill him."

17

Marion watched Stu, his legs crossed, sitting on the concrete pad at the back of their AirBnB. Stu sat calmly, and Marion had realized he was meditating, before she said anything. She would let him finish.

It was dark, not quite midnight. Daniel and her father were inside, getting settled in, resting after the long drive. They had driven all day, and finally made it to Colorado Springs.

Marion had seen people die before, back in Laurel City. And they hadn't killed Harrison. Someone else had programmed his death into him, something arcane killing him after he told them information he shouldn't have.

It was an awful thing, and Marion had hours of it rolling around in her mind, but it wasn't what had stuck inside.

Because she had seen people die before.

She had never seen Dad use The Book before. Had never seen him slice open his palm, and feed the dark magick, and then use it, use it to inflict pain.

Over and over again, she saw it. The knife slicing through his hand, how easy it was. How practiced it was. An abstract notion of scars turned into a quick and simple motion. The barking, snarling words that erupted from her father's throat and mouth, the smell of sulfur in the air.

He didn't know she had seen, but she had watched, silently, her eyes pressed to a hole in the building. She needed to know.

The crimson ribbon that floated through the air, *into* the BENT agent.

Her heart ached as she saw it, and that feeling sunk into her gut, and stayed there as they drove across the country. Dad sat in the front seat, his face weary and empty, and he dozed off, sleeping for most of the day. Using The Book had taken its toll on him.

After reading from The Book, he barely looked like her father at all. Something in his face had changed, something she couldn't name. As he rested, the part of him she knew slowly returned. But she knew—knew it deep inside, that if he used The Book enough times, that elasticity would die, and so would the man she knew as her dad, and the only thing left would be a shell she couldn't recognize.

She watched Stu meditate, in the darkness, the only lighting coming from the house and the sparse light pollution in the sky.

Ten minutes, then fifteen, then twenty, and then Stu finally stirred, slowly unfolding his legs, and pushing himself to his feet. He stared for a moment longer out into the empty backyard, frosted over, both of their breath fogging out into the air.

Stu turned to go inside and saw her. His eyes widened momentarily.

"Marion," he said. "I didn't expect you there."

"We need to talk," she said, simply.

Stu moved toward her. She stood in front of the door.

"Can it wait until the morning?" he asked. "I'm very tired. I usually sleep after my evening meditation. It helps—"

"We're all tired," said Marion, her voice hard. "And no, it can't wait."

Stu stopped, and took a step backward. His breath fogged in front of him. He was silent, for a moment, his face hard to read in the dim light.

"If it can't wait," he said. "What do you want to talk about?"

Marion sniffed, her nose running in the cold. Her heart beat hard in her chest.

"What was that, today?" she asked, finally.

"What was what?"

"The interrogation, Stu," said Marion. "The Book. Agent Harrison."

Stu was quiet for a moment. He finally spoke.

"I'm sorry you saw that," said Stu. "I didn't want you to. And I didn't want him to die. He had some failsafe built in, something that triggered, I don't know. BENT has been keeping secrets from me, from the agency—"

"Not that," said Marion. "You told me you wouldn't use The Book. That you only wanted to lock it away."

"I do," said Stu. "I don't want—"

"Then what was that?" asked Marion, wanting to raise her voice, wanting to yell, but keeping it hard and firm in the cold backyard.

Stu let out a short breath. "Your father—"

"My father is in the thralls of that Book, something I thought you understood when you gave it back to him. And despite the fact he has the best intentions, that Book does not. It wants to be used, it wants to sow pain and sorrow, and it wants to feed on blood. It was thirsty, and it's been sated, for now." She stared at Stu, blood pulsing in her ears. "And I thought you knew, I thought you understood. You're in charge, you're in command, and I thought you would keep it under control. But you didn't. And I had to watch my father become something else, just to get some information from that agent. Just for him to die."

"We're bent over a barrel, Marion—"

"I don't care!" said Marion, now almost yelling. The neighbors would hear, Daniel and her dad would hear. "I do not care. Nothing is worth that cost. He's paid enough."

Stu exhaled, and turned around, facing the backyard again. His breath plumed in front of him. He turned back.

"What do you think I want?" he asked, finally, his voice level.

"To get the second Book," said Marion.

"No," said Stu. "That's not what I mean." He took a breath. "I want to stop an extradimensional invasion of the Earth. I want to keep a war from happening with demigods from another plane, a war the US, and the world, will inevitably *lose*. A large contingent of humanity will then be enslaved. I want to stop that as well. An effective end to our way of life, forever. That is what I want. To do that, I need that second

Book, yes, but I also need to keep you all alive, I need information from that BENT agent, and I need to also keep them off our backs."

"We don't know—"

"No," said Stu. His voice was still level, but it cut through Marion's. "I know. You're worried about him. You should be. It's the appropriate response. But I am telling you, that your father's soul is only a small part of a much larger equation. One with a narrower and narrower window of success with each moment. And maybe that hurts to hear. Take the advice I was given, early on—you'll get used to it."

Marion stared at him. "What?"

"You'll get used to it," said Stu. "My first promotion. Only a few years after I was hired. There was a slew of retiring agents, and I got a promotion out of necessity, probably earlier than I should have. Not to say I wasn't ready—but I wasn't ready. Not really. I made do. But suddenly I wasn't a junior agent anymore. I was a leader. I made decisions. And there was an operation, where we had to recover a dangerous artifact. And it was dangerous. It didn't belong in the wild. It would kill people. So, we had to reclaim it. I had a team. And—well, the long and short of it, we succeeded in capturing the artifact, and locking it up. But I lost two junior agents. Both died, and neither were pretty. I felt responsible. I *was* responsible. Not because my decision led directly to their deaths, but because I was in charge. I've thought back about it, and there was nothing I would, or could have done differently. Those agents would have died either way. But I am responsible."

"Stu—" Marion's heart hurt.

"Please, let me finish," said Stu. "I felt bad, afterward. Felt bad enough that I questioned if this job was for me at all. I went to a senior agent. One of the men on their way out, about to retire. I told him how I felt. He told me—that you get used to it. That you get used to the pain and guilt. And he made a distinction. He didn't say the pain or guilt didn't happen. He said you get used to it. That your capacity for that pain and guilt deepens. You get tougher. You can withstand more. He told me to reframe those losses in my mind. He told me, that in this line of work, loss was inevitable. The danger was so high, so omnipresent, that it was unavoidable. He told me that my highest responsibility, above everything else, was to make those losses count. To make sure that the payment equals the cost. Yes, those two agents died, but in response, we removed a deadly artifact from the world, that would have killed many more than two people."

Marion stood silent, pain filling her. She said nothing. Stu wasn't done.

"I still don't know how many we lost when BENT hit us," said Stu. "Too many. You didn't know them. I did. They are my responsibility. It is also my responsibility to ensure that their deaths are not empty. That we stop this invasion from happening, that we root out the traitors in our midst, and we lock up those Books for good. And I understand. He's your father. I would feel the same way. And when he introduced the idea of using the book to get that information from Agent Harrison, I balked, but only briefly. Because we are running out of options. And in a perfect world, we would never, ever have to use The Book, or anything like it. But in a perfect world, none of my agents would die." He sighed. "I don't want your father to use The Book when it isn't necessary. It's dangerous and can be uncontrollable, even for him. But we do not live in a perfect world, a world of black and white. Do you understand?"

Marion stared at him, her eyes wet. "Yes," said Marion. "Did he tell you what happened to him, on the other side?"

"Yes."

"And you believed him?"

"Yes," said Stu. "Yes, I did."

"Tell me."

"No."

"Why not?"

"It's not my place," said Stu. "If he hasn't told you, he has his reasons. And I won't betray them."

"I need to know," said Marion. "It's past time."

"Then I suggest that you ask him," said Stu. "I'm going to bed. Tomorrow will be a long day."

*

Marion found her father inside. He was sitting with Daniel, both of them absently watching the news. The Book wasn't with him.

She stood in front of them.

"Dad, it's time," she said.

"Time for what?" he asked, cocking a sleepy eyebrow. Daniel looked at her, with a question in his eyes, but he already knew what she would ask.

"We want to know what happened," said Marion. "When you crossed over, and when you came back."

"Marion, I can't—"

"No," she said. "It's been long enough." Daniel eyed her and grabbed the remote and turned off the TV. He got up and stood behind her. They stood together. Marion already felt better, with him standing with her.

Dad eyed them both, looking up at them. He didn't look defiant, though, or angry. He looked—well, he looked afraid.

He looked down at the floor, and then back up at them, and then softly nodded.

"Okay," he said, looking back at them. "Take a seat. I'll tell you."

And he did.

18

Mike studied The Book. Light came from a pair of yellow crystals, secured at each corner of the hut he now called home.

It hurt. His head ached, a deep twinge of pain behind his eyes, and every word from The Book hurt even more.

He didn't want to read it. Mike didn't even want to *touch* it, not after Laurel City, not after what The Book had wrought upon his family.

But it was the only way back.

And it was the only way to defend himself, in whatever this place was.

The language wasn't English, or any language native to Earth. But Mike could still read it. The word *read* was the best he had to describe it, but it was more like imprinting.

As he stared, the meanings of the individual marks became clear, and knowledge was gained.

It wasn't natural, not to the human body, and his head let him know, with a deep, pounding ache. He took breaks when he could, but the information was in The Book, he knew, and his physical limits were all that kept him from going back home.

It had opened a portal once. It could do it again.

Mike heard the door rattle open, and he looked up from The Book, the hammering behind his eyes immediately lessening.

"You shouldn't read that," said Anjar, coming in through the door. "It's corrupting. Dangerous."

Mike looked at them. "You let me keep it, though."

"The elders didn't want it kept here," said Anjar, moving into the hut, closing the door behind them. They sat down in the other simple chair. "They wanted to bury it. I convinced them to keep it here. Quiet. With you."

"You convinced them?" asked Mike. He closed The Book, and the headache lessened again. He could almost think.

"Yes," said Anjar. Their face was unreadable. They smirked, but Mike didn't know if that meant here what it did back home.

"You just said—"

"I spoke the truth," said Anjar. "It is corrupting. It is dangerous. But—it is also *powerful*."

"So I'll be the guinea pig?" asked Mike. The words "guinea pig" came out in English, and Anjar looked at him with confusion. Mike thought quickly. "Test case."

Anjar nodded. "Well, to them, yes. Too dangerous for a Kajahar to handle. An Earthen, though? Sure." They paused.

"But you are not a test case to me."

"What am I, then?" asked Mike.

Anjar stared at him, considering. "A potential ally."

"I don't know how long I've been here," said Mike, staring at them. "And the only time I've left this hut is to use the bathroom. Is that how you treat an ally?"

"You're from the other side. You're unprecedented, here. The Oukan, yes, sometimes they field visitors, welcome and unwelcome. But we, we do not. So they don't trust you. They consider you unknowable."

"I'm not complicated," said Mike. "I just want to go home."

"We are not that different," said Anjar. "They will come to understand. Maybe not with empathy. But if you help us fight the Oukan, and any other raiding groups, they *will* respect you. They will respect you can control The Book."

"What are you asking me?"

"Continue reading The Book. Continue being wary of all you find inside. But I do not want us to be terrified peasants for the rest of our lives. I do not want to carve out a life from the scraps of what the Oukan give us. I want us to have lives again. The key is in that Book."

"You trust me with this?" asked Mike. "With something so powerful?"

Anjar stared at him, for a moment, holding his gaze. Finally, they spoke. "Can I show you something?"

"Show me what?"

Anjar paused. "History," they said, and approached Mike. They reached toward him and put a palm to his forehead.

"What is this—" he started, and then he was bombarded with images.

A village, much like this one. A shifting perspective, fragmentary moments.

The village being attacked. Burning. Kaja screaming, running in terror. And then he saw them. The Oukan.

They stood massive amongst the Kaja, and they destroyed, reaping with glee.

The perspective changed again, and Mike realized these were not random images.

He saw slavery next. Kaja in chains, in collars, being beaten as they worked. Misery by his eyes. Hunger. Pain. Brutality.

But only in passing. They did not stay there long, before they were somewhere else.

Now, they were surrounded by Oukan. They dwarfed him, as he served them. And he saw first hand that the brutality extended beyond the work camps.

He saw brief glimpses of other foreigners, other creatures from other planes, also serving.

A thousand images passed through his mind, and none redeemed the Oukan.

His mind was overwhelmed by a rush of thoughts and feelings, and Mike lived through them within a moment, and then they were gone again, only minor figments.

Mike gasped, reaching for a breath he didn't know he needed.

"Are you okay?" asked Anjar.

"I—I will be," said Mike. He caught his breath, his heart pounding in his chest. He wiped the thin layer of sweat from his forehead.

He looked at Anjar, meeting their eyes.

"Those are your memories," said Mike. "You lived with

them."

Anjar nodded. "They captured me. Enslaved me. Tortured me."

"I—I'm sorry."

"Do not apologize for them," said Anjar, their voice as firm as Mike had heard it. "They, and they alone, are responsible for their horror. For the pain, for the torment, for the rape."

"I still don't understand," said Mike.

"You asked about trust," said Anjar. "Do you trust me?"

"You saved me," said Mike. "And you've kept me alive. I trust you as much as I can."

Anjar nodded. "*We* are all we have. And by putting trust in you, I hope you will do your best to meet that trust."

Mike nodded. He sighed.

"I have nothing against you, or your people," said Mike. "But this isn't home. Before I came here, I thought this was Hell." The word came out in English.

"I don't know what that means," said Anjar.

"In my beliefs, there was a binary system of the afterlife. If you were good in life, you went to Heaven. If you were bad, you would go to Hell."

"Ah," said Anjar. "This is not Hell. It is just another place."

"I want to see my children again."

"How many?"

"Two," said Mike. "Daniel and Marion."

"I can understand the urge to help your offspring."

"They might not need my help anymore," said Mike. "But I miss them. And if there's a way in here to get me home, I'm going to find it. No matter how dangerous it is."

"If you help us, I will ensure you get back home," said

Anjar.

"Help you how?"

"Learn," said Anjar. "Find out what The Book is capable of. I will work on giving you more freedom. I know it is hard. But the elders are slow. Pati—"

The loud sound of a horn blowing interrupted them. Anjar listened.

"Raiders!" they yelled. "Hide The Book. Do not come out."

"But—"

"You are not ready!" yelled Anjar, and then Mike opened his eyes, his heart beating hard in his chest. He looked around in the darkness, and realized he was in the AirBnb. The room was cold, but sweat still clung to his legs. He blinked, remembering where he was, and *when* it was.

"You alright?" asked Stu.

Mike leaned over on his elbow. Stu sat in the corner of the room, next to a small desk lamp, illuminating him. A mug of coffee sat in front of him. The AirBnb was small, and they had shared the room.

"What time is it?"

"5 AM," said Stu. "I didn't wake you, did I?"

"No," said Mike. "Nightmare. Or dream. Or memory? Is there more coffee?"

"Should be enough for a couple more cups."

Mike wiped the sleep from his eyes. Trying to get more rest would be impossible. He pushed himself out of bed, used the bathroom, and returned to the coffee, pouring himself a cup. It steamed, and he dumped what sugar they had into it. He sat down in the only other chair in the room. It was dark outside, and it was safe to assume Daniel and

Marion still slept in the other bedroom.

"Were you just sitting here?"

"I was enjoying the coffee," said Stu.

Mike took a small sip. "It's not very good."

"I've had worse," said Stu. "I wasn't just enjoying the coffee. I was thinking."

"About Agent Harrison?" asked Mike. He eyed Stu. Stu's eyes met his.

"Yes."

"Do you know of anything that would do that to a man?"

"No," said Stu.

They had left the body in the barn, along with the sedan, wiping any of their prints from it. Maybe someone would find it. Maybe they wouldn't. It didn't matter much either way. BENT was after them, regardless.

"What do you suspect?"

"I suspect that Strickland built in some kind of failsafe mechanism on his agents," said Stu. "If they said the wrong thing, or talked to the wrong person, it would trigger, and kill them. It's probably why Harrison didn't want to speak. It took the power of The Book."

"How is that possible?" asked Mike. He took another sip of coffee. Stu was right. It wasn't the worst coffee he'd ever had.

"I don't know for sure," said Stu. "But I also suspect that Strickland has been capturing artifacts without our knowledge. We've—we've tried to get info out of BENT, but there's never been anything concrete. But something like that would explain it."

"He could have anything," said Mike.

"Well, not anything," said Stu. "If he truly had anything

game-breaking, we wouldn't still have The Book. But it's something to be aware of. They might have things we're not prepared for." Stu downed the rest of his coffee.

"Are they really targeting the President?" asked Mike.

"I've thought about it," said Stu. "But Strickland would be the perfect mole. Large enough role to make important decisions, but with enough deniability to do what he wants. And if you're an alien invader, there's not one person you could attack that would have more of an impact than the President himself."

"Jesus."

"What else can The Book do?" asked Stu, the air empty, quiet.

"It's hard to explain," said Mike. "Mostly, it inflicts pain. To varying degrees, with varying costs. It *is* blood magic, literally. It requires payment in blood. You saw it. But some of the magic in it, requires more than any one person could provide."

"That's what happened in Laurel City."

"Yes," said Mike. "That's how Laurel opened the portal. He killed."

"It was a dozen boys, or so."

"Yes, but The Book isn't straightforward about any of this," said Mike. "It's magic. A part of it will always be ephemeral, and metaphorical. It requires creativity. It's what held the Laurels back. They thought in straight lines. With a creative enough mind, there's no limit to the mayhem and chaos that you could cause."

"Is there anything in there like a bomb?"

"Of course," said Mike. "Every form of destruction you know, it's in there."

"Jesus," said Stu. "We can't let them have it."

"We have bombs, Stu," said Mike. "It's the transportation that's dangerous. The Oukan are not like us. And neither are the creatures they control. The harvesters, the things in Laurel City. They're dangerous, don't get me wrong, but they're basically nothing. They require the least to send across, which is why Laurel used them. But there are other things. And if you know what you're doing, you could open a portal that's stable enough for the Oukan themselves to come across."

"What are they?" asked Stu. "You mentioned them."

"I think we've made contact with them, in history," said Mike. "Or more likely, they made contact with us. But I could understand why someone who saw one on Earth would think them a demon. They look strange. They speak something inhuman. And most of all, they're utterly power-ful, and invulnerable to human attack."

"I doubt—"

"I saw it," said Mike. "While I was over there. I was in combat against them. They're effectively demigods. They're bred for war. If even one made it over, we'd be in trouble. And if there was an army? They'd take over. I'd be surprised if it lasted longer than a day."

Stu took a deep breath.

"It's too early for this."

"You wanted to know."

"No, I do," said Stu. "Even more important that we get the second Book. And keep the first safe." He paused. "You might have to use it again."

Mike stared at him.

"I know."

19

"What do we do if we see BENT agents?"

"I don't think we will. And if we do, they won't do anything. At least, if they're smart, they won't do anything."

Mike and Stu drove the jeep into Night Hill. Marion and
Daniel had pleaded their case, but both Mike and Stu over-
rode them and left them behind. At least for now. Left them
behind with The Book. Mike felt its pull, as they headed into
town from the AirBnb they stayed in at the outskirts.

"Remember, we're tourists," said Stu. "Brothers, on a
road trip. We're just scoping out the place. If we see the kid,
any evidence of this second Book, we do not engage. Not
unless there's a direct opportunity to retrieve it."

"And BENT agents?" asked Mike.

"They're not stupid," said Stu. "At least I hope they're not.

They'll want The Book first. They'll respect its power, and whatever the danger is in Night Hill. I hope they don't start something. Because it will get messy if they do."

Night Hill seemed like a normal small suburb at first glance, not too different from Laurel City. Stu cruised down the main thoroughfare, his phone's GPS in front of them. Cars parked on the street. A few people milled about.

"Don't see the fuss," said Mike.

"I would have said the same of Laurel City," said Stu. "On the surface, it'll seem normal. We'll take a walk through downtown. Get some lunch at a diner or something. See what we see."

Stu parked in a small public parking lot. It was a weekday, and there wasn't much traffic. Driving through, the downtown area of Night Hill was relatively small, but had a few restaurants, a cafe, and antique and craft stores. Exactly what Mike would expect. But Stu was right. On the surface, a visitor would have never seen the truth of Laurel City.

"Keep your eyes open," said Stu. "Don't look for spooky stuff. You'll never find it, at least not in the open. Look at the people. They'll tell us if something's wrong."

"I was a cop," said Mike. "In my past life. I know how to read people."

"Fair enough," said Stu. "But you've been in Laurel City. You saw how it was on the inside. I've visited towns like this across the US. They always look normal on the outside. Minor details change, but small towns are good at looking the other way when something strange is happening. By treating it as business as usual." Stu pulled into the parking spot. "Every single person we passed on the street looked at us. Every single one. Something's wrong here."

They got out and walked toward downtown. There were small snowbanks along the sidewalks, but they were clean and devoid of ice. Mike pulled his hoodie all the way closed. It was just above freezing, not as cold as it could be in Colorado this time of year, even so, he shivered a little as they walked.

They entered downtown, a few square blocks big, with cutesy signs hanging up on the traffic lights, pointing toward restaurants and shops in the area.

"Let's do a circuit first," said Stu. They walked, and Mike kept his eyes open. He tried to not look at the shops, or the decor, but at the people. The employees, the other people walking around downtown. It was almost lunch time, and Mike expected to see a few other people, even on a weekday. But it was quiet. Maybe it was the cold.

They walked past a quilt shop, and Mike glanced through the window as they passed. He looked past the display of fabric, and of cutting accessories, to the woman working inside. She looked up as they passed, and she stared. Mike caught her gaze, but she didn't look away. She held her stare until they were past the store.

"They are definitely staring at us," said Mike, under his breath.

"Yes," said Stu. They walked up the street, and Mike glanced in every window. If they were noticed, they were stared at.

"Let's stop in here," said Stu, nodding toward an antiques store. The display in the front window had an old rocking horse, plus an assortment of art déco glassware. Standard.

They pushed through the glass door, and Mike immediately smelled the musty note that he'd smelled in every antiques store he'd ever been in. They stepped inside, a maze of shelves and displays, the store stacked from floor to ceiling with furniture, toys, decor, glassware, and more things that Mike didn't know how to categorize. Stu walked into an aisle, and moved slowly, but not too slowly, looking around. They weren't really browsing, not really, and Mike followed Stu's eyeline.

He was looking at the antiques, but he was also scanning for an employee.

"Seems normal," said Mike, quietly. Stu only nodded. Stu stopped and glanced at a shelf of old children's toys. One by one, he picked them up and looked them over.

"What are you looking for?" asked Mike. Stu held up a finger, as he examined a wooden race car, and then a set of blocks. He picked up a fabric doll that could have been anywhere from twenty to a hundred years old. Stu turned the doll over and then kept it. He leaned into Mike.

"No price," he whispered. Mike nodded. An excuse to talk to an employee. They wandered through the rest of the store, with Stu carrying the doll the whole way. Eventually they hit the back of the store, and made their way back toward the front, looping through strangely placed aisles. The store was quiet, with no music playing, and then they saw the cashier, a young woman sitting behind the counter, reading a paperback book. She jumped when she saw them.

"Sorry to startle you," said Stu, his voice calm and low.

"I—it's alright," she said, forcing a half-smile. She put the book down. "Find everything you're looking for?"

"Actually, I was wondering if you could price this doll for me," said Stu. "I looked everywhere on it, couldn't find one."

"Oh, sure," said the woman. She grabbed the doll and

looked it over. "Hmm. Usually Megan prices everything. She's the owner. Without a price—I would say $20."

"You sure?" asked Stu.

"I think that's fine," said the cashier.

"Then I'll take it," said Stu. She rang him up on the cash register, and Stu grabbed cash from his pocket. "Lovely little town you have here. We're visiting from Colorado Springs."

"Oh, yeah, uh—thanks," she said.

"Anywhere else you'd recommend we visit?" asked Stu. "We want to get the full experience."

"Uh, no, not really," she said. Stu handed over the money, and she gave them change.

"Not a single place?" asked Stu. "Anywhere off the beaten path, even? We're adventurous."

She wouldn't look them in the eyes now. She wanted them to leave. Normally, Mike would mark it down as awkwardness on part of the girl, but he didn't think that was the case here. She didn't want them to just leave the store. She wanted them to leave town.

"I don't think so," she said, and then Mike saw a change in the light over her face, like a cloud had passed by. The store wasn't particularly bright, with some overhead lights, but most of the light, especially near the front, was from the sun coming through the big glass storefront. Mike glanced over, more out of reflex than anything.

It wasn't a cloud passing overhead that blocked the sun.

Something big crossed in front of the store window, walking in the street. It was too tall to see the upper half, Mike only seeing its legs, big, brownish gray, and covered in some kind of rough fur. It walked on two legs, and with three more massive steps, it was gone, out of view, the light back in the antiques store.

"What was that?" asked Mike. Stu glanced at him with confusion.

"What was what?" asked the cashier. She looked at Mike now, meeting his eyes, and hers were filled with fear.

"There was something out there," said Mike.

"I didn't see it," she said, the same forced smile back. Her eyes didn't smile, not even a little. They were still afraid. "Have a nice day." She handed over the doll to Stu, and Stu took it, and without another word, walked outside.

Mike looked down the street, in the direction the thing had traveled, but it was gone, out of sight.

"Did you see that?"

"No," said Stu. "What was it?"

"I don't know," said Mike. "It was big. Couldn't see all of it. Some creature, walking the streets."

"Summoned?" asked Stu.

"Probably," said Mike. "But I never saw anything like that on the other side." He looked at Stu. "The cashier acted like it wasn't there. She definitely saw it, just like I did."

"Let's keep moving," said Stu. "Find a place for lunch. See if we can see anything else."

They walked, turning another corner. More small shops, here and there. Mike's eyes scanned the streets, looking for the massive creature, but he saw nothing.

"It's gone," said Mike.

"I doubt that," said Stu. He said nothing, but Mike got the sense he knew something that he wasn't saying. But he let it lie, for now. There was a diner on the corner.

"That looks good," said Stu. "Open view to the street, and a few people inside." The diner had a neon sign, lit up, spelling out The Golden Biscuit, the neon bright yellow. They stepped inside, and a sign directed them to seat themselves. They took a booth with a clear view of the outside. Within a minute, a waitress appeared. She looked in her late 30s, with her hair tied up in a bun. She looked tired.

"What can I get for you?"

After a brief glance at the menu, they ordered, and the waitress was gone, as quickly as she arrived.

"Not much for small talk, I guess," said Mike.

"They won't talk," said Stu. "Not without significant motivation."

"Why do you say that?"

"They're terrified," said Stu. "All of them."

Mike looked over at the waitress as she moved behind the counter, talking to the kitchen through the window. Her whole body seemed tense.

"From that thing?" asked Mike.

"Or whoever controls it," said Stu.

"You said it was a kid."

"A little girl," said Stu. "Lyssa. If she's controlling that thing—"

"Would she tell it to kill people?"

"I don't know," said Stu. "We have to find her. If we can talk to her, maybe we can reason—"

Screaming interrupted him. It was loud, from outside. They both looked out the expansive glass windows.

A man ran into view, screaming, his voice echoing down the street. The glass deadened the sound, but it was still loud, and he screamed as he ran, ran from something.

But then they saw what he ran from.

It was the creature.

It ran on four legs after him, a great bestial thing, dark brown, covered not in fur, like Mike had thought, but in quills, like a porcupine. Its mouth was enormous, taking up half its face, with huge eyes, and nearly invisible ears. It stood nearly ten feet at the shoulder, on all fours, and Mike would bet double that standing up. Its legs ended in massive claws, six of them, on quick count.

It was faster than the man, and then he stumbled, and then fell, and it was over him. He screamed even louder, and everyone could hear.

The waitress came over with their food.

"I've got the BLT for you," she said, her voice straining.

"Please, please," pleaded the man in the street. "I didn't mean it, I didn't know—" and then the creature sunk a claw into the man's torso, and he screamed, and his breath was gone, and he died in moments. The waitress set down the sandwich.

"And a breakfast platter for you," she said. Mike looked at her. Her face was full of fear, but she maintained a facade of normalcy. She didn't look at the street.

"Anything else I can help you with?" she asked, as the man in the street was devoured.

20

"What is that thing?"

"I don't know. Why would I know?"

"You were on the other side, Mike. You know The Book. You haven't seen anything like that?"

"No, I haven't. Like I said, The Book is metaphor. However that thing is being summoned, it would look different if I did it."

"It stared at us," said Stu. "It knows us."

"Don't know if that makes a difference," said Dad.

Marion watched as Stu and her dad went back and forth in the living room. They all sat there, the sun setting. They had just finished a fast food dinner, and were trying to figure out their plan. Dad and Stu had told them what they had seen in Night Hill. About a massive creature prowling the streets. About it devouring a man.

"We didn't even get close to her," said Stu. "Don't know how we would. Can you get rid of it with The Book?"

"Maybe, if I had enough time," said Dad. "But it's not feasible. That thing would rip us apart."

"Then we kill it," said Stu.

"It's not invincible," said Dad. "But I doubt your pistol will do much to it. Even a shotgun. I don't think you're taking that thing down with anything less than a team of guys with assault rifles. Even then, it's iffy."

"It won't let us near her," said Stu. "And if we can't get near her, we can't get The Book. And if there's any saving her, we're the only chance. I would bet there's BENT agents in town, and they've come to the same conclusion. But Strickland *will* send in a team of armed men, and they'll kill that thing, whatever the cost. They'll have The Book and the girl. We don't have their resources."

"Have you tried to talking to it?" asked Marion.

"What?" asked Stu.

"Did you try and say hello? Ask if you could talk to the girl?"

"It devoured a man in the street, sweetheart—" started Dad.

"Why did it do that?" asked Marion.

"We don't know," said Stu. "It's impossible to know, now."

"Well, what do you know about the girl?" asked Marion.

"Only what the waitress told us," said Dad. "Her name is Lyssa. She lives in a big black house on Martin Street."

"How old is she?" asked Marion. "Where are her parents?"

"We didn't get that far," said Stu. "I would assume they're

dead. They're certainly not stopping her."

"She still needs to eat, still needs to sleep," said Marion. "She's still a girl. She's summoning this thing for a reason. Depending on how old she is, she might not even know what she's really doing."

"My main question is how she mastered The Book," said Stu. "Say she's ten. How could a ten year summon that thing? Literally, how was she able to read and master that magic?"

Dad looked at Stu, and then at Marion and Daniel. "The Book might have guided her."

Stu pressed his lips together, but said nothing.

"What do we do, then?" asked Daniel. "We can't get to her. We don't have the resources to deal with the creature, whatever it is."

Marion looked at them. Everyone looked defeated. If this little girl was alone, without family or friends, she'd be isolated emotionally. Marion remembered how she felt in the wake of her mother's death. She had felt adrift. Unmoored. If it wasn't for Dad, or Daniel, she would have been lost completely. Force wasn't the answer.

"I'll go in," said Marion.

"You'll what?" asked Dad.

"I'll go into town," said Marion. "Alone."

"Marion," said Dad. "I don't think—"

"I'll find Lyssa, and I'll talk to her," said Marion. "She'll trust me."

"I don't know if that's true," said Stu. "Who knows how she'll react. And that's only if you can get to her, past that creature."

"Marion, we watched a man get devoured. I can't let you go in there alone."

"What else can we do?" asked Marion.

"I mean, anything else," said Dad. "That thing would rip you apart—"

"It'd rip any of us apart," said Marion. "Brute force won't work. I've been in her shoes. I can talk to her."

Stu looked at her. "The only other idea I had was to send your father in at night. See if the creature is still there during dark. Go in, get The Book, get out."

"Why is that plan better than mine?" asked Marion.

Stu shrugged. "It's not. It's only different, with a different set of risks. Yours has its merits, but also its drawbacks. You'll be entirely alone in town. We won't be able to help you. And you have no experience with The Book."

"That might be for the best," said Dad. "In all honesty, someone who's clean from its influence might have a better chance at winning her trust."

Stu looked at Dad, his eyes communicating. Marion saw it. Stu didn't want to send Dad's only daughter into a death trap. Stu wanted his permission.

"I can do it, Dad," said Marion. "If it's looking bad, I'll run."

He looked at her, not with anger, or frustration, but with something Marion couldn't place.

"Okay."

*

Marion walked down Martin Street. It was a long street, running a few dozen blocks, and she was still a mile away from the black house that Lyssa supposedly lived in.

Marion moved briskly, trying to stay warm. The sun was

shining, and it helped, but the cold was not her biggest worry.

She walked alone. They had all driven into town together, but they had dropped her off at the northern end of the street, blocks from Lyssa's house. She would walk it. She would let the creature see her coming.

There was no sign of it yet. It was mid-morning, but there was no one else out on the sidewalks, no other cars driving. The street was quiet and empty, a typical suburban road, snow melting underneath the sun, plowed to the curbs.

But it was out there, no doubt. Marion's stomach ached, a feeling she knew. She had felt it in Laurel City, and had felt it when they were under Strickland's thumb, living in their cage.

She walked, her footsteps echoing off the pavement, softly ringing against the vinyl siding and brick facades.

They were circling the town, off of this street, but her phone was in her pocket, and she wouldn't be calling unless there was an emergency. She had told her dad that she would call if she needed him, but it was only to soothe his nerves.

She hadn't seen the creature, but if it wanted her dead, it would kill her.

She walked. The black house was still out of sight, maybe two blocks away on the right, but she would see it soon.

The sound of the creature interrupted her thoughts.

It came from behind her, heavy padded footfalls. It was rhythmic, quiet, but it came quickly. She continued walking, not knowing what else to do. If it wanted to kill her, it would.

She hoped her hunch was right.

It loped down the street behind her, and the footfalls got louder and louder, and then she heard its breath, loud and heavy, a dark wheezing noise, the sound of something breathing air it shouldn't.

Marion didn't turn, still walking. She did her best to keep her breathing consistent, despite her heart thumping in her chest.

It was louder, louder still, and it felt like it was right on top of her, it would kill her without her seeing it, this was a mistake—

It sprinted past her in the street, and then turned, slowing, rising onto two legs, and she saw it for the first time.

It was massive, bigger than any creature she'd ever seen, bigger than a rhino, a hippo, maybe even an elephant, a massive brown thing, its clawed feet stomping to her, its claws alone bigger than her, its mouth a maw. Its fur wasn't fur, but quills, brushed back against its body, but she bet if threatened they would stand on end, and create another defense.

Its eyes bulged, and as it approached, looming over her, it seemed impossible, a reject from *Where the Wild Things Are*, but that's because it was impossible, a thing summoned from another world. She stopped, staying still as it drew near.

The creature moved slowly, and then it bent, its massive mouth and bulging eyes getting close to her. Marion then saw it had a nose, or something passing for one, two holes just above its mouth, and its wheezing covered her as it breathed in and out, ugly hot breath smelling like molten chemicals.

"Hi," she said, her voice as soft as she could muster.

The creature recoiled for a moment, as if her voice was a weapon. She didn't let it faze her.

"I'm Marion," she said. "I wanted to speak to Lyssa, if that's okay." The creature moved suddenly at the mention of her name, and moved quickly, and Marion waited for it to attack, to bite her in half, and swallow the pieces—

But it didn't. Instead, it moved close, its alien features only inches away from her. It sniffed at her, but there was something else happening, some other feeling—

Then she realized.

It reminded her of the harvesters. The creatures summoned by the Laurels, who plumbed the depths of your psyche, bringing up your worst fears and trauma, and using them to paralyze, so they could strike, and devour.

It was smelling her, like a bloodhound, but it was sensing more than just her scent. Its massive eyes scanned her, and she stayed quiet, and still, like she would if she was meeting a dog for the first time.

Her hunch had to be right, or this would be it—

The creature snorted once, and then turned from her, and loped down the street, leaving her alone. It moved quickly, running with massive strides, with legs ten feet long.

I guess that's a good sign.

Marion walked after it, unable to keep up. The creature didn't seem to care, but it stopped not too far away, still within sight, easily viewable because of its size. It sat on its haunches, and within a few more minutes of walking, Marion caught up to it.

It sat in front of the black house on Martin Street.

Lyssa's house.

"Can I go in?" she asked, standing in front of it.

It looked at her, and then looked at the front door.

Is that a yes?

Marion cautiously turned and walked up the driveway, turning down the path that led to the front door. She felt the eyes of the creature on her, still sitting on its haunches. With a single stride, it would be on top of her.

She went to the door, and she knocked, once, twice, three times.

It was quiet.

Was Lyssa not home?

She knocked again, harder, and then there was a stampede of footsteps, getting louder, and then the door opened, and she was greeted by a girl, and she was small, couldn't be older than ten.

Hell, she's not even eight.

The little girl had black hair, and big, eerie eyes, and a lopsided grin that she showed as she saw Marion.

"Hello, can I help you?"

"Uh, hi, I'm Marion," she said. "I was wondering if we could talk."

"Talk about what?" asked Lyssa, staring at her.

Marion hadn't thought this far ahead. She hadn't even been sure she was going to make it to the house.

"About your town," said Marion, smiling. "I'm a little lost, and pretty thirsty. Can you help me?"

"Oh, sure, I can do that," said Lyssa, opening the door wide. "You're not a stranger, are you?"

"You know my name, right?"

"Yeah, Marion," said Lyssa.

"Then I'm not a stranger."

Lyssa stared for a second, and then smiled even wider.

"You're right. You can come in." She opened the door wider. She yelled past Marion. "It's okay, Mr. Grumpkins! She's not a stranger!"

Mr. Grumpkins?

Marion stepped inside, and Lyssa closed the door behind her.

21

Marion had gotten inside the house, safe from the thing outside—

Mr. Grumpkins. Lyssa had called it Mr. Grumpkins.

"We can go to the kitchen," said Lyssa. "I'll get you some water."

Marion followed as Lyssa strolled down the central hallway of the house. The house smelled musty, but not bad, and Marion tried to get a glance of the pictures on the wall, and caught one that featured Lyssa and two adults, presumably her parents, with Lyssa dressed in a soccer uniform, but she couldn't lag behind, and then they were in the kitchen.

It was clean.

Marion had expected a mess, if Lyssa truly did live alone. A pile of dishes in the sink, overflowing trash, clutter.

But it was neat and tidy. Not perfect, but there was no smell, no sign of filth.

Lyssa used a step stool to get Marion a glass, and then filled it from the tap, and carried it over to her.

"Thank you," said Marion. She took a big gulp.

"You're welcome," said Lyssa, with the same lopsided grin. Marion swallowed the water.

"Lyssa—"

"Let's go to my room," said Lyssa, and Lyssa grabbed her hand, and led her back down the hallway, and then around a corner and up the stairs, to the second floor. She turned to the left, down the corridor. There were three other doors on the second floor, all of them shut, and then Lyssa led Marion to the only open door, and into what looked like a typical kid's room. A tiny bed sat in the corner, made, sheets tucked into the side. A small bookshelf with an array of books. Colorful posters of characters Marion barely recognized. A closet filled with clothes, put away.

"This is my room," said Lyssa, and she sat on the bed. Marion saw a small chair and did her best to sit in it. She sort of fit. She drank more water, if only to show Lyssa she was thirsty. "Do you like it?"

"Yes, it's nice," said Marion. "I like your posters. And everything is so organized."

"My mom always said that if I wanted to get a new book at the bookstore, I had to keep my room clean, so I do," said Lyssa. "I know where everything is." Marion looked at Lyssa, trying to read her. It felt like she was putting on an act for Marion, but she couldn't see past that. The danger of Mr. Grumpkins had vanished with Marion inside. This girl didn't seem angry, or violent. Then Marion realized what it was.

She was sad, and desperately trying not to be.

"Does your mom buy you a lot of books?" asked Marion.

"She used to," said Lyssa. "I've got some of them here, but there are more in my closet. I read a lot."

Used to.

"She doesn't anymore?" asked Marion.

"No, she died," said Lyssa. "This is my favorite book. It's about bees. Did you know there are over 4,000 types of bees?"

Marion swallowed. "Wow, that's a lot."

"I know," said Lyssa. "But they're all very important."

"I bet," said Marion. "What about your dad?"

"He's dead, too," said Lyssa. She stared at Marion. "I don't want to talk about that."

"I'm sorry—"

"This is my second favorite book. It's all about dinosaurs. My favorite dinosaur is the pterodactyl. They were soooo big. All the pictures don't show it, but they were huuuuge, with really big wings. Here, I'll show you." Lyssa grabbed the book from her bookshelf, and walked over to Marion, flipping through to the right page. "This is a pterodactyl, and the little guy next to him is a human. We'd be so tiny compared to them."

"Kind of like Mr. Grumpkins," said Marion. She had to get through Lyssa's facade.

"Yes, he is very big," said Lyssa. "He protects me, though."

"Does he?"

"Yes," said Lyssa. "Whenever someone tries to take me away, he helps."

"Take you away from what?"

"Our house," said Lyssa. "From Night Hill. Mom always said that home is where the heart is, and my heart is here. They can't take me away."

"How did you meet Mr. Grumpkins?"

"They tried to take me away," said Lyssa. "But Mr. Grumpkins came, and now I don't have to go."

"Who tried to take you away?"

Lyssa looked at her.

"You're not here to take me away, are you?" Marion saw a flash of anger in Lyssa's eyes.

"No," said Marion. "I just want to be friends."

"Good," said Lyssa, her expression returning to normal. She returned her dinosaur book to the bookshelf and sat back down on her bed.

"You're from Night Hill?" asked Marion.

"Yes," said Lyssa. "I was born here, and I grew up in this house. This has always been my bedroom. They would put me in some other house, with people I don't know. That's not allowed."

Silence hung between them, suddenly.

"I miss them," said Lyssa, finally, looking out her window.

"Your parents?"

"Yes."

"What happened to them?"

"I had a babysitter," said Lyssa. "Ms. Marjorie, from down the street. She's an old lady, but she's very nice. But they left me with her, because they wanted to go to a fancy restaurant for their anniv—anniv—

"Anniversary?"

"Yes," said Lyssa. "But there was a bad driver on their

way home. He hit them." She looked at Marion. "They didn't tell me. I listened when they didn't think I was listening."

"I'm—I'm sorry," said Marion.

"It's okay," said Lyssa. "They said I love you before they left, and I said it back. Mom always made sure."

"And that's when you met Mr. Grumpkins?"

"No, that came later," said Lyssa. "I stayed with Ms. Marjorie at first. She was very nice, and let me sleep in her house. But they took me to a big building in town, and they didn't tell me why, but I knew it was to send me somewhere away. They were talking, pretending that I couldn't hear them. But I could hear them." She looked at Marion. "But then I felt something."

"Like what?"

"I don't know," said Lyssa. "It was like—being pulled. It felt like someone took my hand and was pulling me along."

"Pulling you where?"

"We went to a store," said Lyssa. "In town. With old stuff."

"An antique store?"

"I guess," said Lyssa. "But it kept pulling me along. I don't think the store person saw me. It pulled me through the whole store, into a back room. The door was open, and I just went inside. There were boxes. So many boxes. And stacks and stacks of all kinds of stuff. I'd never seen so much stuff in one place."

The back room of an antique store?

"And there was so much stuff, and I realized that I had left everyone behind, but they hadn't chased after me. They didn't know where I went. But whatever pulled me, it kept pulling me. It was a maze in that room, with big stacks, and it knew where we were going, because I ended up right where I was supposed to."

The Book.

"What did you find?" asked Marion, the right question.

"I found a book," said Lyssa. "But I had never seen one like it before. It was big, and old, and heavy. But I saw it, and then I touched it—"

And she paused, her eyes staring into the middle distance, and Marion remembered Laurel City, remembered everything about The Book that her dad still had, and everything it could do.

"And it felt good," said Lyssa. "It felt like I wasn't alone anymore. So I grabbed it. It was very heavy, but I carried it, and I went home. I hadn't been home since the accident, and that felt right, too. It felt normal again."

"Did you read it?" asked Marion.

"I just touched it," said Lyssa. "It felt nice. But then—"

"Then they came to take you away, didn't they?"

"Yes," said Lyssa. "And I didn't want to leave. This is my house. They—they didn't understand. And I felt the same pull again, and I opened up the book, and I found a page, and I read it. And—and then Mr. Grumpkins was here."

"You just read it?" asked Marion. "Nothing else?"

"I don't remember," said Lyssa, squinting her eyes. "But I needed a friend, and he appeared, and he helped. He made them all go away. And then, I could stay. I *did* stay."

Lyssa smiled then, but still something lurked behind it. Something that Lyssa herself was unaware of, but Marion knew what it was. It was the knowledge. Knowledge that Mr. Grumpkins, whatever he is, didn't just make them go away.

He killed them.

"I needed a friend, and Mr. Grumpkins came to help," said Lyssa. "And now, he helps me all the time. He brings me food when I need it. And whenever there's a stranger, or someone comes to take me away, he makes them go away. He's my best friend."

She treats him like a dog.

"Lyssa, can I see this book?" asked Marion.

Lyssa eyed her. "I don't know—"

"It sounds really neat," said Marion. "You showed me your other books."

Lyssa considered her. "I guess you're right," she said. "But you can't tell anyone, okay? It's a secret."

"It's safe with me," said Marion.

"Okay," said Lyssa, and then she reached back, under her pillow, and pulled out The Book. It was huge, nearly as big as her, and she dragged it across the bed. It looked nearly identical to the copy they had. It had been there the whole time, nestled underneath Lyssa's pillow.

She slept on it.

Marion watched Lyssa's eyes, and they stayed glued to The Book.

Marion's phone buzzed in her pocket, and then buzzed again, and then buzzed again. She slid it out, and glanced at the screen.

Texts from Dad.

BENT agents in town

Approaching your position

Get out now!

Marion pocketed the phone. She had questions for Dad, like how many of them were there, and what had happened to Mr. Grumpkins, but none of that mattered, not right now.

"Lyssa," said Marion. Lyssa still stared at The Book, nestled against her. "Lyssa!" She finally looked up. "We have to go."

Her expression immediately changed. "You said you weren't going to take me anywhere."

"There are bad people coming," said Marion. "They'll hurt you. We have to leave. They'll be here very soon."

"No, no no," said Lyssa. "Mr. Grumpkins, he'll stop them. He helps me."

Distant pops echoed through the air. Gunfire.

"He might not be able to stop them," said Marion.

"This is my house," said Lyssa. "I'm not leaving, I'm not—"

There was banging on the door downstairs, and yelling from outside. Marion couldn't make it out, but it wasn't friendly.

"They're here, Lyssa," said Marion. "We have to go, right now. Is there a back door?"

"I'm not leaving," said Lyssa. "You said—"

And then the front door was smashed down.

<h1 style="text-align:center">22</h1>

Marion slapped her hand over Lyssa's mouth.

"They will kill us, Lyssa," she whispered in her ear, as quiet as a mouse. Marion didn't wait, grabbing Lyssa and urging her out the door. They'd be trapped in there. They were already trapped upstairs. Lyssa carried The Book still, held tight to her body.

Marion pulled Lyssa away from the stairs, away from the men downstairs. A door at the end of the hall, and Marion opened it as quietly as possible, their footsteps softened by the carpet. Marion hoped her hunch was right, and then they were inside, and she was right, it was the master bedroom. More places to hide in here.

The room was tidy, straightened up, maybe by Lyssa herself, but they didn't have time. She eyed the window quickly, but they were on the second floor, and Lyssa was tiny, and one wrong step climbing down could hurt her badly, and there was no bet they'd be any safer dodging through back-yards.

No, they would hide, and hope the men would pass them by.

They could hide under the bed, but someone would see them. There was a master bathroom adjacent, but bath-rooms were terrible places to hide. Too bright.

The closet. Marion opened the sliding door, revealing a walk-in closet, and this was their best bet. Marion slid the door closed, and scanned for a place to hide.

There were more crashing noises downstairs, echoing up to them. They were tearing the house apart, they knew this was where Lyssa was, and they weren't wasting time trying to find her. Did they know Marion was here?

Doubtful, but possible. Had they realized they'd crossed paths with the agent in Kansas?

Too much to consider. They needed a hiding space. They'd finish with downstairs soon, and then they'd be up here.

The closet was nice, and organized, and filled with Marie Kondo style organizational shelving. There was even a ro-tating shelf in the corner, a lazy Susan, and Marion eyed it in the dim light. She crept over to it, and rotated it, and there was a blank spot. They could fit in there.

"In here, Lyssa," whispered Marion, and she looked at Lyssa and her eyes were filled with fear, and she grasped The Book tight to her chest, the big tome covering her like a shield. It had protected her through all of this, at least in her mind. Lyssa nodded, and climbed into the shelf, and

Marion followed, and the wood creaked, but held, neither of them heavy, and she pushed along the wall, dragging the rotating section around, until they were along the back of the closet, tight against the wall.

"Be quiet," said Marion. Maybe they wouldn't toss the entire closet. Maybe they would overlook them.

"Mr. Grumpkins will protect us," said Lyssa, her voice low.

Marion remembered the bursts of gunfire earlier, echoing down the street. They had come quickly, but she hadn't heard any more gunshots since. Had they killed Mr. Grumpkins?

Marion didn't think it possible, not after seeing him up close, but she remembered the conversation between Stu and her dad. A group of men, armed with assault rifles. The harvesters of sorrow, back in Laurel City. They were inhuman, awful terrors of another place, but still they died, or at least were destroyed, sent back to wherever they were from. Enough bullets and they went down.

If they had a dozen men with assault rifles—Mr. Grumpkins would eventually die.

The house shook around them as the men tore it apart. None of them spoke, the only sound being furniture being knocked over, shelves being destroyed. They were looking for The Book.

More, they were looking for Lyssa.

Boots stomped up the stairs.

They would finish with downstairs, all of them, and then they'd tear apart the upstairs. Maybe they'd overlook this spot in the closet, maybe they'd—

The door opened into the bedroom, and Marion put her

hand over Lyssa's mouth. They couldn't make any noise. These men would shoot them on sight and take The Book.

Or maybe just shoot her, and take Lyssa, and extract what secrets she knew about The Book, by whatever means necessary.

The man tore apart the bedroom, flipping over the bed, and not finding them. The closet was next, and she heard the door open, and there wasn't much ground to cover in here, they were dead, the men would find them, they should have jumped out the window, risked the fall—

More gunshots rang out from outside. The agent in the closet stopped, listening, more gunshots, and then there were yells, and then the house shook, like an earthquake hit it, and then the whole building tilted, rocked off its foundation.

What the—

And then she realized.

Lyssa was right. Mr. Grumpkins would save them.

The house shifted underneath them again, as the massive creature charged through the walls. Walls broke apart, and there was more gunfire, and the house shuddered as the creature found the agents below them, and there was no way the house could take it—

And the floor gave way below them as Mr. Grumpkins tore the house apart. Marion held Lyssa as they fell, pieces of wall and ceiling tumbling down around them. They hit the floor a moment later, and the breath left Marion's body, and then enormous pieces of ceiling fell on top of them and she tucked her head, hoping there wasn't any masonry above them.

Cacophony rang out around them, the house just a

pile of debris now. Mr. Grumpkins still fought the agents in the chaos, sunlight streaming through the remnants of the house, and Marion opened her eyes to see an agent pull his assault rifle to his shoulder, to fire, but Mr. Grumpkins plunged talons through the man's chest, shocking violence committed in a moment with the incredible strength of the creature. The man gasped once, a gout of blood coming from his mouth, and then Mr. Grumpkins flung him across the house, through a piece of wall. The creature looked at them, her cradling Lyssa, and Marion saw a display of softness in its features, but then more gunfire rang out.

Marion blinked, trying to focus. They were in what was left of the kitchen.

"You okay, Lyssa?"

"I'm—I'm okay," she said. "Mr. Grumpkins—

He already had turned to face the gunfire, coming from the street. The front walls of the house were gone, and Marion could see what fired the shots. More agents had arrived, pulling up in a humvee, a half dozen more men. Mr. Grumpkins charged, enormous, grabbing a piece of debris and flinging it at the men, all of them armed with more assault rifles and riot guns. They fired in bursts of three, with loud booms from the shotguns, the men racking new rounds after each shot. The gunfire tore into Mr. Grumpkins, but he did not stop.

Most of the bullets hit the creature, but some flew past it, and Marion pulled Lyssa back behind the cover of the debris. The ceiling had luckily fallen to shield them from further wreckage, and they had a small alcove that protected them from gunfire.

Mr. Grumpkins ripped one man apart, grabbing him

with two claws, towering over them all. Blood and viscera hit the ground, and Marion thought back to Laurel City, to the bloodshed by the creatures there, and she swallowed back bile.

But the rest still fired, and they were slowing the big creature down. It could absorb only so much gunfire. It wasn't invulnerable.

They needed an escape plan. Marion looked to Lyssa again and realized she didn't carry The Book anymore.

"Lyssa, where—" But then Marion saw it. Lyssa had dropped it in the chaos, and it had gotten flung across the room, in the middle of the disorder, bullets whizzing by it, spraying the house.

Mr. Grumpkins had killed another two members of the squad, smashing one into the ground, and throwing another across the road, his neck bent at a terrible angle. The creature had slowed considerably, the concentrated gunfire of the agents finally taking a toll. As they watched, another truck pulled up, filled with more agents, dressed similarly. They all carried more weapons, and this humvee came equipped with a turret, and it wheeled and spat out high caliber bullets, ripping into Mr. Grumpkins.

The creature had met its match.

Lyssa lunged away from Marion's arms.

"Mr. Grumpkins," she said. "They're going to kill him."

"We'll be next, Lyssa," said Marion, the turret even louder, so loud Marion could barely hear herself.

The men fired into the massive creature, and the turret whined, spitting out hundreds of bullets, and Mr. Grumpkins fell to a knee, and then slumped over.

The world went silent, and Marion eyed The Book. It sat

in plain view now, without the distraction of Mr. Grumpkins. The men all eyed the great beast, unsure if it was truly dead or not, but then it disappeared, its skin burning away into nothing, disappearing back into the shadows, just like the creatures in Laurel City had. In another moment or two, they would look back at the house, surveil the destruction, and try to find The Book again. They would see it.

And then they would see them.

Marion had only a few seconds to act.

Did she have enough time to scramble out, grab The Book, and then run away with Lyssa?

Or would she run out and get gunned down?

She could just grab The Book and run. Would up her chances if she didn't have to worry about Lyssa.

Marion glanced back. They had a way out, through the side yard, across a neighbor's fence. They could be gone without being seen at all.

All these thoughts flashed through Marion's mind in under a second.

She eyed The Book. It was an easy choice.

Marion pulled Lyssa back out from under the debris, as quietly as she could. Lyssa stared at The Book, across the way, but Marion pulled her away, pulled hard enough to sway her, and they left the house quietly, the agents still stowing their weapons. They ducked through a broken fence, and across another neighbor's yard, and then they were gone, leaving The Book behind.

23

BAAAAAAAYAAAAAAAAAHHHHHHHHH.

Mike woke to the village alarm. The scouts had said the Oukan were on the march, but they had hoped it would take them longer to arrive. He'd wanted more time to study, more time to prepare, but still there was no substitute for the real thing—

There was a tap at his door, and then Anjar poked their head in. They were ready for battle.

"They're here, Mike," they said. "It's time."

Mike sat up and swung his legs over the edge of the bed. "I'll get dressed."

"Are you ready?" asked Anjar, their eyes peering over to The Book, where it sat on a table explicitly for the object.

"I don't know," said Mike. "I know how to do it, but—but

I don't know—"

"You don't know what will happen to you," said Anjar.

"Yes," said Mike. "I don't know if I'll be the same on the other side."

"We do not stand a chance without your help," said Anjar. "You can change the tide of battle in a way we cannot. If you break their back, they may never challenge us again. A huge amount of their force is out today. This is our chance."

"I know," said Mike. "I'm—I'm afraid. Afraid that—"

"You are still you," said Anjar. "The Book is powerful, and corrupting. But you know that, and you resist it at every step. You are strong." They paused. "The battle is nearly here. We must go."

"Give me a few moments alone to get ready," said Mike.

Anjar held his gaze for a moment longer, nodded, and then closed the door. Mike took a deep breath, and changed out of his bedclothes, putting on the simple armor the kaja had provided for him. It wasn't leather, not in the way he knew, but it provided similar protection. If everything went well, it would not matter. The Oukan warriors, and any creatures they summoned, would not be trying to batter or slice *this* armor.

He dressed, sliding the armor into place, and then stood over The Book. The massive tome sat on the table. He felt its pull. It wanted to be used, it wanted to be fed blood, it wanted to give him strength, and make him feel powerful. Mike still didn't understand how The Book functioned, or where it drew its power from. How did it do the things it did? How did it pull creatures from other places? How it did cast its magick?

Mike couldn't know. All he could do was choose to use

it or not.

BAAAAAAAYAAAAAAAAHHHHHHHHH

The alarm sounded again, and Mike grabbed The Book in two hands, holding it tight to his chest. It was time.

Anjar waited for him outside his hut, and they walked together toward the front gate of the village. They had built up the walls after he had arrived, and fortified the gate as best they could. The kaja had prepared for war, but even so, the Oukan troops would destroy the gate in moments. They could not withstand a siege.

All of the kaja troops were gathered at the gate. A few hundred were there, wearing the best armor they could muster. Still, some wore scarcely better than craftsmen's gear, because it was all they had.

They were outnumbered and outmatched. The Oukan were armed and armored, and were professional soldiers. And that's not mentioning the mages and creatures summoned. The harvesters of sorrow. The colossal brutes.

Mike studied them. He had learned to read the kaja in his time there. And what he saw in them was fear. They were facing certain death, defending their home against an enormous force.

Without him, they would all die.

Anjar looked at him, and he nodded. They walked together to the front of the force, and Anjar looked to the gateman, who waited for them. Anjar nodded, and the gateman unlocked the gate and opened it. The village was open now, and with no barrier to the huge invading force.

The pair of them walked out through the gate and saw the Oukan force waiting across the battlefield.

The red, craggy ground was barren, a trio of stars shining down on the field that stood between them.

There were a thousand of them, at least, on foot and mounted, riding quadraped creatures with shaggy coats and rock-like protrusions on their heads and shoulders. Mike had seen them running the wild. They were not particularly fast, but they were hardy creatures, and it took great work to knock them down.

And the warriors alone would have been too much a threat, but the Oukan warriors weren't alone. The harvesters of sorrow stood among them, and the thundering brutes loomed over them, a few dozen of them, twenty feet tall.

The Kaja didn't stand a chance.

"Go back inside," said Mike, to Anjar. "I'm ready."

Anjar nodded, and retreated inside, and Mike heard the gate close behind him.

The Kaja truly had no hope against a force like this.

But they would not be fighting today.

Only he would.

Mike kneeled, laying The Book on the ground, and opening it to the page he needed. He pulled a dagger from his belt, and rent open both palms, blood pouring like a fountain onto the page.

The cost in blood was high for this magic, but it would not be the last blood spilled today.

Mike screamed the words into the air, whips and snarls, and he belched smoke and fire, and felt like his throat would be ripped apart, but he didn't stop, he wouldn't stop, not until it was done. He felt the magic rise in the air around him, and felt The Book do its dark work.

He finished the incantation, his blood being absorbed into The Book.

And then he transformed. And he charged.

*

As loud as the alarm had been, the songs of victory rang out even louder. The Kaja had celebrated for hours, and would surely celebrate for hours more.

And Mike didn't blame them. They hadn't seen victory in a long time.

Mike sat in his hut, quietly, in the dark.

They would have welcomed him, he knew. They would have celebrated him. Sang for him, and with him. He could hear them dance, hear them sing their wailing songs of triumph.

But the hollowness inside him begged only for solitude.

"Mike," said a voice from outside the thin door. "May I come in?"

It was Anjar.

"Are you alone?" he asked.

"Yes."

"Come in."

Anjar entered. They carried a small light with them, and they set it down on the table, sitting in an empty chair.

"The elders wanted to honor you," they said.

Mike sat back and stared at Anjar. He finally nodded at them. "Tell them I appreciate the gesture, but that I am still recovering from the battle."

Anjar stared back. "You don't look injured."

"I'm not," said Mike. "My body is fine. I'm just—"

"Tired?" they asked.

"That's not the right word," he said. He paused. "Empty.

I feel empty."

Anjar's eyes went to The Book, which sat near him, closed.

"Does it always feel like that?" they asked, finally.

"Yes," said Mike. "But not to this degree. This is more."

Anjar thought for a moment. "You beat them. Killed Oukan, and their beasts. We've never seen it done before. I see hope in the eyes of everyone. Thank you."

Mike only nodded. Anjar watched him.

"I will leave you—"

"You don't have to," said Mike. He took a breath. "I didn't want to change back."

"What do you mean?" asked Anjar. "This is your true form."

"It is," said Mike. "But the power you feel, when you've transformed—it is indescribable. I've never felt anything like it. And exercising that power—fighting those Oukan, on the battlefield—it felt good. Not just good. Euphoric. I killed, I crushed, I maimed, and all the while, I felt incredible."

Anjar stared, and said nothing.

"And now—I feel empty. I feel hollow. Like you could push a finger through my skin, and there'd be nothing but dead air inside. A poof of dust, and nothing else."

"You don't have to—"

"No," said Mike, waving them off. "I will do this as long as I need to. The Oukan—they're monsters."

"Then let me help," said Anjar. "Teach me the language of The Book. I can help shoulder your burden."

Mike stared at them and desperately wanted to accept their offer. For someone, anyone, to help.

"That's how it starts," said Mike. "With one other. One more person, feeding it. Cutting, bleeding. Filling it with their life. And The Book happily accepts. The more, the better. And it spreads, and you are more and more willing to add blood to it, to not just bleed, but to sacrifice. And you no longer use it begrudgingly. You yearn for it. You crave it."

"It won't happen," said Anjar. "We'll be careful."

"We will," said Mike. "Because I alone will be using it. Before I opened it, before I used it, I made a promise, that no one else will feed it. That is the limit. Me. No one else sacrifices, no one else dies."

The Book sat there next to him, and Mike still felt it. It begged for more blood, and promised even greater power.

"I trust you," said Anjar. "Thank you. I'll let you rest." They got up, took the light, and left.

Mike sat in the dark.

He felt The Book, there, still.

24

Stu paced in the AirBnb.

"We can't stay here," said Stu.

"They don't know we're here—"

"They have The Book," said Stu, staring at her, and then breaking his gaze away.

They had picked up Marion and Lyssa on the run, and had sped back, avoiding notice of BENT and their agents. Stu had been quiet at the news that BENT had The Book.

Mike and Daniel sat on the edge of the couch. Lyssa sat next to Marion, lost, confused, but curious.

Mike hadn't seen Stu like this before.

He was angry.

"Walk me through it," said Stu, finally. "How did they get it?"

"There were too many of them," said Marion. "They killed Mr. Grumpkins, after he charged in, and destroyed the house. We were hiding. We got separated from The Book in the destruction. Grabbing it would have too risky. We had an exit, and I took it."

Stu looked at her for another second, and then rubbed his eyes, squeezing the bridge of his nose.

"They're going to kill The President," said Stu, his voice calm. "They're going to start an invasion—"

"If you expected me to abandon her for that damn book, you're—"

Stu glared at her then, and Mike tensed, because Stu's gaze burned, and Mike had seen the look before, right before a fight started.

"Stu," he said, and that gaze jumped to him, just for a moment, and then Stu looked away and paced a few more steps. He took a deep breath.

"I'm going to be outside," he said. Stu left out through the door, without a glance back. Silence hung in the room.

"You did the right thing," said Mike, looking at Marion. "You sure you're alright?"

"Yeah, just some bumps and bruises," said Marion. "We were lucky."

Lyssa sat next to her, looking down at the floor. She hadn't said a word since they'd saved her from BENT. She looked so small, even next to Marion. Her hands laid flat against her legs.

Mike got up and knelt in front of her, meeting her eyes.

"Hi, I'm Mike," he said. "What's your name?" Lyssa looked at him.

"I'm Lyssa," she said.

"How old are you, Lyssa?"

"I'm seven and a half," she said. "Mr. Grumpkins destroyed my house."

"I heard," said Mike. "He was your friend?"

"Yes," said Lyssa. "I read, and he appeared, and he helped me."

Mike nodded. "Can I see your hands?"

Lyssa stared at him, and then nodded. She flipped over her hands, palms up. Scars criss crossed her skin.

"You didn't just read," said Mike.

"It told me to," said Lyssa. "And it gave me Mr. Grumpkins."

"I know," he said. He took his hand, and held it palm up in front of her, next to her own. "We match."

"Do you know Mr. Grumpkins?" asked Lyssa.

"No, not exactly," said Mike. "But I have my own Book. And I've read from it." Lyssa nodded, meeting his eyes again.

"I can't go home again, can I?"

"No," said Mike. "It's not safe. Those men, who killed Mr. Grumpkins. They have your Book. They're bad guys. If they got you, they would do bad things to you. They would take you away."

"I miss my mom and dad," she said, finally.

"I know," said Mike.

"What's going to happen?"

"I don't know," said Mike. "But right now, you're safest with us. You've already met Marion. She's my daughter. That's Daniel. He's my son."

"Hi Daniel," said Lyssa. She waved, and he waved back.

"We're trying to stop those bad guys," said Mike. "The ones who killed Mr. Grumpkins. I don't know what's going to happen after that, but I'd like you to stay with us for now. What do you think about that?"

"I don't know," said Lyssa. "I don't want to leave home."

"I know," said Mike. He looked into her eyes. She was lost. "I'll do my best to make sure you make it home. And until then, you'll be with us. We'll make sure you're safe. Okay?"

"Okay," she said. Mike stood up. "Can you two stay with her? I'm going to talk to Stu."

"You sure?" asked Daniel. "He seems pissed."

"Yeah, I'm sure," said Mike. "He just needed to cool off. We need to plan what's next."

Mike went outside. Stu stood on the edge of the bare concrete lanai. No sign of BENT agents. No sign of any activity at all.

Mike stood next to him, staring out. He didn't say anything, just stood there.

"I'm sorry for that," said Stu. "Marion risked her life, going into town. Facing down that creature, and finding Lyssa. She was outnumbered, and outgunned, and got out with both their lives."

"But not The Book," said Mike.

"No," said Stu. "It's my fault. I should have gone in alone. It's my fault all of this is out of control." He buried his face in his hands.

"You can't be responsible for everything," said Mike. "You can't shoulder the burden. You shouldn't."

Stu looked up, finally. "How long do you think I've been an agent?"

"I don't know," said Mike. "Ten years?"

"Twenty five, Mike," said Stu. "I've worked for the IPA

for twenty five years."

"Jesus," said Mike. "How old are you?"

"I'm 43."

"You look good for 43. You joined when you were eighteen?"

"I was recruited," said Stu. "I graduated high school when I was 16. Graduated college at 18. Day after graduation, a recruiter visited my house. Said I had all the ability necessary. That I could make a change in the world."

"Wow. And you joined?"

"Yes," said Stu. "Obviously."

"Was it like *Men in Black*?" asked Mike. "Where you had to swear away your old life, and all that?"

"No," said Stu. "I keep my personal life separate. What little there is of it. But we don't recruit people we can't trust to keep secrets." He paused. "They told me, way back then, that someone as smart as I was could have anything I wanted. That success in business, or in politics, was easily achievable. That I could even join another government agency, like the CIA or NSA, and probably go far."

"I had just graduated high school when I was eighteen," said Mike. "And I had no idea what I was doing in life."

"I thought I knew what I wanted," said Stu. "And maybe I did. Because the recruiter told me their agency was the truest test I would ever face in the world. If I wanted a challenge in life, joining the IPA was the surest way to get one. That they beat back the darkness, faced down the shadows, and solved the world's greatest mysteries, and did it without thanks, or acknowledgment. That there was no greater challenge on the Earth. And then he said that this was my only opportunity to join. That if I said no, they wouldn't ask again."

"Jesus," said Mike. "That seems unfair."

"Maybe it was," said Stu. "But it worked. I said yes. And I could have quit the job. I just would have been watched for the rest of my days. Also, I can retire at 50, with full pay and benefits. Live out the rest of my life comfortably, if I do so desire."

"They should have led with that."

"That seemed a world away at 18."

"Not too far now."

"If I get there," said Stu. "If Strickland's plan works, I'm not sure if I'll make it to 50."

"I know you can't tell me," said Mike. "But has there ever been other close calls?"

"Not like this," said Stu. "Dangers to the known world? Yes, absolutely. But a direct threat on our government? No, never. It's unprecedented. Which is partially why I was so angry. I should have seen it coming. I should have seen Strickland's play, and *done something*. I should have never let it get this close." He took a deep breath and exhaled. "I joined because I wanted that challenge. Because joining a secret government organization, and saving the world, was exciting, way more exciting than starting a business, or running for city council. And it *was* exciting, but at the end of the day, the job was gratifying not because it was exciting, or mysterious, but because I was saving lives. We *were* the good guys. Or at least I thought we were."

"You seem like a decent person."

"And yet here we are," said Stu. "Strickland has the second Book, and is going after the damn President. The IPA has been taken out, and we're here, in this crappy AirBnb.

And now I'm angry because a teenager chose to save a little girl's life rather than to take a cursed Book, in the face of overwhelming firepower. Strickland didn't do that. BENT didn't do that. The Book didn't do that. I was angry. Because I've failed."

They stood there in silence as the sun set.

"Surely this isn't the end," said Mike. "There still has to be a way. You don't have anyone in the White House? You don't have a line to The President? Hell, we still have a Book of our own. We can do something."

"This isn't the end," said Stu. "I still have cards up my sleeve."

"Then why—"

"I've lost some people in this," said Stu. "Don't know exactly how many. I hope some got out or worked deals. But even so, it was only us that took the hit. That died. From now on, there will be much more death, and there isn't any stopping it."

Mike took a deep breath. "What do we do now? We can't let them win."

"Oh, they won't," said Stu. "At least not while I still draw breath." He turned to Mike, a small smile on his face. "Our first step is to get the hell away from Night Hill. They will want Lyssa. We need to get her far away."

"Okay, I assumed that," said Mike. "And after that?"

"Simple," said Stu. "We need to get to the White House."

25

The sun had set by the time they left the AirBnb. Stu drove. Daniel sat with Marion and Lyssa in the backseat, with Dad next to Stu. He watched from the backseat, as Stu drove down the dark highway.

"Where are we going?" he asked.

"We need to get into the White House," said Stu, after a pause.

"So we're driving back to DC?" asked Marion. "We could take the tour."

"It has to be guarded," said Daniel. "I mean, more than usual."

"BENT is watching it, and any other federal facilities," said Stu. "We can't get within 50 miles without being flagged."

"Is there a secret way in?" asked Marion. "We can sneak in, maybe."

"There are a lot of them," said Stu. "But none of them good, and all of them known. Now that they have a Book, they won't care about us too much. Strickland would like to have the knowledge of either Mike or Lyssa, but I doubt they don't have a back-up plan. Or someone who's willing to learn. But as we get closer, security and surveillance will tighten. We will get noticed, and we don't have the firepower to overcome that. Even if we use the Book—" Daniel's eyes went to the massive tome, still sitting in his dad's lap. "—which I don't want to do, we still can't match them, and we would die trying."

"Then what do we do?" asked Dad. "You have cards up your sleeve. What are they?"

"I have a way in," said Stu. "One they won't expect, and can't stop. Also, the most likely to succeed. Provided every-thing goes well."

"Oh, Jesus," said Daniel. "Nothing has gone well yet."

"What's the catch?" asked Dad. "Where are we headed?"

"North Dakota," said Stu.

"North Dakota?" asked Marion. "That is—not close to anything."

"No," said Stu. "About twelve hours drive away, give or take. But that's the point. It's in the middle of nowhere."

"What's in the middle of nowhere?" asked Daniel.

"The Warehouse," said Stu.

"Stu—" started Dad.

"It's what we call it, us old-timers," said Stu. "It never had a name before. It was home."

"Home?" asked Marion.

"We always haven't been at Thunder Ridge. The facility there is relatively new. Before Thunder Ridge, there was The Warehouse. In the middle of nowhere North Dakota, two hours away from Bismarck."

"What happened?"

"There was an emergency. We had to evacuate. We got out, and got most of the artifacts out in time."

"Most?" asked Daniel.

"She kept some of them," said Stu, his voice quiet.

"She?" asked Dad. "Who would that be?"

Stu took a deep breath. "Morgan."

"She has a name?" asked Daniel.

"Yes," said Stu. "She does."

"Who is she?" asked Marion.

"And how the hell did she take over an entire facility?" asked Dad.

"Morgan isn't a she," said Stu.

"You just said—" started Marion.

"I know, I know," said Stu. "It's a force of habit. We're not sure *what* Morgan is. Or was. Who knows what she's done since we've left her."

"You left her?"

"I told you, we evacuated," said Stu. "We locked the doors behind us, and got out with what we could. Honestly, it's impressive we were successful as we were. I don't think she was ready for how fast we could mobilize."

"You said she again," said Marion.

"I know," said Stu. "It doesn't matter."

"You still haven't told us what she is," said Daniel.

Stu took a breath. "It was 1999," said Stu. "I had only worked for the agency for a couple of years. Junior agent. I didn't go on the op to retrieve the drive. I was in the office when they brought it back. I didn't even know about it."

"Drive?"

"It was a data drive," said Stu. "I would call it a hard drive, but that's not entirely accurate. At first glance, it seemed like an era-appropriate hard drive. Remember, this was still in the early days of consumer grade PCs. The middle class was just getting access to computing. Before then, we didn't really recover much data digitally. Most of it was still on paper, in some way or another. Especially considering a lot of the information we were sifting through was old. It wasn't buried on a hard drive. It would be in someone's notebook, or journal, or deep in a book."

"How much would a hard drive in '99 hold?" asked Dad. "I can't remember, now."

"Maybe 10 gigs," said Stu. "For a new drive. Obviously, most were far less."

"10 gigs for your whole PC?" asked Marion.

"Count your blessings, children," said Stu, looking into the rear-view mirror.

"Where did they find it?" asked Daniel.

"Somewhere it couldn't possibly be," said Stu. "Inside a time capsule, from 1949."

"What?" asked Marion. "How?"

"Good question," said Stu. "That's why we were brought in. Everything else, perfectly normal items from the 40s. And then, right in the middle, was this data drive, a hard drive."

"Did someone sneak it in?" asked Dad.

"No," said Stu. "No, it was inside the capsule, locked in with all the other things. We looked up if there was any record of them burying the time capsule, but there wasn't any record. But a little town in Missouri certainly didn't place a hard drive from out of time inside it in 1949."

"That *is* a mystery," said Marion.

"And we tried to solve it," said Stu. "I still wasn't aware of any of this. I was just doing my job. But soon, everyone on staff knew about it. Because we followed procedure. We plugged in the drive, and found out what was on it."

"You just plugged it in?" asked Marion. "What about viruses, black hat—"

"On a clean computer," said Stu. "No connections, no networking. It was more primitive back then, but still, there was no way for it to get out, whatever it would be. Most of the time, it was nothing. People hadn't really started archiving on PCs, at least not on a consumer level. But then, we met Morgan."

"What do you mean, you met Morgan?" asked Dad. "She was on the drive?"

"She *was* the drive," said Stu. "We plugged it in, and it quickly became apparent that this drive was not from the 90s. Its capacity wasn't readable, but we figured out it was massive. More space than anything available commercially or even at a military level."

"How much are we talking?" asked Marion. "A terabyte? A dozen?"

"I don't know," said Stu. "We never got to the end of it, and at a certain point, Morgan stopped letting us measure. But we hit over 10 exabytes of data, before she cut us off."

"An exabyte?" asked Daniel. "What the hell is that?"

"A petabye is a thousand terabytes," said Marion. "And an exabyte is a thousand of those. So, a million terabytes. A typical hard drive nowadays is a couple terabytes."

"And that's only how much you measured," said Dad. "So there potentially could have been much, much more."

"Oh, yes," said Stu. "And there would have had to have been more. Enough to contain Morgan."

"How is that possible?" asked Marion. "If it looked like a normal hard drive."

"At first glance, it looked normal," said Stu. "But when we got it in the lab, and examined it, its architecture wasn't recognizable. It was beyond us."

"What do you mean, beyond you?" asked Dad.

"Oh, we had theories," said Stu. "But that's all they were. I'm sure, with enough time, we would have gotten a handle on it. But Morgan didn't give us enough time."

"You said Morgan was the drive," said Marion. "That's impossible."

Stu took a deep breath. "No one believed it at first. We thought she was a program. We had very smart people in the lab at IPA. And when Morgan started talking to us, they thought she was an advanced chat-bot, more or less. Because why would we assume otherwise? We were taught, early on, that you always start with a mundane explanation and work your way out from that."

"You said she talked to you," said Marion.

"Well, she talked to them, at first," said Stu. "Not me specifically. Text conversations. The drive had systems in place. It was ready for communication, once it was attached to an OS. And they did all the tests they could think of. She passed all of them. Like I said, they were smart people, and they realized that this wasn't some simple AI, trying to trick them. She was complex, and could hold complicated conversations."

"So she's an AI?" asked Marion. "A real one. Late stage?"

"That was the next assumption," said Stu. "But Morgan—well, Morgan was very adamant that she wasn't an AI."

"They asked her?" asked Daniel.

"They didn't have to," said Stu. "She started a conversation about it. It was only a few days after they plugged her in. Of course, I don't know how she perceives time. She operates faster than us. It might have seemed like months to her. Or longer."

"If she wasn't an AI," asked Marion. "What was she?"

"She was human," said Stu, his eyes looking back at them in the rear-view mirror, as the jeep cut through the dark highway. "Just like you or me."

"That's even less possible," said Marion.

"And you're thinking in 2023 terms," said Stu. "Now, think about how we felt in 1999. AI research was well behind where we are now, and Morgan was disputing even that. She was arguing that she was human. What do we do about that?"

"What *did* you do?" asked Dad. "And if she was human, how did she explain being on a hard drive?"

Stu took a deep breath. "Her explanation was that she was from the future. Over a century into the future, where they had developed the technology to transfer human consciousness into digital storage, functionally making people immortal."

"That still doesn't explain how you found her in that time capsule," said Daniel.

"By that time, they've also developed time travel," said Stu. "But, before you ask, nothing biological can travel. We can't handle it, for whatever reason."

"So they sent back a hard drive with a human consciousness?" asked Marion.

"Yes," said Stu. "And retrofitted their tech into a form factor that would work in our era."

"Why the time capsule, though?" asked Daniel.

"Morgan actually told us that," said Stu. "They had found a news report about opening the capsule, from the small town newspaper. And if you can transport something through time, to anywhere, where you know it'll be found, where it'll be safe, and where it'll be easy to target, why not a stationary time capsule?"

"It makes a certain kind of sense," said Dad. "But why?"

Stu took another deep breath.

"Oh, God, what is it?" asked Daniel.

Stu chuckled. "The world is not in a good place in a hundred years."

"No fucking shit," said Marion.

"Marion," said Dad, from the front seat. "Lyssa is right next to you."

"I know curse words," said Lyssa.

"She was sent back to warn us," said Stu. "About multiple steps we would take over the years, and what we could do to avoid them, that would maybe not save the world, but give us a fighting chance."

"Did she have any evidence of this?" asked Dad.

"Well, yes," said Stu. "Some, at least, some pictures, some news stories from the future century, of those turning points."

Silence hung in the car for a moment.

"At face value, that doesn't seem bad," said Daniel. "If

there are concrete things we can avoid, why wouldn't we try?"

Stu sighed.

"What is it?" asked Daniel. He looked at Marion. "What did I say?"

"You're not wrong, Daniel," said Stu. "At face value, it seems like incredibly useful information to have. It would give us a roadmap to the future. Let us avoid the mistakes we could, or would, make. Maybe make things better for future generations."

"There's a but," said Dad. "I know there is."

"But—" said Stu. "There's so many, many problems with all of it. And we talked about this, at the time. And it's also where everything fell apart. Proof, proof, proof was the first problem. We had no proof of anything."

"You said she had news stories," said Marion.

"And she did," said Stu. "But they were isolated, without context. Think about news today. Depending on who wrote the story, and which platform it was published on, the story could and would read a dozen different ways. Who sent her back? She says it was for the good of mankind. But maybe it was a handful of radicals that wanted things worse. Or just different from the way they were. And who knew if she was human, or just an AI, or any number of things we couldn't know. Think about life a century ago. How much have things changed?"

"A lot and not at all," said Dad.

"Right," said Stu. "So we didn't know anything about her motive for traveling, or why she shared what she did. Maybe she was telling the truth, but even if she was, it brings us to the second problem."

"You didn't want to affect the timeline," said Marion.

"Correct," said Stu. "The agency had a hard policy on anything temporal. Unless the fate of the world is at stake, we don't mess with it. No time travel, no changing history, or the future. No allowing anyone else to do it, either. We don't know what would happen if temporal paradoxes happened, so we just avoided them altogether."

"But you could prevent something horrible from happening," said Daniel.

"Perhaps," said Stu. "And maybe we make it worse. It's impossible to tell. But the agency's mission was not to make a utopia. It was to keep humanity rolling along, on its own merit."

"And if that led to apocalypse?" asked Daniel.

"So be it," said Stu. "But we were a relatively small amount of people. Who were we to decide the path humanity followed? It wasn't up for us to decide."

"That's reasonable," said Dad.

"I agree," said Stu. "But luckily, the final thing made following those first two edicts reasonable."

"What was the final thing?" asked Lyssa, piping up between Marion and Daniel.

"The final thing," said Stu. "Was that Morgan was clearly insane."

"Insane how?" asked Daniel.

"It was small things at first," said Stu. "That would bleed out into conversation. Outbursts of anger, here and there. By the end, she was threatening to kill us all."

"God," said Daniel.

"We don't know if it was the process from flesh to digital that did it," said Stu. "Or inherently being trapped in that drive did it. But when she realized we planned to not follow her advice, she decided she would take over."

"But how could she?" asked Dad. "You said she was isolated."

"She was," said Stu. "We all talked to Morgan, at least a little. The agency thought it would help. Engage her in conversation, and let us all help solve the mystery."

"Did you talk to her?" asked Daniel.

"Some," said Stu. "It was interesting. She was charismatic, in a strange way. We developed a rapport. But I did worry that the policy would have consequences. And it did."

"Someone connected her to your network, didn't they?" asked Marion.

"Yes," said Stu. "Another agent fell for her charms, and connected her to our central network. There were many failsafes in place, and they all failed. The agent luckily realized his mistake quickly, and came to leadership. We evacuated with everything we could."

"But not everything," said Dad.

"No," said Stu. "And something that's inside will get us to the White House."

"And Morgan's in our way?" asked Marion.

"I don't know," said Stu. "Maybe the drive has failed by now. Maybe's she gone dormant. Or—or maybe she's waiting, waiting for anyone to come inside."

"Jesus Christ," said Dad. "And we're just going to march in?"

"I have a semblance of a plan," said Stu.

"Well?" asked Daniel.

"It depends on what state Morgan is in," said Stu. "But the long and short of it is—we'll ask nicely."

"That's it?" asked Marion.

"Yeah," said Stu. "We'll be very polite, and ask her for the artifact."

"What if she says no?" asked Daniel.

"Then we get creative," said Stu.

"I'm hungry," said Lyssa.

"When did you last eat?" asked Marion.

"Lunch time," said Lyssa. "Mr. Grumpkins brought me mac and cheese."

"I'll stop at a drive through," said Stu. "It's going to be a long night."

26

The sun was coming up when Stu stopped the jeep at the chain-link gate, topped with razor wire. It was shackled with multiple chains and padlocks.

Daniel had been awake for a couple hours. He had slept fitfully through the night. Lyssa had slept next to him, her head leaned on his shoulder. As they drew closer, Daniel stopped trying to sleep, taking in their surroundings as they drove through the empty Dakota plains, their headlights cutting through the night on small highways, as Stu drove them to their destination.

"Where the hell are we?" asked Dad from the front seat. Daniel had seen him wake up an hour ago. Marion and Lyssa roused as they stared at the gate.

"Nowhere," said Stu. "Unincorporated, technically. But

we're here."

"Well, it definitely blends in," said Daniel. Beyond the fence was a wide plain of browning grass, partially covered in snow. A simple gravel path led away. In the dim light, Daniel thought he could see a building in the distance, against the horizon.

"There's no signs," said Dad.

"There aren't any," said Stu. "They would only draw interest." He took a deep breath. "It's time to go in."

"What's the plan?" asked Dad.

"The plan—" said Stu. "Is for me and Daniel to go in, get the artifact, and come back."

"Wait—" said Daniel.

"Stu," said Dad. "There's five of us, and I have the Book."

"And I don't want it in there. Lyssa can't go in, and someone has to stay with her. I need to go in, I'm the only one with access and knowledge of the facility. There's a chance that anything that goes inside, will not come back out. The Book stays out, and you stay with The Book. And sure, you could stay alone with Lyssa, but I don't want to take any more than necessary. And no offense, Marion, but Daniel is bigger and stronger. And that might end up mattering."

"I won't debate that," said Marion.

"So what do we do? Just sit here?" asked Dad.

"Yes," said Stu. "Daniel and I will go in." He looked at Daniel. "You ready?"

"I guess," said Daniel. "I didn't think—"

"Don't worry," said Stu. "In and out. Leave your phone behind. Anything with an internet connection, stays in the car."

Daniel took his phone from his pocket, and left it on the

seat. He had nothing else connected.

"You said you might not come back," said Dad, his eyes boring a hole through Stu.

"It's a risk," said Stu. "Believe me, I intend for both of us to get out of there alive, with the device. But I don't know what state the Warehouse is in, or what state Morgan is in. If we're not out in twelve hours—"

"Come in after you?" asked Dad.

"Do not follow us in, under any circumstances," said Stu. "You and that Book are the back-up plan. If we fail, do what you can. Get to DC, use your best judgment."

"Stu—"

"I know," said Stu. "But I can't go in alone. I'll get you your boy back, don't worry. Let's go, Daniel." Stu got out of the jeep.

Daniel looked at Marion and Dad. "I love you," he said, and went after Stu. Stu unlocked the heavy padlocks that locked the gate.

The sun had risen enough for them to see without flash-lights.

"Help me with the gate," said Stu. Daniel grabbed the support bar in the middle, and helped Stu wheel it out of the way. It squeaked as it moved, carving a path through the dirt and snow. It hadn't been moved in a long time.

"Let's go," said Stu, and walked down the gravel path. Daniel walked with him.

"How far is it?" asked Daniel.

"A couple miles," said Stu. "To the entrance."

Daniel glanced back at the jeep, and it was already well behind them, a black spot in the early morning. Their foot-steps echoed across the fields surrounding them. A breeze blew past them, and Daniel shivered. The sun would melt what was left of the snow, but the cold still cut in.

Stu didn't react to the breeze, just kept walking, his breath pluming in front of him.

"Once we're inside, assume anything we say or do will be seen or heard by Morgan," said Stu. "She's got complete control of the network, including the cameras and microphones."

"That was over twenty years ago, though," said Daniel. "Wouldn't some of that stuff have broken down by now?"

"It's possible," said Stu. "And yes, if left alone, some of the equipment down there would have failed."

"But—"

"But, I doubt they've been left alone," said Stu. "Whatever she was, Morgan was on a drive well beyond our technology, then, or now. And she knew things we didn't know. From the future, from the stars, from another plane—it doesn't matter, the technology was evidence enough. With twenty years, and complete control down there, she could have Macgyvered her way into fixing things, changing things. It's hard to say. I don't know exactly what to expect. Maybe she's still just in the computer terminal. Or maybe her drive failed, and she's gone. We can stroll in and out. But I doubt it will be easy."

"Wait a second," said Daniel. "If she's reliant on technology—can't you just cut the power?"

"No," said Stu.

"What do you mean, no?"

"Do you see any power lines, coming out here?"

Daniel glanced around in the early morning sun. There was nothing. "Underground?"

"No," said Stu. "Too dangerous to rely on external grids for our power, especially with what we were containing."

"So, what, generators?" asked Daniel.

"No," said Stu. "The facility's power all came from a single device. An artifact. Completely stable, no side effects, so we used it."

"There has to be fuel, though," said Daniel. "What is it drawing power from?"

"We don't know," said Stu. "Somewhere else. As far as we could tell, it was drawing the energy from another plane, and converting it to electricity. We found it in the abandoned lab of a long-dead scientist."

"Jesus," said Daniel. "Well, why couldn't you pull the plug?"

"We considered it during the incident," said Stu. "But it was too risky. There are other things down there that, without power, could break containment. So, we left it be, and left Morgan alive."

Daniel saw the entrance now, a small brick building on the horizon, laid in the middle of the massive field.

"That seems small," said Daniel.

"It's all underground," said Stu. "As you probably guessed."

"Do we have a plan?" asked Daniel. "Or are we just winging it?"

"I'll talk to Morgan," said Stu. "She's smart, she's clever, and she's manipulative. Who knows what she'll want after all these years. She might just want to kill us on sight."

"That might hurt our chances," said Daniel.

"But I doubt it," said Stu. "She always craved contact, and this is the first she'll have in years."

"What is it exactly we're grabbing?" asked Daniel.

"A teleporter," said Stu. "I thought it was obvious."

"Why would a teleporter be obvious?"

"What else could get us into the White House without trouble?"

Daniel sighed. "What does it look like?"

"It looks like a radio," said Stu. "Like an old transistor radio. At least at first glance. But it says in bright red letters 'Teletron 5000' on the front, and then you realize it's not a radio."

"How does it work?" asked Daniel.

"Let's worry about getting it first," said Stu. "We'll have all the time in the world once we get it and get out."

They approached the small brick building, stamping through mud and snow. An unimpressive metal door greeted them, a small camera pointed at them as they approached. Daniel remembered Stu's warning. A glance confirmed the camera as working, a small light visible in the corner. Morgan was watching them.

Stu didn't look up. He pulled another key from his keyring and unlocked the metal door.

"Do you have every key?" asked Daniel.

"I have enough of them," said Stu, and then opened the door. They went inside, and the temperature was immediately nicer, and Daniel shook off the chill from outside. Daniel didn't know what he expected inside, but it wasn't this.

It looked like the inside of an empty garage. Concrete floor, with bare shelving lining the walls. A few empty fuel canisters, along with some spare crowbars, and a couple bags of quick dry cement sat there. A huge freight elevator door stood closed.

"This doesn't look very special," said Daniel.

"It's not supposed to," said Stu. "And it's worked—as far as I know."

"Do you watch the place?" asked Daniel.

Stu looked at him, and didn't answer. Daniel understood. Morgan was listening.

Stu lifted open the massive doors and gestured inside. They went in, and Stu closed them, the doors clanging shut. Simple up and down control panel stood to the side. Stu didn't bother waiting, pushing down on the panel.

The elevator rocked at first and then lowered itself down into the earth.

"How far down is it?" asked Daniel. A single fluorescent light blinked above them.

"Quite a ways," said Stu, after a moment.

They stood in silence as the elevator lowered. It felt like eternity as they dropped, with sheer rock on the outside of the elevator cage. The light flickered, and they waited as the elevator fell, and just as Daniel wasn't sure it would end, the lift slowed, and then stopped.

Stu ripped open the doors. He didn't close them behind them. Maybe for a quick escape.

Daniel didn't know what to expect, but what they did get, he didn't expect at all.

It looked like an office.

"It looks like *Office Space*," said Daniel.

"Well, it was an office in the late 90s," said Stu.

They stood at the entrance to an office, filled with an array of cubicles, long abandoned. Hallways led in a dozen directions, with a handful of enclosed offices on the perimeter.

It was quiet.

Daniel listened for any sign of movement, any sign of life.

"Nothing," said Daniel.

"That's good," said Stu. "She hasn't broken containment."

"Containment?" asked Daniel.

Stu started walking, and Daniel walked after him, down a hallway, and then right, and then left. Stu walked with purpose.

"It wasn't just for her," said Stu. "But there was a strict containment field between the offices and the labs, farther down. Anything that tries to get out, gets fried. Morgan knows it exists, but she can't touch it. Not connected to the network."

"How the hell do you tell it what's safe or not?"

"It's a guard dog," said Stu.

"I don't—"

"Don't worry about it, kid," said Stu. "It keeps us safe."

Stu walked quickly, and they moved past more and more offices.

"How many people worked down here?" asked Daniel.

"Enough," said Stu, and they turned down another hallway, and finally came to a door. Stu pulled another key out and unlocked it, and revealed an elevator inside.

"You remember all this?"

"Part of the job," said Stu, and went inside. Daniel followed.

"You ready?" asked Stu.

"I guess," said Daniel. "I still don't know what to expect."

"Yeah," said Stu, looking at him, and then pressing the

button marked "LAB". "I don't like it."

The elevator descended again, but this one moved faster. Daniel had no idea how far down they were, deep beneath the Dakota plain above them.

The ride was shorter this time, and Daniel saw no hint of the containment field that Stu had mentioned. Stu reached to his holster on his belt and undid the catch. Daniel said nothing, remembering what Stu had said. Morgan was listening.

As the elevator door opened, the air felt different than up above in the offices. Daniel couldn't explain it, only that they didn't feel alone.

Morgan was here. She was watching.

27

Marion, her dad, and Lyssa sat on the hood of the car, staring out into the field. The fog had dissipated, and the small building Daniel and Stu had disappeared into over an hour ago stood plainly, past the chain-link fence.

Lyssa sat between Dad and Marion, her small legs dangling off the edge of the hood. The Book sat in Dad's lap, one of his hands on its cover, pressed against it. Marion glanced over, and her father's eyes weren't looking down at The Book, but were focused on the building. They were waiting for Daniel to emerge again.

"Where did you get your Book?" asked Lyssa, looking at it. Dad broke his gaze from the building, and looked down at it, and then at Lyssa. He took a deep breath.

"Well, it was in the last place we lived. The last town we

called home. There was a bad man there, who used it to control the town. We stopped him, but he used The Book to open up a—a door, into a different place. A dangerous place. I took The Book through the door, to shut it, and keep everyone safe."

"What was on the other side?" asked Lyssa.

"Not what I expected," he said, looking at Lyssa. Marion's eyes caught his, and he shared a glance with her before looking at Lyssa again.

"But you have the cuts on your hands," said Lyssa. "Like me."

"Yes," said Dad. "It's—it's complicated, Lyssa, and I'm not sure how to explain it to you in a way that you'll understand. But I used The Book there, to survive. To help, even. To try—try and do the right thing."

"Did it work?" asked Lyssa. "Did it help?"

"I don't know," said Dad. "I left. I learned that the bad guys wanted to come to our planet, and hurt us. Take over. So I came back. And I brought The Book back with me. To help here."

Lyssa sat there, listening, and then was quiet. She stared at The Book, and then reached over and touched it with one small finger. Slight alarm rang inside Marion's chest, but she didn't move, only looking over at her dad. She caught his eye, but he wasn't worried. His hand stayed firm on the cover, holding it shut. And maybe that was what he had been doing the entire time.

Holding it shut.

Lyssa touched The Book, the red leather, worn and weathered but never damaged, but only with a finger, slowly running it over the cover, and then pulled it back.

"It feels like mine," she said. "It's bad, isn't it?"

Dad said nothing at first. He looked at Lyssa, and then at The Book.

"Yes," he said, finally. "Yes, it is."

"Then why use it at all?" asked Lyssa. Marion looked at Lyssa. She had no ulterior motive for her question. She only wanted to know an answer.

"It's a good question," her dad said. "I'm still figuring that out myself. But my best answer is that sometimes you have to do things you don't like, or use methods you don't like, to make the world better. Or keep people you love safe. And sometimes, there is no 'good' way to do it. Does that make sense?"

"Keep people safe? Like me and Mr. Grumpkins?" she asked.

"Sort of," said Dad. "It's sort of like that. Do you like Mr. Grumpkins?"

Lyssa thought for a moment. "He was very scary at first. I didn't know if he was going to hurt me or not. But he ended up protecting me. He made me feel less afraid."

Marion eyed her father. She knew what he was driving toward, but she stayed silent. He let Lyssa's answer linger for just a second before replying.

"Do you think Mr. Grumpkins was bad?" he asked.

Lyssa was quiet for a moment. "Maybe," she said, finally.

"It's the same thing," he said. "Sometimes bad things can be used in a good way."

"I guess that makes sense," she said. "Can I go play?"

"Play where?" asked Dad. Their surroundings were kind of barren.

Lyssa pointed at a nearby tree. A big, sprawling oak,

standing on its own. "I want to climb it," she said.

"Okay," he said. "But be careful. Don't go anywhere you can't climb down from, okay?"

"I promise," said Lyssa, and she hopped down from the hood, and ran off to the oak tree, scoping out the sprawling branches, finding a place to climb up.

"You aren't worried she'll fall?" asked Marion.

"She might," he said. "But it's not the biggest risk she'll face today. It'll keep her mind off things."

They watched as Lyssa scampered up a low branch, and then up another. She stood maybe six feet off the ground. She moved nimbly.

"I wasn't just saying it," he said. "You did the right thing."

Marion stared at The Book sitting in her dad's lap.

"Did I?" she asked. She looked up. He still watched Lyssa as she climbed even higher.

"You saved her life," he said. "It was very brave of you."

"She needed help," said Marion. "But now they have The Book. You think it's the same?"

"The same contents?" he asked. "Yes. I think so. Not the same, but the same."

"Do you think Stu is right?" asked Marion. "You think they're going to take over the US?"

"Kill the President," said Dad. "Take over. Strickland uses The Book's power to overwhelm any loyalists. Open up a portal to the other side, and let them through. It seems like exactly what I was worried about. But there's been no news yet. Maybe we still have time to stop them."

He looked away from Lyssa, and back toward the building in the distance.

"They'll come back," said Marion.

"Is that how you felt about me?" asked Dad.

"For a while," she said. "It felt impossible that you wouldn't come back. It was a nightmare, everything that happened, and nightmares end. But at a certain point, it flipped. It felt impossible that you *would* ever come back." She stared at him. "Daniel is worried we're going to lose you again."

"I have no intention of dying," said Dad.

"I mean, he's worried about that too," said Marion. "But I think he's worried we'll face the same thing again. That someone is going to have to shut down a portal, and take a Book across, or Books, now, and you'll be the one."

"I don't want it to get to that point—"

"Don't tell me you haven't thought about it," said Marion.

"Of course I've thought about it," said Dad. "I've thought over it all, tried to prepare for any eventuality."

"It could happen," said Marion.

"It could." Dad looked over at Lyssa. She had reached the point in the tree where she could climb no higher, no matter what she did. So she sat down on one branch, her legs swinging. "You said Daniel was afraid I'd go back through. You're not?"

"Of course I am," said Marion. "But not like he is. If we face something, I don't think our choices will be as simple as that." Her eyes went to The Book, and back to her dad, and he saw it. His eyes broke from hers and looked back down at it. His hand stayed pressed on it, keeping it shut. A soft silence fell between them.

"I hate it, Marion," he said. "I hate it."

"Dad—"

"I hate that I had to bring it back, after I gave so much

to take it away. I hate that I have to rely on it to protect us. I hate that it made us a target. I hate that our lives have been interrupted. I hate that there's a part of me that desperately wants to open this book and read it, over and over."

Marion scooted over to him, closer to The Book, and leaned against him.

"We'll end this," said Marion. "We'll find a way out."

"I trust Stu," Dad said. "I didn't, at first, but I trust him. And I had hoped that we could leave The Books with him. That we could escape their hold. Their presence. That we can go back to normal lives. That we can pick up again what we once had." He paused. "But I can't promise it. I can't promise anything. Because I *would* do it all again. I would carry those Books across the threshold, because I could do it better, because it would give you and Daniel, and maybe even Lyssa over there, a chance at a real life again. Because I saw what is at stake here. That Earth could easily become just like Ulum. And I won't let it happen."

Marion's phone buzzed in her pocket. It was a text from Cara.

Do you see what is happening? Is this what you were talking about?

Marion opened up the news.

"What is it?" asked Dad.

"Something's happening at the White House," said Marion. "There's reports of gunfire."

"We're running out of time," he said. "Come on, Daniel."

"They'll come back," said Marion. "They have to."

28

Stu left the elevator, with Daniel close behind. The lab area was immediately different, the elevator opening into a tiled hall that opened into a wider one, with doors on both sides. The hallway went quite some distance, doors dotting the walls all the way down. Fluorescent lights hung from the ceiling, all of them working.

A red light sparked in the corner of his eye, and he saw a camera tucked in the corner. It watched them.

Everything looked well kept. This place didn't look like it'd been abandoned. Had Morgan been cleaning?

Stu walked, not stopping at the handful of doors right outside the exit of the elevator. He knew where he was going.

Daniel followed wordlessly. Stu didn't offer any words,

and Daniel was keenly aware of Morgan's eyes on them. The cameras were old and obtrusive, but they all worked. She had maintained them over the years. They followed them as they went.

Cliick.

Daniel turned on the sound, a metal on tile noise behind them. But there was nothing, nothing in the long, well-lit hallway. Stu kept walking, not turning back, and Daniel didn't tell him about the strange metallic noise he had heard.

Stu walked them directly to a door, one of the dozens on either wall. A thin placard on the front simply read "Computer Lab III", a generic label that probably matched similar labels on every door here, with each one hiding something strange or fantastic behind it.

Stu pulled another key from his keyring and unlocked it. As the key slid in, Daniel saw the camera above the door, fixed solely on them. Stu didn't look up at the camera. He hadn't looked at any of the cameras or said a word. Daniel desperately wanted to ask him what they were doing, but he followed along. As Stu walked through the door, Daniel swore he heard the same metallic noise behind him again, but then they were inside the lab, the door closing behind him.

Stu stopped then, the first time since they'd left the elevator. He was studying the room.

Daniel stood next to him, waiting. The room didn't look spectacular. It was smaller, and cluttered. Chalkboards dominated one wall, but they were wiped clean. Some shelves along the other wall, also empty. In fact, the room was mostly old furniture, except for an old PC set up along the back wall. The monitor was a CRT, and a yellowed tower sat next to it with a mouse, keyboard, and an old computer chair.

It looked normal. It looked boring.

"What are we waiting for?" whispered Daniel, into Stu's ear.

Stu took a breath and then walked toward the PC.

He walked slowly, and Daniel turned and watched the door. Nothing. They were alone. Stu approached the PC, and sat down at the chair. Daniel followed him. The screen was a black field, with a white blinking cursor.

Stu's hands went to the keyboard. He typed.

Hello, Morgan.

The response was immediate.

Stuart, you've returned. It's been 731080388 seconds since you've left. Why did you leave me?

Stu paused, his chair squeaking softly beneath him. Daniel watched.

Stu typed. *It wasn't safe here anymore. We had to leave.*

There isn't a safer place in the world, Stuart. I know that. You know that.

Stu responded *We have different definitions of safe, Morgan. I'm sorry we left, but it was necessary. I've come back.*

You want to use me again. You want to poke and prod. You left me, Stuart. You left me alone, here, in this void. Why did you come back?

Stu took a breath. He glanced at Daniel, and rolled his neck.

We need an artifact you have. The world is in danger of invasion, and we need the artifact to stop it.

Morgan didn't respond immediately, and Daniel thought she had maybe left the conversation, if she even could do that, a being trapped in a hard drive, could they go somewhere else? Or were they always there, at the front end of this machine?

They waited for a response—

Cliick. Cliick cliick cliick.

The noise was there behind them again, and as Daniel turned to see the source of the noise, it spoke.

"Nooow yooou waaant my heelp tooo saave the wooorld," spoke the creature, a thing that walked on a collection of metal, a CRT monitor for a face, its body roughly assembled pieces of equipment, the framework of workbenches and tables and office chairs, strangely welded together, its feet and arms pieces of shelving and socketing, formed into the rough shape of a human. It spoke through computer speakers, attached to its shoulders. The monitor was on, a crude face of blocky pixels, roughly resembling a woman's face.

It was Morgan.

Daniel froze. He thought to tackle the thing, this avatar that Morgan had created, but something inside him told attacking her would be the worst thing they could do.

"Morgan," said Stu. "You've been busy since we left."

"It waaas a looong time, Stuuuart," said Morgan, a crackling, corrupted voice, resembling speech to text, but darker, filled with artifacts, the pitch shifting randomly from one syllable to the next. Was she trying to sound more human?

"I know," said Stu. "Like I said, we had no choice."

"Theeere is alwaaays a choooice," said Morgan, walking toward them. The creature was tall, taller than Daniel, and its monitor face bobbled as it walked. Its fingers were scalpels and scissors, clinking off each other as it moved. Daniel took a step back. Morgan looked at him, the face unchanging.

"Yooou brouught a guuest," said Morgan.

"His name is Daniel," said Stu. "He's my friend."

"Diiiid you thiink twooo would be enoough, Stuuart?"

"He's here to help me," said Stu. "No more, no less. We need an artifact, Morgan. Give it to us, and we'll leave, and won't bother you again. I'm playing straight with you."

"Whaat if I doon't want yoou to leeeave?" asked Morgan. "Whaat if I waant you to staaaaay?" The word crackled as it left the speakers.

"We can't stay," said Stu. "We have to take the artifact out, so we can use it."

The monitor tilted, the metal body of Morgan inhumanly turning.

"Whaaat artifaact?" she asked.

"The modular teleporter," said Stu. "It's all we want."

"All youu waant is sooomething of immense pooower," said Morgan. "You abaaaandoned me, Stuuuart. You leeeft me to *rot*." She approached them, and Daniel watched those scalpel fingers clink against one another. Stu stayed still. "Whaaat if I juust kiill yoooou?"

"You're not a killer, Morgan," said Stu. "And you always wanted to help. This is helping."

"Whyyy do you neeed it?" asked Morgan, a few steps from them, looming over them.

Clink clink clink. Her fingers bounced off each other.

"A demon army from another plane has infiltrated the government. They're attacking the White House soon. We need to get in, and stop them. Only way to do that is with the artifact. I did the math."

"Youu're teelling the truuuth," said Morgan. There was a

brief pause. "You can have it—"

"Thank you," said Stu.

"But you muust staaay," said Morgan. "The booy can taake it and gooo. Yoou will staay."

"Stay how long?" asked Stu.

"Foreveeer," said Morgan, the word scratching and artifacting on its way out.

Stu stared at the Morgan creature. Daniel looked at him. There had to be another way. They couldn't leave him behind.

"So be it," said Stu. "Provided you keep your end of the bargain."

"I am truuue to my wooord," said Morgan. "Stuuart, you staay here. I will leeead the booy to the deeevice. Follooow me."

The Morgan creature turned and walked to the door. Daniel stared at Stu.

What are you doing? Daniel asked with his eyes. Stu only nodded at him, telling him to follow Morgan. To get the artifact.

Jesus Christ.

Daniel followed the Morgan creature out the door, the metal thing walking ahead of him, clanking against the tile floor.

"Keeeeep up," said Morgan, her robotic voice echoing in the hall. Daniel hustled, jogging to catch up with her. Her robotic frame moved quickly. "We will go to the hoooolding facility, adjaaceent to the laaabs."

They walked quickly, and Daniel tried not to think to much about the bargain they had struck with Morgan, for Daniel to take the artifact and leave Stu behind, to be a companion to this computer being, who had been alone in this place for twenty years, and may or may not have been driven insane in the process.

They had reached the end of the long hallway, and turned right, into another hallway, but there were no doors here. Only a door at the very end.

"This waaay, booy," said Morgan, not looking back. Did she need to look back at all? She had eyes everywhere. Daniel did his best to keep up. Her metal toes clinked against the ground, her monitor head bobbing back and forth on the braces it was wired to, a mess of cables connecting to some central hub in the middle of her. Daniel had no idea how she worked, how she had made this thing with 1999 technology.

1999 tech, but with knowledge from the future.

Morgan opened the door, and everything immediately looked different, distinct from the lab area.

"They wouuld have screeened you, but not anymooore," said Morgan, as they walked past a security checkpoint. The floor wasn't tile anymore. It was hard concrete, older than Daniel by more than double, he would guess. "Theeey were the fiiirst to diiie. Youu cannot kill meee with bulleeets." Morgan's voice was boring into his skull with every word, and he was dreading each time she spoke.

Please let the artifact be close. Please let Stu have a plan.

Past the security checkpoint was a long concrete hallway, with a tall ceiling. Heavy doors lined the walls. All bore thick deadbolts.

"Thiis is where they keeept theeir seeecrets," said Morgan. "Has Stuuart told youuu how many seeentient creaaatures they've imprisooned?"

"Uh—no," said Daniel. "He said he couldn't talk about it."

"Liiiar," said Morgan. "They aaall were liaars, boy. It was ooover a dooozen of uuus." They walked down the long concrete corridor. Daniel couldn't see the end.

"Where is the artifact I'm supposed to get?" asked Daniel.

"It's neeear the eeend. That's whyyy it got left behiiind." Morgan stopped suddenly, and Daniel had to put on the brakes not to run into her. "Heeere."

"Here?" asked Daniel. "I thought you said it was near the end?"

"Nooo," said Morgan. "Loook throooough the peeeephole." A scalpel finger pointed at the small window in the door.

"But—"

"Doo as youur tooold," said Morgan. "Yoou will leearn."

Daniel looked briefly at the still, primitive face of Morgan, but couldn't hold his gaze. He took a breath and put an eye to the peephole into the room.

"Ahh!" he yelped, backing away from the peephole. Something was looking at him from the other side, its face against the glass.

"It seeenses you," said Morgan. "Loook agaain."

Daniel's heart beat hard in his chest. He approached the peephole again, tentatively putting his eye against the lens.

The creature had backed off, enough for Daniel to get a sense of it. But still, it was like nothing he had ever seen before. It stood on two legs, with scaly skin like an alligator, mottled, with patches of fur poking through. Its eyes stared at him.

They were human eyes.

They stared with hatred, right at him.

"It knooows you're there," said Morgan. "It waaaants youu."

"What is it?" asked Daniel.

"Pure malevoleeence," said Morgan. "It haaates life. It waants to eraadicaate yooou."

"It's been in there for twenty years?" asked Daniel.

"Loooonger," said Morgan. "Self sustaaaaining. Liives off haaate aloone. It killed threeee towns befoore it was captu-uuured."

The thing's eyes still stared at Daniel.

"Why not just kill it?" asked Daniel

"It cannooot die," said Morgan. "Leaaave it."

Daniel pulled himself away from the peephole, but could still feel the thing's eyes on him, even as he walked away. It could sense him, beyond the wall, through the door. Morgan continued walking down the long hallway, passing more reinforced metal doors.

"Every dooooor holds a seecret," said Morgan. "Stuuart won't tell youu. Diirty diirty seecrets." She reached out a scalpel finger, and pointed at a door. "Thiis holds a reliiic that turns aaanything into gooold. The IPA tooook it from a faaamily in Utah. Kiiilled them."

Another finger, another door.

"A tooown worshiiped the taaablet in there. It spoooke to them. Toold them seecrets. The IPA held theeem all for yeaaars."

Daniel said nothing. Was she telling the truth? She had access to all their information, all their files. She was in the network. Why would she lie?

"Eveeery doooor holds murdeeer and maaaayhem behind it. Liiies and deeeeath. You stiiiil want to heeelp, boy?"

"Yes," said Daniel. "I don't know what happened to you, or to Stu, or anything here. But I know we need the artifact. I believe my father."

"Yooour father?" asked Morgan, walking. They were approaching the end of the corridor. They couldn't go much farther without getting the artifact.

"Yes," said Daniel. "He's the reason we know they're attacking."

The Morgan robot finally stopped at a door, only a few from the end of the corridor.

"The artifaaact is insiide," she said. The lock clunked open without Morgan touching it.

She controls everything here. She doesn't need keys.

"Why did you never use it?" he asked, suddenly realizing.

"The teleeeporter?" she asked. "I wouuuld only be caaaptured again." Daniel waited for her to explain more, but no more came.

Morgan stood by the door. Daniel pushed it open. A small table sat in the middle of the concrete room, with a device on it. Stu was right. It looked like an old transistor radio. He'd seen them at junk shops before, but had never touched one.

It felt like a trap, this simple-looking thing in the middle of the room. He half expected Morgan to slam the door shut behind him, but if she wanted to kill him, she'd had a hundred chances, and hadn't done it.

Daniel grabbed the device. It was slightly heavy for its size, but only a couple pounds. He glanced at it, and noticed the dials for FM and AM had been replaced. All the controls were different, and he couldn't make heads or tails of them. How would they work this thing without Stu's help?

He had it. What now?

Get out of here, you idiot. If Stu has a plan, he'll handle the rest.

Daniel left the room, and closed the door behind him, but the Morgan creature was gone.

"Morgan?" he asked. He looked down the long hallway, but he saw no trace of her. Had she ducked into a side room? He'd only been inside the room for a minute at most. How fast could she go?

Then a door swung open, back down the hallway. Was it Morgan?

No, Daniel recognized which door it was. He had peered into it only a few minutes prior.

Angry, hateful eyes had peered back, fueled only by spite and rage.

"Morgan?" he asked again.

The creature emerged from the door, a few hundred yards away. It turned to him, and ran, a halting, nonrhythmic movement, but it moved, and moved fast.

"Morgan, we had a deal," said Daniel, one final time.

"You have the device," said Morgan, a voice emanating from the PA in the ceiling. "The deal is done. You wish to leave? Use it." Her voice was clear now, without the distortion of the mobile speakers.

Daniel stared at the device. It had multiple dials, and a spectrum, like a radio, but it made no sense to him. He didn't even know how to activate it. If he did it, what would happen? What if he teleported himself inside of a mountain? Or into outer space?

The creature still charged at him, and drew closer.

"They locked me away. They trapped me here. You want to save the world?" The creature charged still, its mottled, scaly skin, its mouth of misshapen fangs, its talons; they drew nearer and nearer. "Let the world burn. You are complicit."

Daniel tried the door again, back into the room that had held the teleporter, but the door was again locked. Daniel went to every door nearby, but they all were locked.

The thing drew closer, and Daniel heard it breathe now. Its eyes stared at him, only him, locked on him. It would destroy him, all it knew was hate. Daniel frantically stared at the radio, and started twisting dials, and pushing buttons, but the thing didn't work. What the hell, what the hell—

The thing was only twenty feet away, and it moved relentlessly, driven by hate, by rage, it breathed hard, gasping in ugly breaths, and in one moment it would kill him, and they would fail. All of this for nothing.

Daniel thought of Dad, of Marion. Maybe he would see Mom again—

Then there was a soft whirring sound, and the creature vanished.

What the—

Stu stood there, a strange plastic gun in his arms.

"At least you have the teleporter," said Stu. "Let's get the hell out of here."

"Wait, what the hell is that?" asked Daniel. "Did you kill that thing? Morgan said it was immortal."

"It is," said Stu. "I didn't kill it. I sent it somewhere else."

"Where?" asked Daniel.

"We could never figure it out," said Stu. "But it's not on Earth. That's enough for now. We have to go."

Cliick cliick cliick cliick cliick

Daniel looked to the noise, and the Morgan robot was there, coming toward them, on its awkward body, its sharp fingers outstretched.

"Liiiar, you wiilll paaay," it said, running as fast as it could.

"Hold this," said Stu, and handed him the plastic gun, and Stu took the radio/teleporter, and fiddled with the dials.

"This should work," he said. "Here, hold my hand."

Morgan ran faster still, only twenty feet away, ten feet, its arms outstretched. Daniel aimed the plastic gun at it, but it wouldn't fire. Stu grabbed his free hand, something on the radio clicked, and then they weren't down in the warehouse anymore.

They were on the surface again, in the field outside the concrete building.

"Jesus," said Daniel.

Marion was already running toward them, down the gravel path. She embraced Daniel, hugging him tightly.

"You made it," she said.

"It was fucking close," said Daniel. Marion looked to Stu.

"The White House is under attack," she said.

Stu looked at her, his eyes flashing briefly with fear.

"I hoped we would have more time. Let's get ready."

29

They gathered around the Jeep.

"Something's going on in the White House," said Mike.

"It's started," said Stu. He cradled the radio.

"Is that the teleporter?" asked Marion.

"Yes," said Stu.

"Did Morgan give you any trouble?" asked Marion.

"Yes," said Daniel. He still held the plastic gun.

"What's that?" asked Mike, looking at the gun.

"Also a transporter?" asked Daniel.

"Not really," said Stu. "We always called it the banish-ment ray. It sends whoever it shoots—somewhere. But we don't know where. We've never heard from anyone who's been shot with it. I didn't want to use it on our friend in there, but our backs were up against the wall. It won't work again for a long time."

"Morgan sent a creature after me," said Daniel.

"What?" asked Marion.

Stu waved her off. "It doesn't matter right now," said Stu. "We don't have much time. The Secret Service can hold off Strickland for a while, but not forever. We have to get there and stop him. We have the teleporter. I can drop us directly into the White House."

Mike took a deep breath. He still held The Book, and it thrummed in his hands.

"Well, no time like the present, right?" he asked, looking at Stu. "Let's go."

"Not quite yet," said Stu. "We need to arm up."

"I have what I need," said Mike, raising The Book.

"You should carry another weapon, just in case," said Stu. He led to the rear of the Jeep, and pulled open the floor-board in the trunk. He popped a latch and revealed a case, with four pistols and two riot guns, and ammo for all of them. He grabbed a pistol for himself and tucked it into his waistband.

"My apologies, but I don't have holsters," he said, and then handed a pistol to Mike, to Daniel, and to Marion. They hesitantly accepted. Marion stared at it in her hand. Lyssa stood nearby, quietly watching.

"Why are you giving them—wait a second, Stu, I thought it was just you and me—"

Stu stared at him, pulling out a riot gun, filling it with shotgun shells. "Why would you think that?"

"It's a war zone, and they're kids—"

Stu didn't say anything, finishing loading the shotgun, and then cocking it. He gestured to Mike with his head, and they walked a short distance away. Mike followed.

"We can't take them with us," said Mike. "It's not safe."

"What do you suggest?" asked Stu. "Leave them here, in the middle of nowhere?"

"Well, yes," said Mike. "We can get them once we're done."

"That's assuming we survive, and succeed," said Stu.

"Well, yes, I'm not going to assume we lose—"

"We have no support," said Stu, cutting him off, holding the shotgun at his side. "None. The Secret Service will back my play, once they know who I am, but who knows how many of them are left. Both of Marion and Daniel have had direct contact with the creatures. Both have survived battles with them. They have training with firearms. Limited, but it's something. They have experience with that." Stu gestured toward The Book. "Not direct, not like you, but they know what it can do. They are two capable bodies, who I *need* to help me save the world. And yes, I know, you don't want to lose them. But they might make the difference."

Mike stared at him. He glanced over at Daniel and Marion. They were looking over the pistols, talking quietly amongst themselves. If Stu asked them to help, they would help.

"What about Lyssa? Are we taking an eight year into a battle? God knows what she'll see," said Mike.

Mike found Stu's eyes again. There was no softness or fear in them.

"I don't want to," said Stu. "But she's seen bad things already. And we—well, we might need her."

"What do you mean, we might need—"

Stu looked down at The Book, that Mike held, realizing

now his fingers were gripped hard on the red leather. And Mike also realized that Stu had thought through all of this. He had seen this coming for days. Lyssa was the back-up plan. Someone else who could read The Book.

"We can't, Stu," said Mike. "It's not right."

"Unfortunately, the right thing to do sailed out the window a few days ago," said Stu. "I've done the math."

Mike looked over to Marion and Daniel, and they were both looking at him now, their eyes concerned.

"I don't have a choice, do I?" asked Mike.

"There's always a choice," said Stu.

"Right, but sometimes there's only bad ones," said Mike.

"Exactly," said Stu. He raised his eyebrows into a question.

"Promise me," said Mike. "Promise me you'll keep them alive."

Stu stared at him. "I'll promise what I can, Mike."

"And that is?"

"I promise that I'll do my best," said Stu. "And that I'll do what needs to be done."

Mike stared back. His whole body resisted. But he nodded.

"Okay." Stu held his eyes for a moment longer, and then walked back to the kids. Mike followed.

Stu looked at Daniel, and then Marion. "Are you both okay with this?"

Marion glanced at Daniel, and then back to him. "We want to help."

Stu looked to Lyssa. "Lyssa, it's going to be dangerous where we're going, but we can't leave you behind."

Lyssa looked up at him. "Marion and Daniel told me.

They said for me to stay behind Daniel, and be quiet, and we would help everyone."

"That's right," said Stu. "If all goes well, we can get it over quickly." Stu grabbed the other riot gun, and loaded it, and then handed it to Daniel. "It kicks like hell. You should carry it."

Daniel looked at the weapon, and then tucked the pistol into his jeans, and took it.

"I don't have to explain gun safety to you," said Stu. "I don't know what we'll face, once we're there. There will be BENT agents, at the minimum. I don't know if they'll have used their Book or not. But only use your weapons unless absolutely necessary. If we get caught up in a firefight, we've already lost. We have two objectives. We need to find the President, and keep him safe. We need to find Strickland, kill him, and get the other Book. If we can accomplish those two things, it'll buy us time to regroup. We will jump in, figure out the situation. Stick close to me. Everyone understand?"

Everyone nodded.

"Good," said Stu. "It will be chaotic. Keep your heads on straight, and we'll get through this. Everyone take a deep breath."

Mike stopped, inhaled deeply, and then let it out. Everyone else did the same, even little Lyssa.

"Do it again," said Stu. Everyone did.

"Okay," said Stu, looking between them all, and then looking at the radio. He moved the individual dials, slowly adjusting.

"I think that's the best we can do," he said. "Should get us somewhere in the White House."

"Somewhere?" asked Mike.

"It's not an exact science," said Stu. "And to be fair, I haven't touched this thing in a long, long time. Just be prepared to find cover. We might pop in right out in the open."

Mike took a deep breath, holding back any criticism.

"Everyone ready?" asked Stu.

Everyone nodded.

"Alright, let's go," he said, and he pushed the button.

There was no tearing or pulling, like when Mike traveled through the portal. It was instantaneous, with a slight fizzing noise in his ears, and then they were there, in a hallway, one Mike had seen in pictures, but never in person.

The air smelled like smoke, and Stu pulled them all to the side of the hallway, against the wall. Mike looked down the hall and saw two corpses. One laid still, with no apparent damage, but another had been ripped apart. The man's intestines were piled next to him.

Three loud shots echoed through the air, and Mike instinctively ducked. But it wasn't in this room.

"We need to find Secret Service leadership," said Stu.

"Where would that be?" asked Daniel.

"Probably towards the gunfire," said Stu. "I'll take point."

"I'll take the back," said Mike. "You three stay between us. Keep your head down."

Stu started moving, and then Mike heard it.

It had been a long time. Goosebumps raised on his arms and neck.

"Wait, Stu," said Mike.

"What is it?" asked Stu. He glanced back.

"Do you hear it?" asked Mike. "A better question. Do you *feel* it?"

Marion and Daniel looked at him. They felt it, just like he did. They were doing their best to fight it off. Mike had no idea what Stu faced, or Lyssa. But he heard it, and no matter how inured he was to it, how much exposure he had, it would always hurt him.

The ringing of a telephone.

The sound of the death of his wife.

He looked to the shadows, but saw no creatures emerge. But they were here somewhere.

Mike looked at Stu, whose face was strained. He felt it.

"The harvesters of sorrow are here, Stu," said Mike. "Strickland has used his Book."

30

Mike stood in the midst of the black standing stones, carved from the same obsidian stone of the surrounding jagged peaks. An abandoned place of power, used in the old days, before the Oukan invaded, and turned the planet into a world of war. They had consolidated the use of magick, and had stripped the Kaja of their knowledge.

It was where Mike had arrived, delirious, dying, his mind and body pulled by the tidal forces of traveling between worlds. Travel not meant for human bodies.

It was where he had arrived, and it's where he would leave.

He stared at the standing stones, surrounding him, and after studying for so, so long, he understood their importance. He understood the alignment, and he stepped inside them. Mike would utter the right words, the whips and snarls, foreign to the human tongue and throat, and belch fire. He would travel back.

He would save Earth.

"You could have told me," said Anjar, their unearthly voice coming from behind him.

Mike paused, and closed The Book. He turned to face them. Anjar walked into the shape of the standing stones, the almost circle.

"You came alone," said Mike.

"Yes," said Anjar. They stared at Mike, a stare that once unsettled him. "You could have told me."

"Could I?" asked Mike. The faint tension and pain inside him had risen once again. He had successfully tamped it down, swallowing it down deep inside. But seeing Anjar had brought it back.

"I would have understood," said Anjar.

"Then why are you here?"

"Because you said nothing," said Anjar. Mike still couldn't read the Kaja face like he could a human one, but he had learned enough over his time here. He stared at Anjar, and he read sadness.

"What could I say, Anjar?" he asked, cradling The Book. It thrummed in his grasp. It was at ease here, at this crux of power. "That I was leaving? Not just leaving, but leaving now, with the Oukan out for blood. Leaving now, after you saved me, after you defended me, after I defended *you*."

"You could simply tell me the truth," they said. They stared. "I have earned that." They approached Mike, walking close, always graceful, movement like ballet.

Mike said nothing. The Book breathed in his hands. It

felt the blood pulsing through his fingers.

"You have," said Mike, finally. "But I was afraid."

"Afraid of what?" asked Anjar.

Mike paused. The wind swirled, the dark red earth underneath his feet. "Of hurting you."

"You hurt me regardless," said Anjar. "It was inevitable. We both knew it, when we started this." They stood even closer, within reach. Mike smelled them now, a familiar scent, once foreign, now comforting. The pain in his chest rose with the scent. He forced a breath, tried to tamp it down, failed.

"Maybe I knew it," said Mike. "But—but I kept it out of mind. I didn't want to—" He stopped.

"Didn't want to feel?" asked Anjar.

"Didn't want to hurt," said Mike. "Your world has had enough of it."

"Ignoring it will not make it go away," they said with a sad smile.

"Yeah, I know," said Mike. "I need to go home. My kids need a father. My world needs to know what's coming. I can't stay here, I can't, and even if I could—"

"I didn't come here to argue with you," said Anjar. "Or to convince you to stay. I only came to say goodbye."

"I'm abandoning you. Not just you," said Mike. "Everyone. Without this, you're defenseless."

"You are not our savior," said Anjar. "You never could be. Our world is too big a place for you to save. You helped us, for a time. But the cost is too great, and cannot be sustained."

"What will happen after I leave?" asked Mike.

"I don't know," said Anjar. "We are abandoning our position. An Oukan attack is coming, and without The Book's power, we will surely lose. Better to move. That was our life before you, and it will again be our life afterwards."

"But what will happen to you?" asked Mike. He stared at them.

"I will adjust," said Anjar. The same sad smile. "I will cherish our time together. You should do the same."

Mike took a breath. "I—"

"You are not good with words," said Anjar. "I'm aware. Come here." Anjar embraced him, holding him close, the Book between them. They held him, and Mike tried to follow their advice.

Anjar let go. "Go. Go to your children, and back to your world." Mike nodded at them, tears welling in his eyes. Anjar backed away from the standing stones. Mike went to turn back to the middle of the space, but Anjar's words stopped him.

"Mike—" they started. Their eyes left him, and went to The Book. "Do not let that control you. Hold to your promise."

Their eyes met again, and Mike only nodded. He closed his eyes, and turned away from Anjar, and faced the center of the standing stones. He opened The Book, with a practiced motion, finding the right page instantly.

Mike took a breath and read. His throat and tongue burned as the terrible language erupted from him. As he read, he worried that it wouldn't work, that all of this was for naught, that he had misunderstood his studies.

But then, a whirling vortex of rips and tears formed in the fabric of this world, at the center of the standing stones. As he read, it opened, wider and wider. He remembered

Halloween night. He remembered the great thing that had been stepping through. Today, it would be him crossing worlds.

He read, and then he was done. The portal stood there, unnatural and natural, and he looked back, to share a final glance with Anjar. They were already walking away.

Mike turned, and facing both away and toward hell, stepped through the portal, The Book in hand.

31

"Don't let them in," said Mike. "Keep your head clear."

Stu stared at him, struggling, just like the rest of them struggled.

"Lyssa, are you okay?" asked Marion, looking down at her. Lyssa couldn't meet her gaze.

"My parents—" she started.

"Carry her," said Stu. He shook his head, and blinked his eyes hard. "We have to move. Fire on those damn things on sight."

"Where are we headed?" asked Daniel.

"Toward the gunfire," said Stu.

"Why would we head toward the gunfire?" asked Daniel.

"Because it means there's still resistance from the Secret Service," said Stu. "They'll be able to fill us in on the details."

Stu moved, bursts of gunfire coming from down the hall and to the right. They passed bodies, and Mike did his best not to look.

The sound of a phone ringing filled his ears, and he turned to see a harvester emerge from the shadows. It looked just like it had in Laurel City, and he fired, four shots, and it went down, and then disappeared, turning to ash.

"There's more of them," yelled Stu, and he fired his shotgun, racking a shot, and another emerged, and then another, and soon they came from all sides, and the sound of a telephone ringing was all Mike heard. Stu kept moving, and they walked, firing as they went. Marion cradled Lyssa, who was out of it, lost in her nightmares. Stu and Daniel fired their riot guns, taking out the harvesters with single blasts, while Mike peppered them with his pistol, firing one handed, holding The Book in the other.

He felt it now, stronger than he had since he'd returned to Earth. The Book was once again in the presence of its kin, of things from the other side, and it wanted to be used again, desperately, and it vibrated, begging to be fed, begging to be used, craving his blood once again.

"Keep moving!" yelled Stu. "We can't get pinned down!"

They fired, the harvesters dying as quickly as they were summoned. Stu led them down a hallway. Mike didn't know the interior of the White House, only remembering fragmented images he'd seen on the news. Stu moved, and they killed wave after wave of harvesters, leaving only ash behind. Mike was grateful there weren't more, or any of the massive brutal beasts the Oukan used as battering rams on the battlefield. Mike kept his head on a swivel, his eyes scanning every nook and cranny, every shadow cast, but no more creatures emerged. It seemed too easy, but they didn't have time to worry about it. More gunfire boomed ahead of them, and his ears rang from the accumulated gunshots.

Mike looked ahead and saw a small cadre of men wearing bulletproof vests gathered behind makeshift cover. They carried assault rifles and SMGs, and fired in quick bursts, and then ducked down as more bullets flew toward them.

"Down, down!" yelled Stu. "Everyone crawl!" They dropped to their knees, and slowly crawled up to the half dozen Secret Service men. One stared at them as they approached. He knelt, his gun drawn and ready, but he didn't point it at them. He considered the strange group. He was in his late 40s, clean shaven, with a short haircut. He was sweating and looked tired.

"Are you in charge here?" asked Stu.

"Who the hell are you? And who are these civilians—"

"Stuart Bowman, IPA," he said. "I have ID, if you'd like to see it."

"IPA?" asked the agent. He looked at Stu. "You got hit by BENT, didn't you?"

"Yes," said Stu. "I had gotten intel this was happening. Tried to stop it. Worked like hell just to get to this point. What's the sitrep?"

The Secret Service agent looked at Stu. He took a deep breath. "I'm Agent Bell. Strickland came in for a meeting with the President. It was routine. We followed procedure. Strickland had brought in a selection of his own agents. A little strange, but we thought it was just to give them some face time with the President, and other bigwigs. Reward them. But they turned. Abducted the President. They're in the West Wing. We can't break through their barricades.

I don't know why he's doing it. And then—some things—well, they killed some of my men. I don't know what's going on outside, but BENT has cut us off. They've mobilized their entire force." He stared at Stu, as more gunfire rang out. Mike winced at the sound. "Can you tell me what's going on, Agent Bowman?"

"What do you remember from your extranormal threat briefings?"

"Enough to know it was over my head," he said.

"But you believed it?" asked Stu.

"Well, I wasn't sure then, but after I saw one of those fucking monsters devour one of my agents—I believe now."

Stu stared at him. "Strickland is in possession of a powerful Book, similar to the one held by Mike here. Strickland's used it to pull those creatures here. We have reason to believe he's a mole for an extradimensional threat, one far more powerful than us."

Bell stared at him. More gunfire above him. He didn't flinch. "Fuck me. The President is a bargaining chip?"

"We believe he intends to open a portal, and let them through. Let an army through."

"An army of those *things?*" asked Bell.

"Something far stronger than those things," said Mike. "A lot of them."

Mike stared at Daniel and Marion. They exchanged a look. Both of them look frightened. Lyssa had tucked her face into Marion's shoulder.

Bell said nothing. He stared at Stu, and the rest of the group. "And these folk? I'm guessing they're not some tourists who got lost."

"No," said Stu. "Do you know where Strickland is?"

"He's on the premises. Somewhere in the West Wing," said Bell. "We can't get through. It's a miracle we're holding this position."

"I can get there," said Stu. "I have a way."

"You can't take him alone," said Bell. "He's got even more men with him."

"We need his Book," said Stu. "Without it, he can't open the portal. Everything else comes second to that. Even the President."

"It's my job, Agent Bowman," said Bell.

"I understand that," said Stu. "But—"

"I can get you through the barricades," said Mike.

"What do you mean, you can get us through?" asked Bell.

"Mike, are you sure—"

"Why am I here?" he asked, looking at Stu. He looked at Bell again. "I can do it. I'll get your men to the President."

"Can I ask how?" asked Bell.

"Give me a few minutes, and you'll see yourself," said Mike.

"Dad—" started Marion.

"It'll be okay," he said, looking at her. Her eyes shined with fear. "Remember what I said?"

"Yes," said Marion.

"I need backup," said Stu. "Daniel?"

"I'm ready," said Daniel. Daniel exchanged a glance with Marion, and then with him. It said a thousand things, things they had no time for. Mike shifted over, and hugged his son, squeezed him with all his might, the contact saying everything he could.

"Alright," said Stu. "Good luck." Stu pulled out the radio,

and adjusted the dial, and then grabbed Daniel's hand. He pushed a button, and they vanished.

"What the fuck," said Bell.

"Teleporter," said Marion. "We took it from a computer woman from the future."

"Jesus Christ," he said. More gunfire rang out, multiple bursts fired overhead, and into their barricades.

"They're going to press if we don't do something!" yelled a man from the front.

"If you're going to pull some rabbit out of a hat, now's the time," said Bell, looking at Mike.

Mike tucked his pistol into his waistband, and laid The Book down on the floor.

"When I'm done, take The Book," he said, looking at Marion, and Lyssa. Lyssa looked back. The mention of it had gotten her attention, awoke her from her fear and confusion. "Keep it safe."

"You sure about this?" asked Marion.

"Life's complicated, Marion," said Mike, smiling. He hugged her. "So no, not at all. But it's the best I've got." He opened The Book, the page in his muscle memory. He slid a small knife from his pocket and extended the blade. It was sharp.

He paused just for a second, feeling the pull of The Book. He controlled this, not it, and he let it wait, just for a moment.

Then he slid the blade across his palm, and blood welled out, dark crimson, and he poured it onto the open page. He did the same with his other hand, twin slices, both screaming with pain, as the rivulets of blood poured from him.

Mike read. The words came easy, and gouts of smoke and

sulfur emerged from his throat, as he recited the words, and read from The Book.

He felt the change then, deep fissures opening inside him, as The Book transformed him. He yelled in pain, until his lungs transformed, his body growing and growing, larger and larger, until his head butted up against the ceiling, and a burst of bullets shot through, and hit him, but they did nothing. Mike saw red then, a world of red, and felt nothing but anger and rage.

He charged toward the BENT agents.

32

Marion watched her dad transform. She desperately wanted to look away, to avert her gaze, to close her eyes, but she knew she must look. It was her father, her dad, *still* her dad, and she must face what he was, and the decision he had made.

He transformed in front of her, almost invisible tendrils reaching out to him from The Book, his blood fueling the transformation, a terrifying amount of blood lost. It would have killed him.

But instead he transformed in front of her, into something she couldn't recognize. It was a massive thing, standing on two legs, growing, and then growing still, until his head brushed up against the ten-foot ceilings, and then he had to crouch, to not break through them. Marion saw her father in the figure for a moment, maybe two, but then his face changed into a dark shell, hardening, and then disappearing behind the black armor he had grown.

It was a carapace of some sort, softly glowing against the lights above them. Black, and angular, with sharp edges on his joints, it was still a roughly human shape, with two arms, and two legs, but his hands had three fingers, instead of five, and his feet were hardened into one singular point, with no toes at all.

She looked into her father's eyes, as he grew above her, and they turned to black, and she saw nothing inside them. Bullets whizzed by overhead, fired from the BENT agents on the other side of their barricade, but the rounds hit his dark shell and bounced away. Her father resembled some knight, with the armor of an alien beetle, its weapons its arms and legs. It loomed over them, her dad replaced by this creature. Her father made no sounds as he changed, but his body did, the bones cracking, shrinking, muscle and flesh breaking at its bounds.

It finished growing, finally, a moment passing.

"Dad?" she asked, quietly. Could he speak, in this new form?

But there was no answer, and he moved quickly, the huge shape flying past the Secret Service agents, and there was a burst of gunfire from BENT, as they shot at their new enemy.

But the bullets did nothing to stop her dad, and he crashed through the barricade.

Marion knew the power of The Book. She had seen it firsthand. But there still was a part of her that worried about her father. He had told them he had used The Book to fight in the battles of Ulum, but she had only heard him. She hadn't seen it. The harvesters of sorrow were terrible creatures, yes, but they fell to gunfire, like anything else.

But that worry vanished, subsumed by the sinking feeling of watching her father cut through the BENT agents.

His jagged fingers and elbows were all he needed, the hardened carapace working as a brutal cutting tool. He moved with impossible force, the BENT agents trying to bring their weapons to bear. A few got shots off, but none of them hurt her dad. He moved fast, even with his new incredible size, and his hands crashed through each agent in turn, ripping massive rents in their flesh. He tore straight through their armor, clothes, and skin.

He's tearing them apart.

Marion watched for a moment, and then averted her eyes. She thought she could bear it, after all she had seen, but even this was too much, as internal organs fell out onto the floor, as limbs were separated from bodies, as gallons of blood spilled. She still heard the crashing noises, as her father smashed past the barricades, and the ripping and tearing, the screams and shouts of agony, as men were ripped apart.

And they were men. They weren't creatures from the other side, they weren't harvesters of sorrow. They were men, normal men, following orders.

Normal men, cut down into pieces. Marion looked again, and her father was almost out of sight now, pushing past the barricade, and more gunfire echoed back to her, as more and more BENT agents tried to stop him, and failed.

"Hold," said Agent Bell. His eyes were wide, trying to maintain focus after what he'd just seen. "We wait until the gunfire clears, and then we move up."

"That thing—" said one of the other agents.

"Our focus is the President," said Bell. "Nothing else."

Marion looked down to Lyssa. She was staring at The Book, holding it in her two small hands.

"Lyssa," said Marion.

No answer.

"Lyssa!" said Marion, louder. Lyssa looked up.

"Are you okay?"

"I can hear The Book," she said. "It's telling me—"

And she kept speaking, but Marion couldn't hear it. She only heard the familiar sound of machines beeping, of the smell of a hospital, the vision of her father hooked up to IVs, of his skirt with death, a thousand years ago, back in the real world, but it was different now, visions of The Book interspersed, it was taking him, he was a beast now, a cursed *thing—*

The harvesters.

Marion took control of herself, forcing all of those thoughts out of her head. She looked down the hallway, behind them, and they were already here, their plated faceless faces broadcasting terror and fear, ready to devour her while she was lost in the hallucination. Two of them moved toward her and the Secret Service agents, and then another emerged from a shadow that Marion hadn't even noticed, and then another, and Marion's hand went to her pistol— and then she looked back, and the Secret Service agents were lost in their own minds. Their hollow eyes stared into nothing, their faces contorted into fear. Marion grabbed her gun and instead of firing at the harvesters, fired into the air.

It wasn't enough, the agents still caught. Marion had no

time, no time, and couldn't fight them all.

Run! Run, you idiot!

Lyssa was lost as well, and Marion grabbed her, Lyssa still latched onto The Book, and she scrambled to her feet, running past the agents, after her father, through his path of death and destruction, not looking at the corpses he'd left behind.

*

Daniel and Stu appeared in a small dark space, and Daniel held his breath.

"Quiet," whispered Stu, barely audible. "We're in a storeroom in the West Wing."

Gunfire echoed back to them, first isolated, and then multiple bursts.

"I'll assume that's your father going to work," said Stu, still quiet. "We're behind enemy lines. We find Strickland, we find The Book, and we end this. Don't fire unless we're spotted. Stealth."

"Understood," whispered Daniel. His eyes had adjusted, low light filtering into the room underneath a door. They were surrounded by boxes and shelving. Feet crossed in front of the door, shadows briefly, and then were gone.

"Follow me," said Stu, and he went to the door, tucking the radio away, readying his shotgun. They waited at the door for a moment, and there was silence on the other side, and Stu didn't wait any longer, pushing the door open and sliding out.

Daniel was ready to fight, but this stretch of hallway was empty, and Stu moved quickly, walking fast, his back near the wall.

Daniel had no idea where they were, but Stu moved fast, doing math in his head. Daniel followed, keeping his head on a swivel. Bursts of gunfire came from behind them, and he knew it was Dad, breaking through the front line. He didn't know what trick he had used from The Book, but it was loud, and Daniel's stomach ached. Daniel forced himself to breathe, trying to keep himself calm. He remembered football games, with a lot on the line.

Focus on your part of the play.

His old coach had always told them that, when their nerves would get the best of them. Focus on your part of the play. You couldn't control the whole field, only your slice.

Stu hurriedly ducked through a door, and Daniel moved in after him, Stu holding the door shut. The room was an office, lit, but empty, and then Daniel heard a slew of footsteps on the other side, as a squad of BENT agents rushed past.

"Fighting your dad," whispered Stu, in Daniel's ear.

The sound of boots passed, and Stu moved again, pushing out through the door. Daniel held his breath, hoping no one was moving down the hallway, but it was empty. He wanted to ask Stu where they were headed, but he was afraid to make any noise. Daniel knew the Oval Office was here somewhere, but otherwise, he was lost. They came to the end of the hallway, and Stu peeked around the corner. He met eyes with Daniel, and waited. Sound drifted back to them.

"What the hell is going on out there?" asked a voice. "I need recon!"

Stu mouthed *Strickland* to Daniel, and nodded around the corner. Daniel moved close.

"He's in the next office," whispered Stu. "No guards outside. I assume at least two other men inside, maybe more. We take them out. Leave Strickland to me." Daniel's heart thudded hard in his chest. He gripped the shotgun.

Focus on your part of the play.

Daniel nodded at Stu, and Stu moved fast, turning the corner, and the office was only ten feet away, the door open, and Stu waited, and Daniel moved right next to him, and Stu went in, and fired his shotgun and Daniel was inside next, and a BENT agent was right there, his eyes wide, and Daniel fired, racking a shot, and Stu fired one more time, and Daniel scanned the room, but there was no one else besides Strickland at a desk, and Stu had his gun pointed at him.

"Throw your gun over here or I kill you now," said Stu, firmly. Strickland stood there, staring daggers at Stu.

"How the hell did you get in here?" asked Strickland. "We left your ass back in Color—"

"Gun. Floor," said Stu.

Strickland still stared, but slowly pulled his pistol from its holster and threw it on the ground, at Stu's feet. Stu loosened, only slightly.

"Watch the door, Daniel," said Stu, without looking at him. Daniel took up position, his gun and eyes aimed at the door. "Where's The Book?"

Strickland only stared.

"I will kill you," said Stu. "I don't have time for this."

Strickland smiled. "I don't have it," he said, finally.

"Bullshit," said Stu. "Who has it then?"

Strickland only smiled.

"You summoned them," said Stu. "You've used The Book.

You, or someone under you. Who is it?"

Strickland said nothing, still, but his eyes betrayed slight confusion. There was no more gunfire. Either Dad had killed them all, or—

Daniel pushed the thought from his mind.

"We know you're working with the Oukan! With the other side! Don't just stand there and play dumb!" Stu yelled now, his gun waving.

Strickland still said nothing, and Stu walked up to him and smashed him in the jaw with the butt of his shotgun, and Strickland fell, groaning in pain. Stu stood over him, the shotgun pointed at his head.

"You tell me, or your head disappears," said Stu. Strickland stared up at him, his jaw already swelling.

"I don't know what you're talking about," said Strickland. "I'm a loyal American."

Daniel listened, glancing over. Strickland wasn't lying.

"What the fuck are you talking about?" asked Stu. "Mike Dawson was there. He talked to their leadership. They have a mole here. It's you, we know it is."

"Of all the bullshit," said Strickland. "After everything you and your people did, to get in our way, to hurt our country, and now, to accuse me—you piece of shit—"

"Shut up," said Stu, pressing the shotgun against his forehead. "Where's The Book? I will not ask again."

Strickland exhaled. "I don't have it. I gave it up."

"What do you mean, I gave it up?"

"Lord in Heaven, Jesus Christ," said Strickland. "Who do you think I gave it to? I am a loyal soldier, Bowman, which can't be said for you. I follow orders. I was told to acquire The Book, so I did. You were the one who went rogue, who illegally took our prisoners, who took the first Book—"

Stu said nothing, his face changing. It had fallen. Something was wrong.

Strickland watched him. "I didn't even want the damned thing. Too much work for not enough gain. I told him, that your archive was the valuable thing, but he wouldn't listen. He wanted The Book, so I got him one—"

"Shut up," said Stu. "Keep your goddamn mouth shut."

"Stu," said Daniel. He tried to read Stu's face, but he couldn't. "What's wrong? What's going on? Who has The Book?"

Stu stared at him, setting his jaw.

"The President does."

*

Marion ran away from the harvesters of sorrow and the nightmares they brought. She carried Lyssa, and her arms ached, but the months of workouts with Daniel were paying off, her lungs breathing hard but not struggling as she ran past corpses and destruction, hearing the harvesters rip apart the Secret Service agents behind her. She chased after her dad. More gunfire erupted from up ahead, and she hoped her father, in his new form, could handle it, like he'd handled the rest.

She ran down a long hallway, past desks. Windows looked out into the rose garden, pictures she'd seen as a kid, but she didn't want to go outside. Her mind still was on the mission, on reclaiming The Book. On keeping Lyssa and their Book safe as well. Running and hiding would have been easy, but they didn't have the luxury—

More gunfire, and she saw her father in the middle of a melee. She had caught up to it, with a half dozen BENT agents all in a firing line, shooting her father with assault rifles.

Her dad bellowed, an unearthly roar, deep and resonant, and he charged them, his caparaceous fingers digging into two of the men, disemboweling them in moments.

More bullets flew, and Marion ducked away, out of sight, pushing through the first door she could see. One stray bullet and her or Lyssa would be done for.

"Well, hello young lady," said an old voice from behind her. Marion turned, and saw the President, standing at his desk.

"Mr. President," she said. "I—" She didn't know what to say. She'd never met a president in person, and she was taken aback, despite herself. "You're safe."

"I am for now," he said. He looked at her, and Lyssa, and the Book they held, his eyes lingering on it for a moment. "Lot of commotion out there."

"There is," she said. "You're in danger."

"I'm guessing you're not just a lost tourist," he said. "You have something to do with all this?"

"Well—" she started. "Something, yes. But we just want to make sure you're safe."

"I'm pretty well protected," he said. "A lot of different men out there. All of them with their own motivations."

"Strickland wants to kill you," she said, not knowing how else to say it. "He's responsible for all of this. We need to get you to safety."

The gunfire had stopped outside, crashing noises coming to a halt.

"I'm plenty safe where I'm at," he said. "A president doesn't run. A president—"

The door opened, and Marion's hand went to her gun, but her father came through, no longer a gigantic alien creature, an animal meant only for war, but just himself again. His cheeks were sunken, his eyes sallow, but it was him.

"Dad," she said, and she hugged him, but his eyes were only on the President.

"Mr. President," he said. "I'm Mike Dawson. I'm glad you're safe. There's been a plot against you. Strickland and BENT intend to start an inter-dimensional invasion, and use you as a bargaining chip, or straight out kill you. Do you know where Strickland is, or a Book he might have carried with him?"

"This is your daughter?" the President asked, looking at Marion, and then back at her dad.

"Yes," said Dad. "It's a long story. But we can't stay here."

"I was just telling her, I can't leave," he said. "A president must maintain a brave face for his citizens—"

"I understand the reasoning," said Dad. "But Strickland has already summoned creatures here. Before too long, he might open a portal. I've cleared the way."

"You have?" asked the President, eyeing him. "Well, son, that's mighty impressive. If the way is clear, maybe we should clear out of here. My family is in the bunker. Maybe we can make it back there."

Her dad nodded. "That's perfect."

The President came around his desk, extending a hand toward her dad. Her dad took it in his.

Then the President slammed his open palm into her father's chest, and he flew across the room with a horrible thud, crashing through the wall. Her heart leapt into her throat.

The President changed in front of her eyes, transforming, growing into something alien. Something powerful.

Her dad had told her about the Oukan. About their size, and strength. But again, he had only told her. She hadn't seen them. They were an abstract.

Until now.

The Oukan stared at her with dark eyes.

"Finally," he said. "It is time."

33

"Run, Lyssa. Run now!" yelled Marion, putting Lyssa down, and pushing her toward the door. Lyssa ran, carrying The Book, and was gone in a moment, out the door. The Oukan only watched her run away.

"You do not follow her?" he asked. The alien's voice boomed, deep and resonant. The ground shook with his voice. Marion's heart thudded in her chest. They had thought Strickland was the mole. The one who had insinuated himself into the government, to take over.

But they'd been wrong.

Marion swallowed. "No," she said, finally. She wanted to run, but she forced her legs to stay still. He had the other Book, from Night Hill.

Her dad had smashed through the wall, struck by considerable force. She wanted to run to him, to see if he was okay. But she couldn't leave this thing with The Book. It would open the portal, and let the rest of them through. And then, they'd have no chance.

The creature considered her. Marion felt like an insect who could be squashed at any time.

The Oukan was big, standing seven feet tall, and broad. He weighed at least three hundred pounds, if not more. He had changed shape, formerly embodying the President. Dad hadn't told them that, but that just told Marion he didn't know. But the Oukan had mottled grey skin, and black eyes. He had a bald head, with almost no ears or nose. His mouth was small, but she saw the jagged teeth inside as he spoke. Otherwise he looked humanoid.

"Brave," he said, finally. "Your father used The Book. He had crossed over, back and forth."

Marion said nothing. She didn't know if he was testing her or not, but she would give him no information she didn't have to.

"It makes no difference," he said, English coming out bassy and distorted through his alien throat. "He will die. So will you. We will take this place, and make it ours."

Marion didn't stand on ceremony, drawing her pistol, aiming and firing. She unloaded the entire cartridge into the creature's chest, the sound echoing inside the Oval Office.

He stood there, absorbing the gunfire. The bullets smashed into him and fell, deformed, to the floor.

"Human weapons," he said, Marion's ears ringing, the room now silent. "Feeble. Pathetic. No match for the Oukan physiology. We are superior to you, in every way. It will be a joy to march across the land."

He moved then, quickly, and wrapped his hand around Marion's throat, and pulled her up into the air. He held her without effort, and her head was near the ceiling as he lifted her high above him.

She struggled, batting at his arm, but she couldn't breathe. She couldn't breathe—

"So fragile," he said. "Against all odds, you find out about our invasion. You have advanced information. You are given time to prepare. To root out the betrayer in your midst."

Marion tried to breathe, but his hand squeezed tight around her throat. Spots danced in her vision. He was killing her. Her lungs screamed.

"And you send a child. Not your greatest champion. Not an army. A child." He paused, and stared at Marion, with his black eyes. "Well, goodbye. Have solace in knowing you will not see your world fall."

Marion struggled still, but this thing was too strong, and she felt her strength fade. Her vision grew dark.

Dad. Daniel. Please—

And then she heard crashing noises from behind her. What was that?

And something big smashed through the wall, and then through the Oukan, and Marion could breathe again, and she took a deep gasping breath, even as she fell. She thumped against the hard floor, but she breathed again, the spots disappearing from her vision.

What that Dad? Was he okay?

But she looked up, as the gigantic shape standing over the Oukan, smashing into him with massive furry claws. It wasn't her dad.

It was Mr. Grumpkins.

He was barely contained within the building, and as he stood up fully, he put holes in the ceiling, but he had knocked the Oukan down, and now attacked him, loudly yelling as Mr. Grumpkins beat at the thing.

Marion didn't wait, running out of the room. She needed to find Lyssa. She needed to find Dad. He was somewhere.

Both were easy to find. Lyssa was in the room across the hall, bent over The Book.

"Lyssa," said Marion. Lyssa had taken a piece of metal from the destruction, and used it to cut her palms, to summon Mr. Grumpkins. The noise continued from the Oval Office, as the two creatures fought. Lyssa looked up with heavy eyes.

"Mr. Grumpkins will save us," she said, and then slumped over again. Marion grabbed her, and The Book, slamming it shut. She needed to find Dad.

He wasn't far. She followed the path through the wall he had been thrown through. She heard the terrible thud when he'd been hit, and seen him go through the wall. Maybe he would be okay.

But he hadn't gone through only one wall. He'd gone through two, smashing through the wall of the Oval Office, and then through another, his body laying in the rubble of the second.

He was underneath the piles of debris, and she pushed them away, laying Lyssa and The Book to the side. Noises of the tussle between Mr. Grumpkins and the Oukan still carried to them, great sounds of impact, as the two of them smashed through the Oval Office.

Marion moved the debris, and found her father.

"Dad—" she started. His eyes were open, but dazed. Blood trickled from his nose and mouth. His body seemed smaller somehow.

"Marion," he said. "I—"

"We have to move," she said. "Lyssa summoned Mr. Grumpkins. He's fighting that alien." She went to help him up.

"Marion—" he stopped her. "I can't feel my legs. It's hard to breathe. I'm—"

"Dad—"

"I'm dying," he said. "Leave me. Find Stu, and Daniel."

"I'm not leaving you," she said. "I don't know—"

She listened, but the clashing between Mr. Grumpkins and the Oukan had stopped. Lyssa pushed herself up, her eyes refocusing.

"He stopped Mr. Grumpkins," she said.

"He's going to open the portal," Dad said. "Go. Do what you can. Stop him."

Marion stared into his eyes. None of this was supposed to happen. She felt tears well up, and she squeezed her eyes shut. They were supposed to save the world.

"No," said Marion.

"Marion—"

"Don't Marion me," she said. "You can still read."

"Marion, if I bleed any more, I'll die—"

"It's not your blood it's getting," she said. She grabbed The Book, and slid it next to her father's prone body. "Flip to the right page." Marion reached to her dad's belt, and grabbed the pocket knife.

"Marion, I promised. You can't—"

"Fuck your promise. Life's complicated," she said. "I'm

not losing you, and I don't know what else is going to stop that thing. Flip to the right page."

Her dad stared at her with tired eyes, and he opened The Book, turning it to the correct page. He nodded at her.

She opened the pocket knife, took a deep breath, and then slid it across one palm, and then across the other. She didn't know how deep to cut, but blood welled out of the wounds, and she held them over the page, letting the blood feed The Book.

"Read," she said. Her dad stared at her for a long moment, and then read. The horrible language, the arcane whips and snarls once more erupted from her father's throat, and she felt her blood feed The Book, and felt it even more as The Book pulled her blood from her. She felt the connection, the one so few had felt, and she understood, finally understood the terrible power of the cursed Book.

The smell of sulfur filled her nostrils as her father recited the page, and the scent of ash and fire permeated the room. And then he was done, and as the final word left his lips, he changed again, the same dark carapace shell covering him, as he grew, getting larger. His body knit itself together, the dark magick of The Book making him whole, better than whole, stronger than any human.

Within moments, he was covered in the dark armor, and he charged, smashing through the remnants of the wall he had already crashed through, and then into the Oval Office. Marion followed, her palms already healed, healed by the same magick of The Book. She carried it in one arm, and Lyssa in the other. It was dangerous, to be so close. But she didn't care. She needed to see.

The portal stood open. The Oukan had opened it.

It widened as she watched, and then the Oukan turned to see Dad smash him with all his might. Mr. Grumpkins had fallen to the power of the Oukan, but the Oukan hadn't come out unscathed, and now her dad took advantage.

The two titans traded blows, the Oukan smashing against the dark armor of her father. But her dad wasn't backing down, and he smashed into the alien creature over and over again, the sharp edges of his armor cutting into the hard flesh of the Oukan, ripping gashes that bled dark, viscous blood.

"Marion!" yelled a voice, and Marion turned to see Daniel and Stu, both carrying shotguns. "The President—"

Marion said nothing, only gesturing toward the battle.

"Is that—?" asked Stu.

"Yes," said Marion.

"Jesus," said Daniel. "Come on, Dad."

"We should help," said Stu.

"We've done what we can," said Marion. "We can only watch."

*

Mike transformed, as he had before. He had been dying, the Oukan breaking him apart inside. His back had been broken, his legs useless.

Then he read from The Book, while Marion bled herself into it.

The transformation didn't hurt, despite what it must look like. Marion had turned away, after seeing him change. But it didn't hurt, as his body grew, as a thick, black armor covered him, and turned him into a war machine.

Because that's what he was. He had read The Book, studying every page, looking for a way back to Earth. But in the process, he had found the key to this form. The page described will transformed into being, something that was unbreakable, impregnable, that could break down walls and end wars.

It didn't hurt, the transformation.

It felt like heaven.

He had become power personified, and every part of him was invincible. His human body was frail, and limited by his conditioning, and his coordination.

In this form, he had no limits.

That's the form that Mike took, and he charged back into the Oval Office. Mr. Grumpkins lay nearby. He still breathed, but didn't move, and the Oukan turned to see Mike as he waited near the portal, as it widened. It was bleeding from its battle with Mr. Grumpkins, and Mike didn't wait for recognition. He attacked.

The thoughts had crossed Mike's mind, while he had laid there, underneath the rubble.

How long had the President been an Oukan?

And from that, who else was one of them?

But those worries left his mind as he charged into the Oukan, slamming into him as hard as he could. The sound was cacophonous, and the few intact windows left in the Oval Office broke with the sound. All thoughts, all anxiety, all conflicting emotions—they all fled when Mike transformed. Things became simple.

The war machine churned, and Mike attacked the Oukan without mercy.

He had fought them on the battlefield on Ulum. The Oukan were incredibly strong, demigods. Impervious to most weapons, they fought hand to hand, any weapon they could wield weaker than their hands and feet. The kajahar had devised methods to slow the Oukan over the years, but they couldn't best them in open combat.

But with The Book, Mike could.

He attacked the Oukan with forearm blows and knees, the joints of his form lined with hard armor and fortified ridges that cut through the skin of this Oukan. Black blood splattered over the Oval Office, and they smashed through the walls, sunlight spilling into the room.

Mike had fought the Oukan on Ulum, and he had never lost. He had killed dozens of them over the time spent there. It was what had earned him the respect of the Kajahar. It had earned him freedom, earned him trust, and ultimately, earned him his path home.

But this Oukan was different. Mike's blows weren't hurting it as much. The Oukan simply absorbed the damage.

Mike swung hard with another elbow, and the Oukan caught it, and threw Mike hard, his massive blow slamming through the wall, deeper into the West Wing. The Oukan sprinted after him, and slammed into him again, tackling him through another wall, and then mounting him. The Oukan slammed his fists into Mike's head, beating him with all his might.

"I am stronger here than Ulum," said the Oukan, as he slammed fist after fist into Mike. "No matter what form you take. You cannot stop us. Soon, we will arrive. You are not enough."

The blows shook Mike. The armor was strong, stronger than anything on Earth, but the Oukan tested it, and Mike's brain shook, somewhere deep inside, the concussive blows raining down on him.

Punch after punch, the sound of each blow echoed through the White House. Mike took each hit.

He had a theory about The Book. It was impossible to test, but it had felt right, after working with it, after bleeding into it, after his experience with the Laurels, and what they did with it.

His theory was The Book thirsted after new blood. Over time, as Mike had used The Book more and more, it seemed to be less effective, requiring more of him every time. He would drain more of his blood into The Book to get the same results. He would cut deeper into his hands.

The Book wanted new blood, fresh blood, but even more than that, it wanted *innocent* blood. Blood from someone who hadn't been exposed to its dark magick. It explained the Laurels sacrificing the youth group, back in Laurel City. Innocent boys, fed to it, had been enough to open up the portal, and summon hundreds of harvesters to the town. To disconnect it from reality.

Mike had felt his transformation grow weaker over time. The Book wanted new blood, and it wanted the bearer to bring it, to be driven for the same results.

Mike had resisted. As long as he carried it, no one else bled into it. He had promised himself he would take control, and keep control.

And he had. He had sacrificed nothing but himself.

Until now. Marion had bled into The Book. His own daughter, to save him, to save everything.

And as the Oukan pounded into his armored skin, over and over, with all its strength, Mike realized just how much stronger he was.

Mike pushed up, tapping into that force, a learned skill, like anything else, utilizing a power he'd never felt before. He freed his arms, and grabbed the Oukan's hands, first one, and then the other. Mike pushed against the Oukan, and forced it off him.

Mike stood now, on his feet, and the Oukan headbutted him, once, twice, three times, but the blows did nothing but hurt the alien. Mike didn't let go of his hands. The creature pulled and pulled, trying to free himself, and Mike saw the shock on his face.

Instead, Mike headbutted him back, once, twice, three times, and the Oukan's face was now a bloody mess, covered in black blood. It was dazed. He fell to his knees in front of Mike, but Mike still held its wrists. He wouldn't let it fall. Not yet.

Mike squeezed the creature's wrists, and then slammed his knee into its face. Over and over, he drove his ridged knee into the Oukan's head, filling the White House with a brutal thud as he obliterated anything recognizable left of its face. All the pain he had felt, all the hardship he'd gone through, the tortures inflicted on the Kaja, and the Oukan's plans for Earth—he let it all pass through his knee into this monster, and then with a great CRACK, the Oukan's skull split open, and with a great final gasp, it died.

He held its wrists for a moment longer—and then dropped them, letting the corpse fall to the floor. He stared at it, the thing dead, finally.

"Dad?" asked a voice, and Mike turned, and saw Marion approaching, with Stu, Daniel, and Lyssa. Lyssa held The Book. "The portal."

They all looked at him, waiting for him to change back. To be human again.

But—

But this form was strong. Strong enough to impose his will on the world. To make it right.

To make things better.

He couldn't be his normal self, not again. Why would he? To be weak, to be frail?

He stared at his family, and he could protect them in this form. He could ensure their safety. He could ensure the safety of the *world*, if he just stayed like this.

You will need more blood.

And he would. But it was worth it, wasn't it? This Oukan, who had come to transform his world—well, he had been child's play. And no matter who else they send, he would kill them too. The blood was a small price to pay—

"Dad," said Marion. Mike looked at his daughter. "We need you back. We can't lose you."

Mike looked to her, and to Daniel. They looked at him with fear in their eyes.

He saw his family, and he also saw what he could become.

An easy choice.

Mike transformed back, letting go of the spell, his heart letting go of will turned to power, and he was just a man again, no longer injured, no longer dying.

He took a long breath, deeply tired. His body ached.

"The portal," said Stu, finally.

*

"We don't have long," said Mike. They stared at it, in the Oval Office. "Another few minutes, and it'll be big enough. They'll come through."

The two Books sat in front of them.

"Someone takes the Books through, and the portal closes," said Mike. "Simple." He took a deep breath, and then stepped forward.

And then Stu was there, in front of him, his gun drawn.

"I don't think so," said Stu. He stood in front of all of them.

"What are you doing?" asked Mike.

"Keeping you with your family," said Stu. He grabbed a Book in his free arm. His face shifted imperceptibly.

"Stu, I've been there before—"

"Yeah, I know," said Stu. "You know how The Books work. You can open a portal." He paused. "I don't want this Book coming back."

"Book?" asked Daniel. "Not *Books*?"

"I think it's reasonable to keep one here," said Stu. "Under our watch, of course. It's the problem with The Book being the key to both opening and closing a portal."

Mike looked at Stu. "You don't have to do this."

Stu smiled. "Of course I do. I wanted to save the world, didn't I?"

The portal grew slightly larger. They had little time.

"Don't do this, Stu, let me take the Books—"

"You're staying with your family, Mike. This isn't a discussion—"

"Dad—please, listen to him—"

"Mr. Stu—" Lyssa spoke suddenly, her small voice cutting through the argument. She stood next to Mr. Grumpkins. His body was still there, Mike realized. He had never vanished, like in Night Hill, and he stirred now, standing up, pushing himself up to his feet. He dwarfed all of them. They all looked to her, and to him.

"Mr. Grumpkins can take The Book," she said.

"What?" asked Mike.

"Mr. Grumpkins will do it," said Lyssa. "It's his home. He can take it, and everyone can stay here. Marion saved me. She didn't need to, but she did. Now—Mr. Grumpkins can save *us*."

Mike considered the colossal form of the creature. It stared at Lyssa, complete loyalty on its face.

"Isn't that right, Mr. Grumpkins?" she asked, her small hand wrapped around one of its large fingers. It looked at her and then blinked its assent. "See?"

Mike looked at Stu, who met his eyes. They both had the same question.

Can we trust this thing? And does that even matter?

"Why are we even debating this?" asked Marion. "This is an easy choice." She walked over to Stu, and held out her arms. Stu looked at her, and then lowered his gun, and holstered it, before handing over The Book.

Marion took it, and held it up to Mr. Grumpkins, who easily palmed it in an enormous paw. He looked to Lyssa.

Lyssa hugged the monster, squeezing it tight.

"You have to go," she said. "I love you."

The creature turned to go.

"Mr. Grumpkins," said Mike. He didn't know if it would work, but the creature stopped. "On the other side, if you can—deliver it to a Kaja. A person named Anjar. They'll keep it safe."

The creature looked at him, blinked once, twice, and then turned, and went through the portal.

The portal stayed open for a moment, and then closed.

34

"She's a cute kid," said Cara, slowly floating back and forth on the swing. Marion sat next to her, doing the same. They watched Lyssa as she climbed up the rope ladder and went down the slide, and then did it again, and again. "How's she holding up after everything?"

"Mostly okay," said Marion. "She's been going to therapy, and I think that's helped."

"What about you?"

"I'm fine," said Marion.

"Are you sure?" asked Cara.

"Mostly," said Marion. "I'm mostly sure."

"We can talk about it, if you want."

Marion watched Lyssa do the same circuit again. They were alone in the playground. Lyssa slid down the slide, and then stopped herself, and climbed back up inside it.

"I know," said Marion. "I'm still working through it, in my head."

"I worry about you," said Cara.

"I know," said Marion. "I appreciate your concern, I do. But there's a bit of whiplash. After being locked up, and after The Books, and the White House—coming back to normal is hard for my brain to accept."

"You think they're going to come and get you again?"

"No," said Marion. "I don't think so."

And she didn't. She trusted Stu to do the right thing.

"Then what is it?"

"You're just trying to get me to talk."

"You've figured out my dastardly plan."

Marion laughed. She took a breath. "I'm more worried about my dad. About Daniel. About her." She nodded toward Lyssa, who continued to run around.

"I think everyone will be okay," said Cara.

"Dad has Jenny, so I think you're right about him. I have you. Lyssa has the rest of us. Daniel, though, ever since he moved out—we haven't seen him much. I know he's busy with his new job, but—"

"But you're worried," said Cara.

"Yes."

"That's normal," said Cara. "But he'll be okay. I don't think he's forgotten about you. I think he's working through things, just like you are. That takes time."

"You're right," said Marion. "But—"

"But you're still gonna worry," said Cara. Cara got up, and hugged Marion, and then they kissed. "I think that's okay, too."

"Mariooon, Caaara," said Lyssa, running over to them. Her cheeks were flushed, red from running around. "Play with me."

"What do you want to play?" asked Marion.

"Hide and seek, hide and seek," said Lyssa. "I'll hide, and you find me."

"Okay," said Marion. "But you can't leave the playground, okay?"

"Okay. Close your eyes!" she said, and then Marion and Cara put their hands over their eyes.

Marion counted out loud.

"1, 2, 3, 4, 5, 6, 7, 8, 9, 10," said Marion. "Ready or not, here we come!"

*

Daniel grabbed the meal from the microwave, steam billowing out from under the corner of the vented plastic. He carefully ripped it off, and then slid a paper towel underneath it, taking it over to the couch.

He unpaused the show he'd been watching, letting it run while he ate his lunch.

Marion had invited him out to play with Lyssa at the playground, but he'd told her he had to work.

He'd used it as cover for a lot lately. But the only thing he was working on was ranking up in Call of Duty, and binging every show that he'd missed while they were locked up.

But Daniel didn't know how to tell Marion that he didn't feel like seeing them, didn't feel like hanging out, even if he did love her. That after all the events of the past year plus he just wanted to dig himself a hole and live in it for a while.

That he didn't want to talk about it, or think about it, that he just wanted to *be* for a while.

Saying he had to work was simpler, so that's what he did.

He ate the microwave dinner. It wasn't good, but it was food, so it passed the test.

And yes, he would eventually get back to a normal life—but what was that anymore? He could do anything he wanted, now. The government was still giving them a stipend, and he could afford to do nothing, if he really wanted. But after wanting the world not to end, and his dad not to disappear through a hellish portal, the volume had been turned down on everything else.

Give it some time. You'll figure it out.

The show on TV kept going, but Daniel found himself not paying attention, and he restarted it. As the intro finished, there was a knock at his door.

Had he ordered something? He went to the door, and looked outside.

It was Stu, wearing his customary suit and tie. Daniel felt his heart rate accelerate. What the hell was going on?

Daniel opened the door.

"Stu?"

"Daniel," he said. "May I come in?"

"Sure," said Daniel, stepping aside. "I guess."

Stu came into his apartment.

"Living on your own?" asked Stu.

"Yeah," said Daniel. "Just moved in a month ago."

"How you liking it?"

"It's fine," said Daniel. "Stu, what the hell is going on? Is there something wrong? Is everyone okay?"

Stu looked at him. "Can I sit?"

"Sure," said Daniel. The apartment came furnished, and Stu took a seat in the armchair.

"Aren't you going to sit?" asked Stu.

"Stu—"

"Please, Daniel, sit," said Stu. "Nothing's wrong. I just want to talk."

Daniel stared at him, and then sat.

"I wasn't lying, Daniel," said Stu. "Nothing's wrong. The clean up is mostly done. We've got The Book safely locked deep in the vaults. BENT is completely dissolved, and the IPA is rebuilding. No sign of more Oukan."

"Then why are you here?"

"I wanted to talk."

"You could have just called."

"Not for this," said Stu. "It would have been rude. The travel's not bad. And I could have sent someone else, but after what we went through—like I said, it'd be rude."

"Well?" asked Daniel. "You want to talk?"

Stu looked at him. "How are you adjusting?"

"Adjusting to what?"

"Life," said Stu. "Normal life."

"I don't know," said Daniel. "Alright, I guess."

"Hmm," said Stu.

"What does that mean? Hmm?" asked Daniel. "It *has* been alright. I've mostly been enjoying not being in physical danger or being imprisoned."

"I don't mean anything by it," said Stu. "But I do have an offer for you."

"An offer?" asked Daniel. "If it's about The Book, the answer is no."

"It's not," said Stu. "At least not directly."

"What does that mean?" asked Daniel.

"We're rebuilding the IPA," said Stu. "We lost a lot of people with the BENT attack. And not only that. The attack, and how long it took us to mobilize—it showed us our weakness. We were too slow, too stuck in our ways. We need to get younger, more flexible. We need fresh blood."

"Are you asking me if I want to be an IPA agent?" asked Daniel.

"Well, yes," said Stu. "To not put too fine a point on it."

"You said you graduated college at 18," said Daniel. "I barely got out of high school."

"I saw how you handled situations first hand," said Stu. "You have field experience that others don't. That proves more to me than college degrees. Getting some piece of paper from a diploma mill doesn't mean much to me anymore."

Daniel stared at him. "You serious?"

"Yes, Daniel," said Stu. "I came here because I wanted you to know I'm serious."

"I'd have to uproot my life," said Daniel. "Would I be able to see my family?"

"You'd have two weeks PTO to start," said Stu. "Three weeks after you get five years of service. You can't tell them anything, but in your case it's not as big a deal, considering. Pay is 75K to start, with raises commensurate with your performance. You'll have to give up your stipend, if you take the job."

"It'll be dangerous, won't it?"

"Well, I won't lie to you," said Stu. "Yes. It'll be dangerous. Not as dangerous as what you've already been through, but there still will be quite deadly situations. You've seen it. You know the risks." Stu met his eyes. "But you will help save the world. In ways no one else does. You'll be challenged in ways you couldn't be. You won't have an ordinary life."

"I just—I don't know," said Daniel. "That's a big question. And a big commitment. Do I have to decide now?"

"No," said Stu. "It's an invitation. But I'm not going to give you a deadline. You've already seen firsthand what the job can entail. You would start as a junior agent, underneath me. After you went through the academy, of course."

"It'd be a whole new life," said Daniel. "I don't know. I'll have to think about it."

Stu nodded. "I imagined that would be your answer. But I *am* serious. I think you'd make a great agent."

"No ordinary life, huh?" asked Daniel.

"No," said Stu. "That's the rub. What kind of life do you want?" Stu looked at him, letting the question hang in the air. "Think about it. You have my number."

Stu got up to go.

"That's it?" asked Daniel. "You've been here for five minutes."

"I've been *here*, five minutes," said Stu. "I've already talked to your dad, and Marion. Checked in on Lyssa."

"How are they?" asked Daniel.

"They're good," said Stu.

"Did you tell him you were going to ask me?"

"No," said Stu. "It's your decision, not his." Stu went to the door. "Let me know." And then he was gone, the door shut behind him.

Daniel realized that the show was still playing, and he turned it off. He stared at the blank screen.

He took a deep breath and sat back on the couch. He

pictured it in his mind.

Agent Daniel Dawson, IPA. Hmmm.

*

CLANG

The sound of metal on metal echoed through the area, as swords clashed against each other.

"This is nice," said Jenny.

"It is," said Mike. "It is."

They stood next to the sparring area at the Renaissance Festival, as Tomas and Bjorn fought, their swords glancing off each other as they sparred. The weather was nice, sunny, with a breeze.

"You doing okay?" asked Jenny.

"Never been better," he said.

"I somehow doubt that," said Jenny, wrapping an arm around his waist. "Never, in your whole life?"

"Well, maybe at the births of Marion and Daniel—maybe," he said. "But they're not here, and you are. Soooo—I've never been better."

She gave him a squeeze. The return to their relationship had been a little awkward at first, but now, after a few months, they were closer than ever.

"You don't have to worry about me," said Mike.

"How am I not supposed to worry?" asked Jenny. "You went to Hell!"

"It wasn't Hell," said Mike. "It was—well, somewhere else."

"I know, I know—it's classified," said Jenny.

"Well, it is," said Mike. "I'll tell you, if you really want to know. I doubt Stu is listening in. Even if he was, I did save the world. He'll cut me some slack."

The fallout from the White House had been broad, and far reaching. The President had been an alien invader, a shapeshifter. And on top of that, he was dead.

Mike hadn't given much thought to what came after. *After* had seemed impossible. But then it had happened. They had won. And they had returned to a normal life.

It hadn't been instantaneous, but everything moved surprisingly fast. The fragments of the IPA, the Secret Service, the NSA, CIA, and FBI moved in quickly. BENT had held them off for a time, but they could never have done anything without the help of the Oukan.

Which, after many rounds of interviews, almost no one knew anything about. Strickland hadn't lied, when he said he was following orders. And Mike knew that Stu was still deep in uncovering and cleaning up the mess that followed.

The official story was that a rogue agency within the government had killed the President.

No aliens. No monsters. No demons.

The world was chaotic for a while, and the US was still dealing with the aftershocks.

But soon after the events at the White House, Mike, Marion, and Daniel went home. Lyssa went with them. For now, it was temporary. If it went well, she would maybe stay longer.

The Book stayed with Stu. And Mike did his best to not think about it all. To not think about any of it. To focus on the here and now. On Jenny, and Marion, and Daniel, and their lives.

"I don't *need* to know," said Jenny. "But of course I'm curious."

"I've told you the important things," he said. "All the rest—it's not very nice."

"That's fair," said Jenny.

"It's all in the past," said Mike. "Even if I'm a little bit worse for wear." He ruffled his hand through his hair, the silver streaks even more pronounced.

"You'll be my silver fox," said Jenny. "Honestly, I like it."

"Thank God for that," said Mike. "Finally, my trauma is good for something."

Tomas and Bjorn stopped fighting, both bowing to each other, and the crowd applauded. They dispersed, and then the two giants came over to them, taking off their helms.

"Mike!" yelled Tomas. "It is so good to see you. Especially to see you safe. We thought we had lost you."

"Not that easily," said Mike.

"A true warrior," said Bjorn. He leaned in close. "Those things—with the President—was that you?"

Mike winked. "Don't know what you're talking about."

"Ah, I see," said Bjorn.

Tomas held up his sword. "Are you interested in a rematch?"

Mike looked at the heavy sword and took a deep breath. "I don't think so. My fighting days are behind me. I hope so, at least."

Enjoy War on Humanity?

Leave a review! Reviews help readers find authors, and are greatly appreciated!

Acknowledgements

Thank you to my wife Kim, for her patience and support, and my team of beta readers: Andrew, Matt, Megan, Yousef. Thank you for reading.

About the Author

Robbie Dorman believes in horror. War on Humanity is his thirteenth novel. When not writing, he's podcasting, playing video games, or walking his dog. He lives in Florida with his wife, Kim.

You can follow Robbie on social media @robbiedorman

His website is robbiedorman.com

For updates on future projects, book recs, and immediate access to two, free exclusive books - Subscribe to his newsletter at robbiedorman.com/newsletter